DOUBLE JEOPARDY

Novels By Sheldon Siegel

DOUBLE
JEOPARDY

A MIKE DALEY/ROSIE FERNANDEZ THRILLER

SHELDON SIEGEL

For Randy Short, Bob Stumpf, Paul Sanner, and Stew Baird, who provide excellent company, wise counsel, thoughtful observations, and occasional ideas for plotlines during our weekly hikes on Mount Tamalpais in Marin County.

THE "HORNY TEENAGER DEFENSE"

The Honorable Robert J. Stumpf Jr. arched a bushy gray eyebrow over the top of his aviator-style glasses, flashed a charismatic smile, and spoke to me in a commanding baritone leaving no doubt that he was in charge of his stuffy courtroom in Department Seventeen on the second floor of San Francisco's crumbling Hall of Justice. "What a pleasant surprise, Mr. Daley. I didn't expect to see the co-head of the Felony Division of the Public Defender's Office at an arraignment this morning."

I returned his smile. "I didn't expect to see the Presiding Judge of the San Francisco Superior Court, Your Honor."

"One of my colleagues is ill today," he said.

"One of mine is, too."

"I guess we're even."

It was ten a.m. on Monday, February twenty-fourth, 2020. I had first appeared before Bob Stumpf in this very courtroom when I was a rookie Deputy Public Defender after he had just been promoted to Presiding Judge. Almost thirty years later, the Hall of Justice had been condemned because of earthquake safety issues, asbestos-laden walls, faulty plumbing, and an overwhelmed electrical system. The courts and SFPD's Homicide Detail were still open, but the District Attorney's Office, the Public Defender's Office, the Southern Police Station, the Medical Examiner's Office, and most of the administrative staff had moved to more hospitable quarters elsewhere in town. The old jail on the sixth and seventh floors had been mothballed and replaced by a newer building next door, and the cafeteria in the basement had long-since closed.

Judge Stumpf remained one of the few constants at the Hall. At seventy-five, the lanky native of Southern Indiana and one-time backup center on the USF basketball team was appointed to the bench by Jerry Brown during his first stint as governor, and he showed no signs of slowing down. His gregarious manner and incisive wit made an appearance in his courtroom more pleasant than an audience before some of his more taciturn colleagues, but he became impatient if you weren't prepared.

He looked at the prosecution table. "I didn't expect to see you either, Mr. Erickson."

"We had a scheduling conflict. I am also pinch-hitting for one of my colleagues."

"It's always good to see you, too."

"Thank you, Your Honor."

Andy Erickson had just turned forty, and he was also overqualified for this morning's proceedings. The Chief Assistant to the D.A. was a St. Ignatius High School alum (also my alma mater) and a University of San Francisco and USF Law graduate. Over the last fifteen years, the deft political operator had patiently climbed the ladder to his current slot one step from the D.A.'s spacious office. If anyone asked, Andy always insisted that he had no plans to run for his boss's job, which meant that he was, in fact, planning to do so. I didn't always get what I wanted from him, but he was fundamentally honest, and he didn't play games in court the way that he did in the D.A.'s Office.

Judge Stumpf inhaled the eighty-five-degree air and glanced at the gallery, which was filled with A.D.A.s, Deputy P.D.s, and a smattering of private defense lawyers who were trying to maintain a little space between themselves because of a recent uptick in cases of a novel Coronavirus that had found its way to the U.S. from a place called Wuhan Province. He turned to his long-time bailiff. "Please call our next case."

"The People versus Brian Chan. Arraignment. The defendant is present."

My client was standing next to me at the defense table, eyes down, manner sullen. In his ill-fitting orange jumpsuit, the baby-faced eighteen-year-old native of the Sunset District looked like a middle schooler. His mother, Gladys, sat behind me in the gallery. She and Brian and Brian's younger sister lived in a cramped apartment at Forty-seventh and Irving, two blocks from the ocean. Gladys made ends meet by cleaning houses—including the one at Twenty-third and Kirkham where I had grown up and where my mom had lived until she passed away almost two decades earlier. I had known Gladys for years.

I whispered into Brian's ear. "Remember what we talked about. I want you to be respectful and look the judge in the eye. When he asks you for your plea, I need you to say 'Not guilty' in a clear and polite voice."

He responded with a nod as his eyes remained locked on the floor.

I turned around and gave Gladys a reassuring wave. Her eyes were filled with the unmistakable look of fear.

Judge Stumpf pointed at Brian. "You understand why we're here, Mr. Chan?"

He spoke a little too loudly. "Yes, Your Honor."

The judge turned to Erickson. "Charge?"

"Misdemeanor indecent exposure under California Penal Code Section 314."

"How do you wish to plead, Mr. Chan?"

Brian cleared his throat. "Not guilty, Your Honor."

"Thank you." The judge typed a few strokes on his computer, then he turned to me. "I presume that you would like to set a trial date?"

"Yes, Your Honor."

If Brian had been charged with a felony, the next step would have been a perfunctory proceeding where the prosecution would be required to present just enough evidence to convince the judge that there was a reasonable chance that Brian had committed a crime. Since he was charged with a misdemeanor, we would move forward directly to trial.

"Your Honor," I said, "this is my client's first arrest. Before we get to scheduling, I was hoping that we could discuss a couple of issues."

Erickson spoke up before the judge could reply. "Your Honor, if Mr. Daley wishes to talk about pre-trial release, I think we can work something out as long as the defendant is willing to stay with his mother and wear an electronic monitoring device."

"That's acceptable to us," I said, "but I wanted to talk about a few other items."

The judge's curiosity was piqued. "I'm listening."

Here goes. "Your Honor, the facts do not support the charge against my client."

"Facts are facts, Mr. Daley."

"Yes, they are." *Well, sometimes.* "In the circumstances, however, the facts simply do not support charges under Section 314."

The judge gave Erickson a quizzical look. "Perhaps you could enlighten us?"

"Of course, Your Honor."

Erickson rifled through a stack of papers on the table in front of him and speed-read some handwritten notes. If my guess was correct, he had volunteered to cover this arraignment at the last minute, and he knew almost nothing about the case.

He looked up at the judge. "Your Honor, the defendant exposed himself on the 45."

"The 45?"

"The 45 Union Stockton."

Judge Stumpf's blank expression suggested that Erickson was speaking a foreign language. It also delineated the fundamental difference between judges and public defenders and, by extension, the unwashed masses that we typically represent. Everybody in court other than the judge knew that Erickson was referring to the 45 Union Stockton MUNI line, the heavily trafficked bus route between Chinatown, Union Square, and the Cal Train Station down by the ballpark.

Erickson continued in a deferential voice. "It's a MUNI bus, Your Honor."

"I see."

"The defendant boarded at Union and Stockton at approximately eleven-ten last night. At the end of the line, the driver and two other passengers noticed that the defendant was, uh, gratifying himself."

Very deftly described, Andy.

The corner of Judge Stumpf's mouth turned up almost imperceptibly, but he didn't reply.

Erickson pointed at Brian. "The defendant became belligerent. The driver summoned her supervisor and a nearby police officer who placed the defendant under arrest."

The judge's voice filled with resignation. "And here we are."

"And here we are," Erickson repeated.

And here we are.

Judge Stumpf turned to me. "Does your client dispute any of these facts?"

Not really. "With respect, I would like to add a little context, Your Honor."

"You have thirty seconds."

"Brian just turned eighteen. His mother is a single parent who cleans houses in the Sunset to support Brian and his younger sister. Brian is taking classes at City College while working two jobs to help his mother make ends meet. This is the first time that he's ever been arrested. In fact, it's the first time he's gotten into trouble."

"What does he do, Mr. Daley?"

"He's a handyman."

The judge's eyes twinkled. "In more ways than one, it seems."

So it seems. I gave the judge a conspiratorial nod to acknowledge his little double entendre. "Brian was heading home from an eight-hour shift at his second job in Chinatown after he had completed an eight-hour shift at the Botanical Garden at Golden Gate Park."

"Commendable industriousness. He must have been very tired."

"He was. He got on the 45 and was going to transfer to the N-Judah streetcar at Market Street, but he fell asleep and missed his stop."

Judge Stumpf rested his chin in his palm. "This is all very interesting, Mr. Daley, but I fail to see how it changes anything regarding your client's case."

"I was just getting to that." I picked up a volume of the California Statutes, flipped to a page that I had marked with a Post-It, cleared my throat, and read aloud. "Section 314 of the Penal Code says that it is illegal for anyone to 'willfully and lewdly expose his person or the private parts thereof, in any public place, or in any place where there are present other persons to be offended or annoyed thereby.'"

Judge Stumpf held up a hand. "A MUNI bus is a public place, Mr. Daley. And other people were present. It's hardly a stretch to think that they were offended or annoyed."

"Agreed, but my client did not expose his person or his private parts."

The judge turned his gaze to Erickson. "Is this true?"

Erickson frantically scanned his notes. "It seems that the defendant was, uh, fingering the area around his, uh, genitals."

"In other words, he was grabbing his crotch?"

"Yes."

"His pants were still on?"

I answered for him. "Yes, Your Honor."

Erickson tried again. "It was still lewd behavior."

I shook my head. "I think we can all agree that Brian's behavior was inappropriate, but under the exact language of the statute, it wasn't illegal because he didn't expose himself."

The judge gave Erickson a wry smile. "I find Mr. Daley's statutory interpretation pretty convincing."

So do I. "Your Honor, I would also note that Section 314 specifically states that the accused must have acted willfully, which requires conscious intent."

Judge Stumpf's bemused grin turned into a full-blown smile. "You're arguing that he grabbed his crotch by accident?"

Yup. "I'm saying that he did so without conscious intent."

"How do you figure?"

"He was asleep when the bus got to the end of the line." I looked over at Brian, then I turned back to the judge. "When the driver woke him up, she noticed that Brian was, uh, holding his private parts. He couldn't have been doing so intentionally because he was asleep. Since he didn't act with conscious intent, he didn't act 'willfully,' as the statute requires. As a result, there is no basis to charge him under Section 314, and the charges should be dismissed for lack of probable cause under Section 991 of the California Penal Code."

"That's a novel argument, Mr. Daley."

Yes, it is. "It's a straightforward reading of the actual words of the statute, Your Honor."

"I'm not sure that I'm buying what you're selling, Mr. Daley."

Neither am I. "Your Honor, I have a teenage son. I recall that you have three grown sons, all of whom are lawyers, and several teenage grandsons. We did some things when we were their age that were careless, foolish, or even flat-out stupid. It was usually without malicious intent, and, given a second chance, we wouldn't have done it. This is one of those cases."

"You're saying that I should dismiss the charges because this was little more than a teenage indiscretion?"

Exactly. "Yes, Your Honor. Nobody was hurt."

The experienced jurist took a moment to gather his thoughts before he spoke to Brian. "Are you sorry about what happened, Mr. Chan?"

"Yes, Your Honor."

"Are you willing to apologize to the bus driver?"

"Yes, Your Honor."

He looked over at Erickson. "You and Mr. Daley might be able to work something out, right, Mr. Erickson?"

"Possibly." He looked over at me. "Did you have something in mind, Mr. Daley?"

"Yes, Mr. Erickson. Brian will deliver a written apology to the bus driver and do ten hours of community service at the Lady Shaw Senior Housing Center in Chinatown. Upon completion of those tasks and assuming there are no additional, uh, indiscretions, you will dismiss the charges."

"He'll agree not to ride MUNI for a month?"

"Fine."

The judge held up his hands in triumph. "Gentlemen, I think we have a resolution." He turned to his bailiff. "Please call our next case."

My shirt was sticking to my back as I walked down the sauna-like corridor of the P.D.'s Office at eleven-fifteen the same morning. The fluorescent lights flickered as I unbuttoned my overcoat and approached the back of the shaved head of my secretary, executive assistant, process server, occasional bodyguard, and friend, Terrence "The Terminator" Love, who was sitting in his cubicle outside my office.

"Morning, T," I said.

He spun around to look at me and responded in a high-pitched voice. "Morning, Mike."

Now approaching sixty, Terrence was a former heavyweight boxer whose career ended after a handful of fights because he was too good-hearted to hit anybody too hard. At six-six and a muscular three hundred pounds, the recovering alcoholic was my very first client when I was a baby P.D., and he became a reliable customer. A decade ago, I hired him as the receptionist at the two-person law firm that my ex-wife and I were running at the time. It was part of a probation agreement that I had brokered with one of Judge Stumpf's more understanding colleagues. To his credit, Terrence hadn't touched a drop of booze ever since. He became indispensable to our practice, and we brought him with us to the P.D.'s Office when we moved back here.

"Can we turn the heat down a little?" I asked.

"Afraid not, Mike." He smiled broadly, exposing his signature gold front tooth that he received from the on-site dentist during one of his stays in jail. "We tried adjusting the thermostat. Leo did his usual dance with the furnace. Nothing."

"Can he turn it off?"

"With a sledgehammer."

Probably not an ideal solution. "Did you call Maintenance?"

"Yes. They're backed up at the Hall of Justice, so they're going to send somebody over next week. It's the best that we can do unless you can find us some extra money in the budget to replace it."

"Unlikely, T."

"I figured, Mike."

Twenty years ago, the P.D.'s Office had moved into a repurposed auto repair shop on Seventh Street, a half block south of the Hall of Justice. At the time, it was a substantial upgrade from our ratty old digs where the heater worked sporadically, the asbestos-laden walls were covered in lead-based paint, and the plumbing worked when it was in the mood. Two decades of deferred maintenance later, our no-longer-state-of-the-art facility needed a tune-up.

"How did it go in court?" he asked.

"I got Brian off with community service and a promise not to take MUNI for a month."

"Not bad. How is he going to get to work?"

"The P.D.'s Office bought him an Uber gift card." I winked. "I charged it to 'office supplies.'"

He smiled. "Judge Stumpf actually bought the 'horny teenager defense,' eh? That's one of your more imaginative efforts, Mike."

"Thanks, T. It's nice to know that the magic tricks are still working." I pointed at the closed door behind him. "Is the boss here?"

"She's in her office."

Rosita Carmela Fernandez had just won re-election for her second term as the Public Defender. In addition to being my former law partner and current boss, she happened to be my ex-wife and the mother of our two children.

"Is she by herself?" I asked.

"She's on a conference call with the Mayor's Office and some department heads about the Coronavirus thing."

"They're saying it's no worse than the flu."

"Evidently, it could be worse."

"You okay?" I asked.

"I've had a little sniffle for a few days, but otherwise fine. You?"

"I'm okay. Anybody else looking for me?"

"Nady."

Nadezhda "Nady" Nikonova was one of our best young attorneys.

"Did she mention what it's about?" I asked.

His expression turned serious. "No, but I think it's important. She seemed upset."

I pointed at my office. "Could you please ask her to come see me?"

"You okay?" I asked.

"I'm fine." Nady sat in the chair opposite my desk, her intense blue eyes locked onto mine. "Max and I need to go down to L.A. right away. I think my mom has the virus."

Oh crap.

Nady was a brilliant, creative, and driven woman of thirty-five. When she was a kid, she had accompanied her single mother to the U.S. from Uzbekistan. They found their way to cousins in L.A., where Nady picked up English on the fly, became an excellent student, and graduated at the top of her class at UCLA and, later, Berkeley Law, also my alma mater. She began her career working for a downtown firm where she spent countless hours poring over endless documents for mind-numbing real estate deals. I had liberated her three years ago, and she quickly found representing criminals more to her liking. Her husband, Max, was a partner in the antitrust group of the megafirm of Story, Short & Thompson in Embarcadero Center.

"How serious are your mom's symptoms?" I asked.

"She has a cough and a fever. I talked to her a few minutes ago. She didn't sound good. My cousin is driving her to the emergency room."

I pointed at the door. "Go now. You can pick up Max on the way."

She tugged at her shoulder-length hair. "I have a bunch of active cases."

"That's why we have cell phones. Call me from the road. I'll deal with everything. Do you have somebody to look after Luna?"

"We'll take her with us."

"Good."

Luna was a fourteen-year-old Keeshond mix who spent most days sleeping under Nady's desk since I had declared the P.D.'s Office a pet-friendly workplace, much to the chagrin of my bureaucratic masters at City Hall.

"You sure that you have time?" she asked.

"I'll make time. I'll get continuances on everything."

"Lenny Garcia's murder trial starts a week from today."

Garcia was a homeless Army vet who lived in the sprawling tent encampment at U.N. Plaza near City Hall. He was accused of giving OxyContin pills to a young runaway named Annie Parker, who lived on the plaza. The pills were laced with fentanyl, a synthetic opioid that's fifty times more potent than morphine. For the last decade, the cheap and deadly drug has become widely available in San Francisco and other big cities. In certain instances—especially among those with little experience with the drug—an overdose can be fatal.

"I'll get a continuance," I said.

"Judge Powell won't allow it. He's already extended us twice."

Gordon Powell was a smart but cantankerous jurist from a prominent Gold Rush family who lived in a mansion down the street from the Gettys on Broadway's Gold Coast.

"There are extenuating circumstances," I said.

"Lenny has been in jail for over a year. We won't be able to get another trial date for at least nine months."

"I'll figure something out." *At least I'll try.*

"There's something else, Mike. Lenny is being held down in County Jail #5."

It was the warehouse-like facility in the hills of San Bruno about halfway between SFO and the ocean.

She added, "They aren't taking precautions for the virus. A couple of people have already been infected and one died. Lenny is scared to death that he's going to catch it."

"How complicated is the trial?"

"Not very. Jury selection will take longer than the presentation of the evidence. There will be just a few witnesses."

"What's our narrative?"

"Lenny didn't give the decedent the tainted pills."

"Why do they think he did?"

"He gave her some of his real Oxy pills that he got from the V.A. to help her with pain. His name was on the pill bottle. So were his prints."

"If he didn't give her the tainted pills, who did?"

"I don't know. Lenny claims that she must have gotten them from somebody else and put them in the bottle that he had given her. There were a half dozen fentanyl-laced pills in the bottle when the police found it."

Not good. "Any other prints?"

"The decedent's. And a couple of unidentified prints."

"DNA?"

"Nothing identifiable except for Lenny and the decedent."

"Any evidence that somebody else provided the pills?"

"We have some possibilities." She frowned. "No slam-dunk winners, however."

There never are. "Anything else?"

"The decedent had a heart condition. Our medical expert will testify that she could have died of a heart attack unrelated to the fentanyl. He's already prepped."

"Good. You can fill me in on the details while you're driving to L.A."

"I will." She stood up, headed toward the door, and stopped abruptly. "Mike?"

"Yes?"

"Thanks."

2

"ASK FOR A CONTINUANCE"

The Public Defender of the City and County of San Francisco knocked on the open door to my office. "I heard you got Brian Chan off."

"He has to write a sorry letter, do community service, and stay off MUNI for a few weeks."

"Well done." Rosita Carmela Fernandez flashed the perfect smile that I still found irresistible more than a quarter of a century after we'd met in the file room of the old P.D.'s Office and twenty-three years after we'd gotten divorced. "Judge Stumpf bought your 'boys will be boys' argument?"

"Judges will be judges, Rosie."

Her grin broadened as she tugged at the sleeve of her Dior blouse—an upgrade from the days when she wore jeans and denim work shirts to the office. "It's one of the more creative legal theories that you've cooked up over the years."

"Justice was served."

At fifty-four, Rosie's jet-black hair no longer fell to her waist. Nowadays, it was cut in a stylish bob and flecked with a few strands of gray. Her smoky voice was a little raspier than it was when we were young P.D.s. A regimen of Pilates, spin classes, and aerobics kept her fit.

"I'll have Terrence issue a press release to announce your great victory," she deadpanned.

"That won't be necessary."

At seven-forty-five on Monday night, the P.D.'s Office was buzzing as our colleagues were catching up on matters that they didn't have time to address during the day. The heater was still going full blast, so my workmanlike office was sweltering.

I was tempted to toss my stapler through my dirt-encrusted window to improve the ventilation, but that wouldn't have been an especially enlightened solution.

"You're here late," I observed.

"I've been on conference calls all day. The Mayor's Office asked the department heads to make contingency plans for everybody to work from home for the next few weeks."

"This Coronavirus thing is more serious than I thought."

Her smile disappeared. "Yes, it is."

Rosie and I had met at the old P.D.'s Office when I was a rookie P.D., and she had just been promoted to the Felony Division. I had decided to go to law school after a difficult three-year tenure as a priest—much to the chagrin of my dad, a San Francisco cop. Rosie had just spun out of a brief and unsatisfying marriage to a law school classmate who drank too much and cheated on her. Our daughter, Grace, was born a year later. The demands of a baby and our jobs collided, and we called things off when Grace was two. Nowadays, Grace was a USC film school alum and a production assistant at Pixar. Our son, Tommy (named after my dad), was a freshman at Cal, my undergrad and law school alma mater. He came along a few years after Rosie and I split up. Old habits.

After the divorce, I spent five years working at a big firm at the top of the Bank of America Building to pay the bills, alimony, and child support. Rosie started her own criminal defense practice and took me in after I got fired for not bringing in enough clients. We'd been working together ever since—first at our two-person firm on Mission Street, and, more recently, back here at the P.D.'s Office. We were co-heads of the Felony Division for a few years before Rosie ran for her first term as P.D.

She took a seat in the creaky wooden chair opposite my metal desk across the room from my IKEA bookcases and second-hand worktable. The only item of Twenty-first Century vintage was the laptop on my credenza desk next to Grace's graduation photo from USC and Tommy's graduation photo from Redwood High School in Larkspur.

"Kids okay?" I asked.

"Fine." She reported that Grace was finishing production on a new film, and Tommy was trying to decide whether he wanted to spend fall semester in Prague. "It's good being our kids."

"It is. And your mom?"

"Also fine, but she's worried about the virus, so she's being extra careful."

We were firmly in the sandwich years where every conversation began with a check-in on our kids and our aging relatives. Rosie's eighty-five-year-old mother, Sylvia, still lived in the two-bedroom bungalow in the Mission around the corner from the apartments where my mom and dad had grown up. My parents, two brothers, baby sister, and I squeezed into a two-bedroom apartment on Garfield Square Park before we moved to a three-bedroom house in the foggy Sunset.

"Is she staying home?" I asked.

"Yes. She's ordering food online. My brother is bringing her fresh fruit and vegetables."

Rosie's older brother, Tony, ran a produce market on Twenty-fourth Street, a couple of blocks from Sylvia's house and down the block from St. Peter's Catholic Church.

"Do you really think that's necessary?" I asked.

"It's better to be careful, Mike. According to the Mayor's Office, it's likely to get worse before it gets better. At the very least, they're going to recommend that people wear masks."

I took a moment to process her answer. "Are you okay?"

"Fine, but worried. I don't want you or Mama or the kids to get sick. And I'll feel terrible if somebody from the office catches the virus. How are you feeling?"

"Fine."

She pointed at her heart. "Your ticker good?"

"Like new."

A year earlier, my doctor discovered that I had developed an extra heartbeat called a ventricular bigeminy. It's fairly common even among people like me who aren't overweight, have low cholesterol, exercise pretty regularly, and don't smoke. My cardiologist did a high-tech procedure called an ablation where she sent a little probe into my heart, did a detailed map, and zapped the spot causing the extra beat. I was in and out of the hospital the same day, and I didn't feel a thing. Thankfully, the procedure was successful, and my heart was back to normal.

Rosie gave me a skeptical look. "Dr. Dey told you not to overdo it."

"I'm fine, Rosie. It was just a routine little procedure."

"It wasn't open-heart surgery, but there is no such thing as a 'little' heart procedure." She invoked the "don't even think about disagreeing with me" tone that I had learned to obey. "I want you to be careful, Mike." Her voice softened. "Why are you here so late?"

"Nady had to go down to L.A. Her mother is in the hospital. Nady thinks she may have the virus."

Rosie frowned. "Thanks for jumping in on short notice."

"It's what we do."

"Anything big?"

"Lenny Garcia's murder trial starts Monday."

"Ask for a continuance."

"I was on the phone with Nady for the past three hours. She had everything ready to go. It's going to be a short trial. Just a couple of days and a few witnesses."

"Ask for a continuance," she repeated. "Going to trial is not in our client's best interests."

"He's been in jail for over a year. If we ask for a continuance, he won't get his day in court for at least nine months, maybe longer. He's down in San Bruno. They're already seeing virus cases. One inmate died."

"It's better than going to trial with an attorney who hasn't had adequate time to prepare."

"The longer he's in jail, the better the chance that he won't make it out alive."

"Do you have a judge?"

"Gordon Powell was assigned when it looked like we were going to trial in November."

Judges are assigned by the presiding judge of the criminal court shortly before trial. In this case, Judge Powell was given our case immediately before the original trial date.

Her voice filled with sarcasm. "Wonderful."

"He isn't bad, Rosie."

"He isn't great, Mike. Ask him for a continuance."

"I will, but he may not grant it. We've already been extended twice."

"He can be reasonable, and you can be very persuasive."

I folded my arms. "It's the ultimate case of double jeopardy, Rosie. There's the trial and the virus."

"We can't help that, Mike."

"Yes, we can. I'll take it to trial."

"Who's the investigator?"

I lowered my voice. "It was Tom Eisenmann."

She scowled. Eisenmann was one of our best investigators. Unfortunately, he had passed away six months earlier from pancreatic cancer.

"I can't spare anybody," she said. She lowered her voice. "I don't want you looking for witnesses in the Tenderloin until we get a handle on this virus."

"I'll get Pete to help."

My younger brother, Pete, was a former cop who was now a private investigator.

She shook her head. "I don't want him to get sick, either."

"I won't make him do anything he doesn't want to do. We'll be extra careful."

"You and your brother always say that. Then you play cops-and-robbers in the worst neighborhoods. I want you to ask for a continuance."

"I will, but if Judge Powell doesn't agree to it, I'm going to have to take this to trial."

"Understood. Have you talked to our client?"

"I'm going to see him in the morning."

"I want you to try to talk him into asking for a continuance."

"I will."

Her expression softened. "You want a ride home?"

"I'll take an Uber later. I want to look at Nady's files before I meet with our client."

3

"I DIDN'T KILL HER"

The razor-thin young man with the shaved head, pockmarked face, intense brown eyes, and U.S. Army tattoo on his forearm glared at me across a metal table bolted to the floor. "Who are you?"

"Mike Daley. I'm the co-head of the Felony Division of the Public Defender's Office."

Lenny Garcia scowled. "Where's Nady?"

"She had to go down to L.A. to deal with a medical emergency. Her mother is sick. It may be the Coronavirus."

His expression softened. "When is she coming back?"

"I don't know."

His voice filled with resignation. "Figures."

At nine-forty-five the following morning, a Tuesday, we were meeting in a windowless attorney-client consultation room on the ground floor of County Jail #5, the warehouse-like structure perched on San Bruno Mountain above a quiet suburban neighborhood ten miles south of downtown San Francisco. The building opened in 2006 and replaced the Depression-era jail a few miles away. It's a Twenty-first Century facility where a few dozen guards in high-tech pods monitor about eight hundred prisoners. It is known for progressive programming and, more important, functional plumbing. It's the nicest facility in the San Francisco jail system.

"You staying healthy?" I asked.

"So far." He dropped the attitude. "I don't have any symptoms. A couple of people got the virus. One guy died."

"Is the jail taking any precautions?"

"Not really. I keep to myself. Does this mean that you're my lawyer?"

"Yes."

"Are you any good?"

"I've been doing this for almost thirty years."

"You could have been bad for thirty years."

True. I didn't think it would be helpful to mention that the *State Bar Journal* once proclaimed that Rosie and I were the two best public defenders in California. "I trained Nady."

"If you're as good as she is, I'll be okay. Are you going to handle my trial?"

"Looks like it."

"Do I have any choice?"

"Not unless you want me to ask for a continuance."

"Do you think that's a good idea?"

"Yes."

"How soon before I could get a new trial date?"

"At least nine months. If they shut down the courts because of the virus, longer."

"Not interested."

"It would make sense to wait until Nady gets back."

"You haven't been locked up for over a year."

"She's more familiar with your case."

"Not interested," he repeated.

"I would encourage you to think about it."

"I just did. Every day that I'm here increases the odds that I'll catch the virus. If Nady can't do it, you're my guy."

I leaned back in the uncomfortable chair. "Nady told me a lot about you, but I'd like to know more." *And I want to get you talking so that maybe you'll start to trust me. More important, I want to know if I can trust you.* "Why don't you tell me a little more about yourself."

"I didn't kill Annie Parker."

"We'll get to that shortly."

His eyes narrowed. "I didn't kill her."

"We'll talk about it in a minute. Nady said you're from the Mission."

"I am."

"So am I. St. Peter's Parish. My parents grew up on Garfield Square. There were a lot of Irish people in the neighborhood in those days. We moved to the Sunset when I was seven. Where did you live?"

"We moved around a lot." He recited a series of addresses on Folsom, Bryant, and South Van Ness. He said that his parents were from Mexico. "My father was killed in an accident when I was twelve. My mother died of cancer a few months after I came back from my second tour in Afghanistan." He said that his older sister was a nurse and a single mother who had cut off contact with Lenny a few years earlier. "Perlita and I haven't communicated since I checked myself out of detox." His voice filled with resignation. "I can't blame her. It isn't easy dealing with a brother who lives on the street, drinks too much, and is addicted to painkillers."

"How did you get addicted?"

"After I graduated from Mission High, I volunteered for the Army and did three tours in Afghanistan. The third time I took a hit from an IED. I still have some shrapnel in my right leg."

"I'm sorry."

"So am I." He said that after his rehab and discharge, he came back to San Francisco. "My parents were gone. My sister was working too hard and married to an asshole. Most of my friends from high school had gone to college and weren't living in the neighborhood anymore. My buddies from the Army lived in other parts of the country."

"Not much of a support system." I asked him if he was able to find work.

"At times. I worked in an auto body shop, but it went out of business. I worked at a carwash for a couple of months, but I couldn't stay on my feet all day. I tried driving for Uber, but I didn't make enough to pay for an apartment. I kept asking my doctor at the V.A. for higher doses of the painkillers, and he tried to help me. They worked for a while, then I built up tolerance. I got addicted to Vicodin, Percocet, and, finally, OxyContin."

"I know people who've gotten hooked on that stuff. It's tough to get off."

"It's almost impossible." His voice turned thoughtful. "Ever had a bad toothache?"

"Yes."

"After a day or two, you would have taken anything to make it go away, right?"

"Right."

"Multiply that pain by twenty and try to live with it for a few years. You reach a point where the painkillers are the only thing keeping you alive. It's completely destructive."

"I'm sorry, Lenny."

"It is what it is. Now do you understand why I was living on U.N. Plaza?"

"Yes." I leaned forward. "We have resources at the P.D.'s Office. After your trial, I'm going to make sure that you get services and support to find you a decent place to live."

"What makes you think that you can get me off?"

"Because you just told me that you didn't kill Annie Parker."

"You believe me?"

Not necessarily. "You wouldn't lie to me, would you, Lenny?"

"No."

"You didn't lie to Nady, did you?"

"No."

"Good to hear. Because I have only one non-negotiable rule: you need to be absolutely truthful with me. I'll find out if you're lying. And if you do, you'll make my life a lot harder, which means that your life will be a lot harder. Understood?"

"Yes."

"Do you want to reconsider anything that you've told me?"

"No."

"Good." I placed a pad of paper on the table in front of me. "Tell me everything you know about Annie Parker."

4

"SHE WAS JUST A KID"

"How old was Annie?" I asked.

"Nineteen," Lenny said. "She was just a kid."

"How well did you know her?"

"Not well." He took a sip of water from a paper cup. "Before she moved to U.N. Plaza, she was living in an SRO on Larkin that her pimp paid for."

"SRO" refers to a single-room-occupancy hotel, a low-end rooming house in a rough part of town.

Lenny was still talking. "She got into a fight with the pimp, and he took her money and beat her up. She couldn't pay her rent, so she moved into a tent on the plaza." He said that she had been living there for a couple of months before she died.

"Do you know the name of the SRO?"

"The El Camino."

"Did she mention any friends or acquaintances?"

"A woman named Patty came to see her a couple of times. Annie told me that Patty lived at the same hotel and worked for the same pimp." He said that he didn't know Patty's last name, and he didn't know if she was still living in the neighborhood.

"You know the name of her pimp?"

"Marcus Strong. I never met him."

"Bad guy?"

"*Really* bad guy." He said that Strong preyed on young women who came into town looking for new lives. "It's an old story. He'd give them money, find them a place to live, and treat them nicely for a while, then he'd control their lives."

"Did he ever come see Annie at the plaza?"

"Once or twice. She said that he asked her to come back to work for him. She didn't want to do it, but she needed money."

"You think he gave her some tainted pills?"

"I don't know. Strong was in it for money. He wouldn't have killed her if she was profitable. It would have been bad for business."

"Maybe he didn't know the pills were spiked with fentanyl."

"Maybe. Even if he did, I have no idea how you're going to prove it."

Neither do I. Then again, Strong would be a thoroughly unsympathetic witness. If I can make a good enough case that he might have given Annie Parker some tainted pills, I might be able to get one or more jurors to reasonable doubt. "Any idea where I can find him?"

"Woodlawn Cemetery in Colma. He got knifed in an alley about six months ago."

"Do the cops know who did it?"

"Not as far as I know. Nobody's been arrested."

"Any possibilities?"

"Nady asked me the same thing. A lot of people didn't like Strong, but I have no idea who killed him."

Crap. Then again, it opens up some possibilities for Lenny's defense. If all else fails, we can blame Annie's death on the dead pimp.

I asked him about Annie's background. I had gone over the basics with Nady, but I wanted to see if Lenny could provide more details.

He balled his hands into fists. "She grew up in Modesto. Her father had five kids with five different women. He disappeared when Annie was a baby. Her mother was addicted to crystal meth. Annie lived with her grandmother for a few years when she was a kid, but the grandmother died. She ended up shuttling between foster homes. She got tired of it and took a bus over here. Strong found her near the bus station and offered her money and a place to stay. He set her up with customers. She had a bum shoulder from a car accident, so he gave her Oxy for the pain. I think he got her addicted to painkillers. When she tried to run away, he beat her up and cut off her supply of Oxy."

A lot of runaways come to cities looking for opportunities, excitement, and a chance to start over. In some cases, they find their way into the sex and drug trades.

I asked him if there was anybody else that we should try to find.

"A guy on U.N. Plaza named Brian Holton knows everybody. He's lived there for years."

Nady had included Holton's name on our witness list. "Was he dealing?"

"Not as far as I know, but it wouldn't surprise me. The cops probably talked to him. I'm sure that he denied selling drugs."

"Any chance he gave Annie some spiked pills?"

"It's possible. There's a lot of tainted stuff out there."

"Is he still living on the plaza?"

"I don't know. I've been living here for a year."

We talked for another hour about potential suspects, but he couldn't provide any additional names. Finally, I got to the heart of it. "Tell me what happened."

"Nothing."

I eyed him and waited, hoping he would be inclined to fill the void.

Finally, he did. "I went over this with Nady a dozen times."

"I want to hear it from you. Why do the D.A. and the police think you gave Annie Parker some tainted pills?"

"I didn't."

"I know the homicide inspector handling your case. He doesn't arrest people unless he has evidence that they're guilty."

"I didn't kill Annie."

"Who did?"

"I don't know."

"The Medical Examiner concluded that she died of an overdose. They found a pill bottle next to her body with pills laced with fentanyl."

"I didn't give them to her."

"Your name was on the bottle. So were your fingerprints."

"It was my bottle. I'm going to tell you what I told Nady. The day before Annie died, I gave her a bottle with three of my Oxy pills. They didn't contain fentanyl. I had taken the rest of the pills myself. I got them from the V.A. I had a prescription."

Presumably the V.A. wasn't handing out tainted pills. "Why did you give her some of your pills?"

"I felt sorry for her. She had a bad shoulder, and she was in terrible pain."

"You didn't need them?"

"I had an appointment with the V.A. to get a refill the next day."

"You just gave her the pills?"

"If you saw a dog who got hit by a car, wouldn't you try to help him?"

Yes. "She couldn't get a prescription?"

"You think she was covered by Blue Shield? She didn't have insurance, and she couldn't get an appointment at the Tenderloin Medical Clinic."

"You're saying that somebody else gave Annie some tainted pills that she put inside the container that you gave her?"

"Yes. Or maybe the person who gave her the pills put them inside the bottle himself. There were some unidentified prints on the bottle."

The good news is that you aren't making up a far-fetched story to cover your tracks. The bad news is that it looks terrible.

I put down my pen. "You appreciate the fact that the optics aren't great?"

"I do." He lowered his voice. "I didn't give her tainted pills, Mike."

"Who did?"

"I don't know."

And I have less than a week to find some unknown suspect. "Where should I start, Lenny?"

"Find out what you can about Marcus Strong. Talk to Brian Holton. And see if you can find Patty."

5

"OUR WITNESS LIST IS A LITTLE THIN"

"How's your mom?" I asked.

Nady's voice was hoarse. "Not great. She's in the ICU with Coronavirus symptoms, but they haven't gotten the test results yet."

"Have you been able to see her?"

"Only on Facetime. They won't let anybody inside the hospital."

At eleven-forty-five on Tuesday morning, I was driving north on 280 past the cemeteries in Colma. The sky was overcast, and a heavy drizzle whipped across my windshield. My head throbbed, and my throat was scratchy. Just another day in the life of a Public Defender.

I pressed my phone against my ear. "Is she, uh, breathing on her own?"

"Thankfully, yes. Hopefully, they won't have to put her on a ventilator."

Hopefully. "Is there anything that I can do?"

"You take care of my cases, and I'll take care of my mother."

"Deal." I summarized my conversation with Lenny. "He doesn't want a continuance."

"The curtain goes up on Monday."

"I'll be ready." *Well, I hope so.* "Our witness list is a little thin."

"I included everybody that I could think of who might be able to help our case, but I didn't find any hard evidence that somebody other than Lenny gave Annie the spiked pills."

Defense attorneys generally load up our witness lists with people who might have something relevant to say. While many potential witnesses never testify, you never know when something might pop up that will help us down the road.

"Lenny said that he didn't give Annie the pills," I said, "but it's damn near impossible to prove a negative."

She sighed. "Our best argument may be that her irregular heartbeat killed her. That would create doubt about causation and improve our chances of getting one juror to reasonable doubt."

True. It might not get us an acquittal, but it would get us a hung jury, and the D.A. would have to decide whether to start from scratch. I asked her if she had been planning to put Lenny on the stand.

"Only if things looked desperate. He's smart, reasonably articulate, and somewhat sympathetic. On the other hand, he can be volatile. An experienced prosecutor like Andy Erickson could get him to contradict himself on the stand or, worse, lose his composure."

"Did you have any other potential suspects in mind?"

"Our best bet is Annie's pimp, Marcus Strong, but he's dead. There's also a guy named Brian Holton who lives on U.N. Plaza. Some people thought that Holton was selling drugs, but I couldn't get any corroborating evidence, and Holton, of course, denied it. He's never been arrested for dealing."

"Did you find anything solid connecting either of them to the tainted pills?"

"No."

Crap. "What about the unidentified prints on the pill bottle?"

"They didn't match Strong or Holton. The police didn't find any matches when they ran it through their databases. Our investigator didn't get any matches, either."

"You told me that they found semen on Annie's panties."

"They did, but it wasn't Lenny's or Strong's or Holton's. It means that she had sex with somebody else before she died. It doesn't prove that the guy she slept with gave her the spiked pills."

"Were you able to get DNA from the unidentified prints on the bottle?"

"Not enough for a conclusive test. It's possible that it's the same guy who slept with Annie, but impossible to prove unless you match the unidentified fingerprint, which seems unlikely in the next six days."

True. "Did you talk to the dead pimp?"

"I tried, but Strong refused to talk to me. I don't know who stabbed him. As far as I can tell, the cops don't, either. You can try to blame him for Annie's death, but the evidence is thin."

"You put Holton on our witness list."

"I did, but he said that he didn't give Annie the spiked pills. I didn't necessarily believe him, but I found no evidence that he did."

"I can still throw him under the bus."

"True enough, but it may be hard to sell it to the jury."

"Any chance Holton knows who gave Annie the spiked pills?"

"There's a chance, Mike, but he didn't share it with me. Last I checked, he was still living on U.N. Plaza."

"Lenny also said that I should talk to a woman named Patty, who lived in the same SRO and worked for Strong."

"Her last name is Dawson. I talked to her briefly. She said that she didn't know anything about Annie's death, and she didn't want to get involved."

"You think she had anything to do with Strong's death?"

"I don't know."

"You think she may have given Annie the tainted pills?"

"I don't know that, either."

"Do you have contact info for her?"

"Afraid not, Mike. She was using a burner phone, and she's no longer living at the El Camino Hotel."

"Any idea where I should start looking?"

"U.N. Plaza."

6

"I'LL SEE WHAT I CAN DO"

The gregarious bartender's blue eyes twinkled, his round face transformed into a broad smile, and he spoke to me in a phony Irish brogue. "What'll it be, lad?"

At eight-thirty the same night, I was sitting on a stool at the otherwise empty bar that my father, Tom Daley Sr., had helped the bartender's grandfather, Big John Dunleavy, build six decades earlier. Big John was my mother's younger brother.

"Have I ever ordered anything but a Guinness, Joey?" I asked.

"Nope." He tossed his dishtowel over his shoulder and pulled out a mug. "I figured that maybe you'd like to try something different every once in a while, Mike."

"Not gonna happen anytime soon."

"Didn't think so." My cousin drew a perfect Guinness and slid it across the bar. Then he poured one for himself and lifted his glass. "To your health, Mike."

"To yours, Joey."

I looked around the homey Irish pub at Twenty-third and Irving, around the corner from the house where I had grown up. Except for the flat-screen TVs and the Wi-Fi password written on the blackboard beneath the list of beers, Dunleavy's Bar and Grill looked the same as it did when I came here as a kid, and later tended bar when I was in college.

"It's quiet tonight," I said.

Joey nodded. "Business has been off since the Coronavirus thing started. The City may ask the bars and restaurants to shut down inside seating for a few weeks."

"You gonna be okay?"

"I'll be fine." He pointed at the kitchen where he cooked the fish and chips using a secret batter invented by his grandfather. "I'll switch to takeout." He winked. "It'll be just like the old days: food out the front door, booze out the back."

"Big John would have been proud."

"Big John would never have shut down."

My cousin, Joey, was thirty-five. He almost got married to his college sweetheart, but it didn't work out, and he hadn't gotten close since then. At six-four and two-forty, the onetime offensive lineman at St. Ignatius was still imposing, although he was getting a little soft in the middle. His bright red hair had turned mostly gray, and his jowls had expanded along with his girth. Joey got a business degree from State and started helping Big John run the bar. Eventually, my uncle turned over the day-to-day operations to him. Big John was a savvy businessman whose holdings included the bar, a house around the corner, and a condo in Palm Springs. Dunleavy's had put Big John's children and grandchildren through college.

Joey dropped the brogue. "I don't think I ever got around to thanking you for taking Big John to Ireland."

"It was our pleasure."

My uncle was born and raised in San Francisco and had never left the U.S. before Rosie and I took him to see where our ancestors had lived in County Galway, our beautiful homeland on the West Coast of Ireland. Even though the weather was cold and rainy, Big John had a great time.

"He was a trouper," I said. "He never admitted that he was tired. I just wish that he could have stuck around a little longer."

A few days after we got home, Big John was sitting in his usual spot behind the bar and counting the day's receipts at closing time. He poured himself a shot of Glendalough twenty-five-year-old single-malt Irish whisky, downed it in a satisfying gulp, placed the shot glass on the bar, then he leaned forward and passed away of a heart attack.

"I'm glad it was quick," I said.

"Me, too." Joey shrugged. "He thought the cancer was going to get him this time."

Big John was about to start chemo treatments for a recurring bout with prostate cancer.

"Maybe," I said, "although he beat it twice before. It's probably better that he didn't have to deal with the Coronavirus, either—especially if you have to shut down for a while."

"Big John always said that Dunleavy's doesn't close."

Even after Big John's wife, my Aunt Kate, died about twenty years ago, Big John took pride in the fact that he never closed Dunleavy's.

We looked at the photo of my uncle above the bar and raised our mugs in a silent toast.

I took a draw of my Guinness. "I don't think I ever got around to thanking you properly for the party that you and Big John threw for Grace and Chuck."

He waved me away. "That was all Big John."

"That was mostly you."

Big John (with a lot of help from Joey) threw an engagement party at Dunleavy's for our daughter and her fiancé. It was reminiscent of the party that he threw for Rosie and me almost thirty years earlier. Big John invited three hundred of his friends, relatives, and regulars, who drank copious amounts of Guinness and Irish whisky and consumed a week's worth of fish and chips. The fire marshal should have shut us down, but he was one of the guests, so he looked the other way. It was the last party that Big John threw at Dunleavy's.

"I'm sorry that Big John won't be able to attend the wedding in December," I said.

"He'll be with us in spirit."

"That he will."

The front door opened, and the most decorated homicide detective in SFPD history let himself inside. Roosevelt Johnson hung his overcoat on the rack and took the stool next to mine. He greeted Joey and me with the melodious baritone that was raspier than it was when he was walking the beat in the Tenderloin with my father six decades earlier.

"Good to see you, Mike," he said.

"Good to see you, too, Roosevelt."

Without a word, Joey poured him a cup of coffee and brought out a takeout order of fish and chips. We took a few minutes to catch up. Roosevelt reported that he was healthy, but an old knee injury was slowing him down. His wife, Janet, had passed away a couple of years earlier. His eldest granddaughter was expecting his first great-grandchild. It brought back memories of the days that Roosevelt's family used to come over to our house around the corner almost every Sunday night for dinner.

He arched an eyebrow. "I heard you picked up Lenny Garcia's trial. Are you going to get an acquittal?"

"I'm not wildly optimistic."

"Hung jury?"

I never tried to BS Roosevelt. "Maybe."

He shook his head. "The Tenderloin was a mess when your father and I worked there. Nowadays, it's a disaster. Seems it's all drugs and homeless."

"It's tough," I acknowledged. "You can get fentanyl on every corner."

"Did your client give that young woman the tainted pills?"

"He said that he didn't."

He gave me the skeptical look that I had seen countless times. "You believe him?"

"Until I have reason to disbelieve him. Do you still have any sources down in the Tenderloin?"

He let out a hearty chuckle. "I've been retired for more than ten years, Mike. My contacts in the TL are old and cold." He turned to Joey and thanked him for the fish and chips. "My granddaughter is waiting for me. I don't want my soon-to-be great-grandson to be hungry."

Joey smiled. "It's good to see you, Roosevelt."

"Good to see you, too." He turned my way. "Say hi to our Public Defender. And give my best to your brother." He put on his coat, picked up his fish and chips, and headed out the door.

Joey pointed at my empty mug. "You want another?"

"No, thanks. I gotta go back to work. You got coffee?"

"Sure." He poured me a cup of Folgers. "I didn't know that you picked up the Garcia trial."

"It's an emergency." I explained that I was pinch-hitting for Nady.

"Is that why you're meeting Pete tonight?"

"It is." I glanced at my watch. "He should be here any minute."

A moment later, the back door opened, and my younger brother, Pete, walked in. He was stockier than I was with a full head of gray hair and a matching mustache. He hung up his rain-drenched bomber jacket, tugged at his denim shirt, and took a seat next to me at the bar.

He nodded at our cousin, who immediately poured him a cup of black coffee.

"Thanks, Joe," he rasped. "You okay?"

"Fine. You?"

"Not bad."

That represented a lengthy conversation for Pete. At fifty-five, he was a quarter of a century removed from his days as a beat cop in the Mission. He got fired after he and his partner broke up a gang fight with a little too much enthusiasm. Pete was still bitter about it. He got his private investigator's license and became one of the City's most tenacious P.I.s. His first marriage to a lawyer at my old law firm was a bad fit that ended quickly. His second marriage, to the chief financial officer of a different law firm, was now in its eighteenth year. Pete and Donna have had their ups and downs, but they've stuck together. Their daughter, Margaret, was named after our mother. She was a top student at Archie Williams High School in Marin County.

My brother looked at me. "You wanted to talk?"

"I need your help. Nady's mother is sick. I picked up the Lenny Garcia murder trial."

"The homeless guy who allegedly gave spiked pills to the young hooker, right?"

"Right." He still knew a lot of people at SFPD and kept up with the gossip. "Trial starts Monday. I want to hire you to do some legwork. Standard rates."

"What about the investigator from your office?"

"It was Tom Eisenmann."

His eyes turned down. "Sorry, Mick."

"Me, too. You got time?"

"Happy to help, but six days is tight, and I'm not doing field work until the virus blows over."

"You're that worried?"

"Donna and I aren't taking any chances. We still have a kid at home. The schools are talking about doing classes online. Donna's firm is making plans for employees to work at home."

"So you're staying at home?"

"We made a deal. Donna will continue to work, and I'll make sure that Margaret does her homework." He winked. "I get along a lot better with Margaret than her mother does."

When Grace was in high school, she and Rosie spent four stressful years engaged in a cold war where I reluctantly played the role of Switzerland. Rosie and I got a lot smarter when Grace turned twenty-five.

"I'd rather have you working from home than hire somebody I don't know," I said. *And I have no better options.* "Do you have contacts in the Tenderloin?"

"I have contacts everywhere, Mick."

"I need you to find an alleged drug dealer named Brian Holton who lives on U.N. Plaza."

"I'll see what I can do."

"I need you to find out who stabbed a pimp named Marcus Strong."

"That may be harder, but I'll see what I can do."

"And I need you to help me find a woman named Patty Dawson, who also worked for Strong. She was neighbors with the decedent at the El Camino Hotel on Larkin, but she's no longer living there, and she didn't leave a phone number or a forwarding address."

"And you need this ASAP?"

"The trial starts Monday, Pete."

He let out a throaty chuckle. "I'll see what I can do, Mick."

7

"YOU'RE JUMPING TO CONCLUSIONS"

"Thank you for seeing me on short notice," I said.

The District Attorney of the City and County of San Francisco nodded. "We always try to cooperate with the P.D.'s Office."

Right.

DeSean Harper sat behind a standard-issue desk in his functional office in the new D.A.'s suite in a refurbished industrial building at the base of Potrero Hill, about a mile south of the Hall. While his surroundings lacked the grandeur of the more spacious old digs at the Hall, the utilitarian building was wired for Twenty-first Century technology, and the Assistant D.A.s had private offices. More important, the plumbing was new, the heating and air conditioning worked, and there was no lead-based paint. The walls displayed photos of Harper with City politicos. The IKEA-style bookcases were filled with legal tomes which Harper used as a backdrop for his TV appearances. If he needed to look something up, he would use the laptop on his credenza.

He nodded at Andy Erickson, who was sitting in the chair next to mine, then he spoke to me in a crisp baritone. "I understand that Nady's mother is ill."

"It's probably the Coronavirus, but they don't know for sure."

"I'm sorry to hear that." His voice was sincere. "Please give her my best."

At nine-fifteen the following morning, a Wednesday, Harper was doing me a favor by granting me an audience. The alum of Cal and Harvard Law School had grown up in the projects near Candlestick Park. He was a couple of years older than I was, but three decades working in the trenches as an A.D.A. had taken a toll. He weighed more than two hundred and fifty pounds, and his closely cropped hair was completely gray. The gifted prosecutor had moved into the top slot when his longtime boss, Nicole Ward, had won a hotly contested election for mayor. Unlike Ward, Harper was more interested in putting bad guys away than running for higher office or appearing on cable news. He had announced that he would not run for re-election, which set off the customary frenzy among his subordinates and other politically ambitious lawyers who were quietly taking measurements to see if their furniture would fit in Harper's office.

I pointed at the framed photo of Harper and his daughters on his credenza. "Kids okay?"

"Everybody's fine."

His older daughter was an associate at the same megafirm in Embarcadero Center where Nady's husband worked. His younger daughter worked for Google.

He took a sip of coffee from a white mug bearing a picture of the scales of justice. "I understand that you're pinch-hitting for Nady on the Lenny Garcia murder trial."

"Correct."

Erickson spoke up. "I take it that you'll be asking Judge Powell for a continuance?"

"No."

"We won't object to an extension."

"My client has instructed me to proceed."

"You think that's wise?"

No. "It's Lenny's decision. I'm following his direction."

Harper spoke up again. "If I were in your shoes, I might reconsider."

You aren't in my shoes. "There are extenuating circumstances that make the decision more complicated." I pointed at the N95 mask on his desk. "There have been several cases of the virus down in San Bruno. One inmate died."

"They haven't determined whether his death was related to the virus."

"Lenny doesn't want to delay his case to find out. This is going to be a short trial. We'll be able to resolve his case in the next two weeks."

Harper frowned. "I trust that you aren't setting up a claim on appeal that your client's representation was inadequate. You're more than qualified, Mike."

Nice to hear. "We've always played it straight with each other, DeSean." *Well, most of the time.* "I'm not going to start playing games now."

"Good to know." He stood up and extended a hand, signaling that our conversation was coming to an end. "Thanks for coming in. Please give my best to Rosie and convey my thoughts to Nady. Andy will see you in court on Monday."

I remained seated. "I was hoping that we could discuss a couple of issues."

He lowered himself into his seat. "What did you want to talk about?"

"When will I see any final additions to your witness list?"

Erickson spoke up again. "You'll have it by the end of business tomorrow."

"Thank you." I told him that I wasn't likely to add any additional names to the list that Nady had provided, but I reserved the right to do so. "Any additional evidence that you'd like to provide?"

"No."

I didn't think so. The prosecution is obligated to disclose evidence that might tend to exonerate the accused. As a result, contrary to what you see on TV, there are relatively few genuine surprises at trial unless something new materializes at the last minute.

"You'll let me know if anything comes in?" I asked.

Erickson responded with a terse, "Of course."

"You're really going to proceed on a first-degree murder charge?"

Erickson nodded.

"There's no premeditation."

"Your client got into an argument with the victim on the night before she died. He accused her of stealing his cell phone. One of our officers witnessed the fight and was able to de-escalate the situation."

"It wasn't a fight," I said.

"She had a different view."

Nady told me that there was a witness to an alleged argument between Lenny and Annie Parker. Lenny assured me that it wasn't a big deal. "Lenny said your witness was exaggerating."

"Then you can put her on the stand to explain what happened."

"He apologized."

"After Officer Carter threatened to arrest him."

It would be her word against his. "It doesn't establish pre-meditation for murder."

"We think it does. We're prepared to let the jury decide who's telling the truth."

I had known Erickson long enough to believe that he wasn't bluffing.

"Besides," Erickson continued, "your client admitted that he gave Ms. Parker the tainted pills."

"Lenny admitted that he gave her some of his legitimate Oxy pills to help her with her pain. He had a prescription from the V.A."

"He gave her pills spiked with fentanyl."

"You have no proof that he did."

"His prints were on the bottle."

"It was *his* bottle. There were also unidentified prints. Somebody else gave her the tainted pills."

"You can try to sell that part of the story to the jury."

"There were traces of semen on her clothes. The DNA didn't match my client's."

"It means that she had sex with somebody else before he gave her the pills."

"Maybe the guy she had sex with gave her the pills."

"You can try that on the jury, too."

"You're jumping to conclusions."

"I'd rather try to sell our story to the jury than yours."

So would I. "She had a serious heart condition."

"The Chief Medical Examiner ruled that she died of an overdose."

"First-degree murder is a stretch," I said.

Harper finally spoke up again. "It's analogous to the John Belushi case."

In some respects, it was. Belushi died after a woman injected him with a lethal combination of heroin and cocaine known as a "speedball." His body was found in a bungalow at the Chateau Marmont Hotel in West Hollywood.

"The woman who gave Belushi the speedball pled to involuntary manslaughter," I said.

"The D.A. at the time of Belushi's death originally charged her with first-degree murder. After he lost the election, his successor cut her a deal for involuntary manslaughter. I thought it was wrong at the time, and I still do."

"I disagree."

"I figured you might."

I took a moment to gather my thoughts. "Why are you doing this?"

"It's a legacy issue," Harper said. "I'm retiring in eleven months. During my tenure, the Tenderloin has become a lawless, dystopian shooting gallery. People are dealing drugs with impunity. The streets are flooded with fake pills—mostly laced with fentanyl. We had more than four hundred overdose deaths last year. They're selling poison on the streets, and the residents believe that we aren't doing anything. I understand their frustrations. There aren't enough police to arrest everybody. There aren't enough EMTs to save everybody. And there aren't enough social workers to get the homeless off the streets, even if we had enough beds to house them."

I looked over at Erickson. It may have been a "legacy" issue for Harper, but it was potentially a ticket to the D.A.'s Office if Erickson used Lenny's case to burnish his bona fides with the law-and-order crowd.

"Making Lenny Garcia an example isn't going to fix the problem," I said.

"No, it won't," Harper replied, "but you have to start somewhere. Ninety-nine times out of a hundred, we can't identify the person who supplied the bad drugs, so the cops can't make an arrest, and we can't prosecute. This is a rare instance where we know who supplied the fentanyl. I want to send a message to the dealers that there will be consequences."

"Nobody has ever questioned your toughness."

"It's also a message to Annie Parker's friends and family that her life meant something and that we haven't forgotten her."

"It's a stretch, DeSean," I said.

"It's a start, Mike."

I stood up and put on my coat. "Thanks for your time." I turned to Erickson. "I trust that you have no objection if I talk to Ken Lee?" Lee was the lead homicide inspector.

"Fine with me, but he has no obligation to talk to you."

8

"HE GAVE HER SPIKED PILLS"

"Got a sec?" I asked.

At ten-thirty the same morning, Inspector Kenneth Lee walked past me in the hallway outside the Homicide Detail. "Can't talk."

I started walking with him. "Just a couple of minutes, Ken."

He kept moving. I noted that the limp from an injury sustained when he was an undercover cop in Chinatown was becoming more pronounced. Now pushing fifty, he was wearing his customary charcoal Men's Wearhouse suit. His closely cropped hair was more silver than black. The scar running across his left cheek was bright red.

"Please?" I said. "Nady's mother is sick. It's probably the Coronavirus. I'm covering the Lenny Garcia murder trial."

He stopped abruptly. "Is Nady's mother going to be okay?"

"Not sure."

"Give Nady and her mother my best."

"I will."

I wasn't surprised that Lee asked about Nady and her mother. The Hall of Justice is like a small town. A lot of people pass through, but the cops, prosecutors, defense attorneys, judges, clerks, and bailiffs know each other. Word spreads quickly when somebody is hurting, and most of the regulars are sympathetic. Even though Lee and I had faced off in court countless times, I've always respected his work, and it's never gotten personal.

"Kids okay?" I asked.

"Yes. Yours?"

"Fine."

His older daughter was a sophomore at Cal. His younger daughter was a senior at Lowell High School. He shared custody with his ex-wife, a parole officer.

"You think they're going to shut down Cal?" I asked.

He shrugged. "I wouldn't be surprised if they do classes remotely for a few weeks."

"Our office was told to make contingency plans for everybody to work remotely."

"So were we."

"How can a homicide inspector work remotely?"

"I can't. It will be even more chaotic than usual." He smirked. "At least I can deal with some of my daily headaches from the comfort of home."

It would be an overstatement to say that I liked him, but I didn't dislike him, and he usually played by the rules. At forty-eight, the Chinatown native had been an inspector for a dozen years. He began his career working undercover in the congested neighborhood where his parents owned a spice shop. He was promoted to Homicide after he brought down one of Chinatown's deadliest gangs. He was trained by Roosevelt Johnson. Lee had worked alone since Roosevelt retired.

He stopped in the quiet hallway outside the courtrooms on the second floor. On a normal Tuesday morning, the high-ceilinged corridor would be buzzing with prosecutors, police officers, sheriff's deputies, defense lawyers, witnesses, and courtroom junkies. Things had become much quieter since the virus started spreading.

Lee took a seat on the uncomfortable built-in bench next to the stairway door. "I take it this means that you're going to ask for a continuance on the Garcia case?"

"Our client doesn't want one."

"You think you can get up to speed by Monday?"

I don't have any choice. "I already am."

"To what do I owe the pleasure of your company this morning?"

"I was hoping that I could persuade you to provide a few more details about your case."

"You've read my report?"

"I have."

"Then you know everything that I know."

Not quite. "What makes you think Lenny gave her the spiked pills?"

"He admitted it."

"No, he didn't."

"He admitted that he gave her pills."

"He gave her a few real Oxy pills that he got from the V.A. He didn't give her the spiked ones."

"His name was on the bottle along with his prints. There were a half dozen pills spiked with fentanyl inside. If you can sell your version of the story to a jury, more power to you."

"Why would he have done it?"

"He got into a fight with the decedent the night before she died. He accused her of stealing his cell phone."

"It was a mistake. He apologized."

"Right."

"He told me that he gave her some real Oxy pills because she was in terrible pain. He was trying to help her."

His expression turned skeptical. "Maybe he didn't like her. Maybe he was reckless or just a jerk. At the end of the day, it doesn't matter. He threatened her the night before. He gave her illegal drugs. She died after she took them. That's murder."

"She had an irregular heartbeat that could have killed her."

"Dr. Siu did the autopsy herself and concluded that she OD'd on fentanyl."

Dr. Joy Siu was San Francisco's highly regarded Chief Medical Examiner. "Our medical expert came to a different conclusion."

"Dr. Siu usually gets it right."

"Not this time. I trust that you have no objection if I want to talk to her?"

"Be my guest, but she's under no obligation to talk to you."

"You'll never prove your case beyond a reasonable doubt."

"That's Andy Erickson's job." He lowered his voice. "Everybody knows there's a fentanyl epidemic in the Tenderloin. Hundreds of people have died over the last couple of years. Most of the time, we can't figure out who supplied the poison. This time we did."

"Did you consider any other suspects?"

"Of course." His voice filled with exasperation. "There are dozens of people within a six-block radius of U.N. Plaza who could have sold the tainted pills to the decedent."

"You only arrested one of them."

"That's because your client's name and fingerprints were on the bottle."

"I understand that there were unidentified prints on the bottle, and there was semen on the decedent's panties."

"It proves that she had sex before she died."

"Maybe the guy she slept with gave her the tainted pills."

"We didn't find a shred of evidence that was the case." He held up a hand to signal that our conversation was coming to a close. "We didn't pull your client's name out of a hat, Mike. We didn't file charges until we got the autopsy results and matched the fingerprints to your client. Andy Erickson thinks there's enough evidence to prosecute and convict. That's good enough for me. If I were in your shoes, I would talk to Andy and see if you can cut a deal. Your client has never been arrested for anything other than shoplifting and possession. Maybe Andy will cut you a break and let him plead out to manslaughter."

"I already talked to him. That isn't an option."

"Then we'll see you in court on Monday."

9

"THE TOXICOLOGY WASN'T COMPLICATED"

"Thank you for seeing me on short notice," I said.

The Chief Medical Examiner of the City and County of San Francisco nodded. "You're welcome, Mr. Daley."

I've known Dr. Joy Siu for almost a decade. The first few times that we met, I told her that she could call me by my first name, but Dr. Siu isn't a first-name person. She was wearing a surgical mask as she sat on the opposite side of a glass-topped table in a windowless conference room on the second floor of the new Medical Examiner's facility in a warehouse-like building about halfway between the ballpark and Candlestick Point. The state-of-the-art examination rooms and expanded morgue were a substantial upgrade from her outdated quarters in the basement of the Hall of Justice.

I adjusted the face covering that I was asked to put on when I entered the building. "How long do you think these masks will be necessary?"

"Too soon to tell. As you know, I'm a proponent of following the science."

"So am I."

From her pressed lab coat to her meticulously applied makeup to her precisely cut black hair, Dr. Siu embodied exactness. Now pushing fifty, the Princeton and Johns Hopkins Medical School alum and former researcher at UCSF was a world-class academic and an internationally recognized expert in anatomic pathology. The one-time Olympic figure skating hopeful spent about a quarter of her time consulting on complex autopsies around the world.

"I understand that you were in the U.K.," I said.

"I was working on a case in Salisbury. I was supposed to stay in London for a few extra days, but I came home early because of the virus. All City departments have been asked to make contingency plans for everybody to work at home for a few weeks. Obviously, my team will need to come to the office from time to time to conduct autopsies." Her brown eyes darted toward her laptop, then they returned to me. "How can I help you?"

"My colleague, Ms. Nikonova, was called down to L.A. because her mother has contracted the virus. I will be handling Lenny Garcia's trial."

"I've heard."

"I understand that you performed the autopsy on Annie Parker."

"I did. She died of a fentanyl overdose."

"Would you mind explaining your conclusion?"

"It's in my report, which I provided to Mr. Erickson, which, I presume, he gave to you."

"He did."

Her eyes narrowed above her mask. "Then you know everything that I know."

No, I don't. "How were you able to determine that Ms. Parker died of an overdose?" I was fishing for a preview of her testimony.

"The toxicology wasn't complicated. There was enough fentanyl in her system to kill someone three times her size."

"She had a heart condition."

"Unrelated to the overdose." She pulled down her mask. "Fentanyl is fifty times more potent than morphine, Mr. Daley. It's cheap and easy to produce, so it's being cut into other drugs. It's also put into fake pills that are pressed to look like the real thing. A lot of people don't know that they're ingesting it until it's too late. It's especially deadly for people who aren't regular users."

"Like Annie Parker?"

"Exactly."

"And her heart condition?"

"Her medical record indicated that she had an irregular heartbeat. If she had sought treatment, it's something that could have been controlled with medication and perhaps a minor intervention. It was an issue, but it didn't kill an otherwise healthy nineteen-year-old."

Our medical expert came to a different conclusion. "Was she pronounced at the scene?"

"Yes."

"Time of death?"

"Sometime between two and seven a.m."

"Can you narrow it down a bit?"

"No."

Medical examiners are loath to lock themselves into tight time frames. "I understand that you found semen on her clothes."

"I did."

"I understand that the DNA from the semen didn't match my client's."

"It didn't." She held up a hand. "The fact that she had sex with someone other than your client doesn't absolve your client of responsibility."

"Unless the guy she had sex with gave her the tainted pills."

"That's beyond my scope of knowledge. You're free to present evidence to that effect to the jury."

Unfortunately, I don't have any. "Defensive or other wounds?"

"None."

"We have reason to believe that her pimp beat her up more than once."

"There were no visible bruises or other injuries. She didn't die of blunt force trauma."

"Photos?"

"In my report."

"Any other wounds of any nature?"

"No."

"My client claims that he gave her some of his own Oxy pills that he got from the V.A."

"I understand that Inspector Lee has verified that your client had a legitimate prescription. The police found a pill bottle next to Ms. Parker's body with your client's name and fingerprints. It contained a half-dozen pills pressed to look like OxyContin. In reality, they were fake pills laced with enough fentanyl to kill a healthy young woman. It isn't my place to predict how a jury will react to a set of facts, and I don't give advice to smart attorneys like you. On the other hand, if I were in your shoes, I wouldn't base my defense on the theory that the decedent died of anything other than a fentanyl overdose."

Neither would I. "Any more non-advice that you'd care to pass along?"

"I would head down to the Tenderloin and see if you can identify somebody else who may have given Ms. Parker some pills." She stood up. "Please give my best to Ms. Nikonova and her mother. And take care of yourself. It looks like this virus could be quite serious."

"Thank you, Dr. Siu."

"I'll see you in court, Mr. Daley."

10

"THIS STUFF HAS TO STOP"

The imposing sergeant scratched the stubble on his face, looked across the dented metal table in the interrogation room in the basement of the Tenderloin Police Station, and spoke to me in a world-weary voice. "How's Pete?"

"Status quo," I said. "Same wife, same kid, same house, same job. He didn't have enough stress in his life, so he's teaching his daughter how to drive."

"I didn't realize that she was already a teenager. Time flies."

Sergeant A.C. Brown was about my age. He was the eldest of five sons of a single mother who worked maintenance at City College. The native of the Bayview had avoided the gangs in the southeast corner of town and applied for the police academy the day after he graduated from Balboa High. He finished near the top of his class and spent a couple of years working at Mission Station with Pete before he transferred to Bayview Station. Smart, streetwise, and driven, Brown developed a reputation for toughness and community service. In 1991, he was recruited to the new Tenderloin Task Force, which was created to address drug trafficking in the TL. The unit was originally housed in the basement of the historic Hibernia Bank Building at the corner of Market, McAllister, and Jones. In 2000, the City built a fortress-like bunker three blocks north at Eddy and Jones.

We exchanged stilted gossip for a few minutes. The twice-divorced Brown had married young and started a family when he was twenty. He was a grandfather four times over; his eldest granddaughter was a junior at Galileo High School.

"She wants to be an influencer," he said. "I told her that she could do whatever she wants after she graduates from college."

"Good call, A.C." I looked around the windowless room. "How are things in the TL?"

"Getting worse. More fentanyl. More homeless. More shoplifting. More guns. This stuff has to stop. It isn't sustainable." He scowled. "There are a lot of hardworking people in the neighborhood. They're afraid to let their kids go outside."

"Keep fighting the good fight."

"I'm trying, but there aren't enough beds to house the homeless, and there aren't enough services to deal with the drugs and mental health issues. I've been playing 'Whack-A-Mole' for three decades. When we lighten up on the drug dealers, things go crazy. When we arrest them, the D.A. puts them back on the street later the same day. In too many cases, he doesn't prosecute them. It's a revolving door. Unless things change, my successors will be doing the same thing thirty years from now."

I could only offer a cliché. "You do what you can."

"It isn't enough. You didn't come over here at five-forty-five on a Wednesday afternoon to discuss community policing. I heard you picked up the Garcia case."

"I did. I heard that you were the first officer at the scene."

"I was."

"You're on the prosecution's witness list. I was hoping that you might give me a hint as to what you're going to say."

"You know the drill, Mike. I can't tell you anything beyond what's in my report."

Sure you can. "Who found her?"

"A guy named P.J. Jenkins, a City Ambassador who works for Urban Alchemy."

Urban Alchemy is a nonprofit started in Hunters Point. The City contracts with U.A. to hire and train people to do outreach in high-crime areas such as the Tenderloin. It has grown to about a dozen branches in other U.S. cities. Many of the employees are ex-felons, recovered drug users, and formerly homeless. While the program has not been without issues, the results have been mostly positive.

"What do you think of Urban Alchemy?" I asked.

"It isn't going to solve all of our problems, but it's a solid program run by well-meaning people. Unfortunately, they don't have the manpower or the resources to address the underlying problems."

"How did Jenkins end up in Parker's tent?"

"He'd met her a couple of times. He walked by her tent on his regular rounds. When he didn't see her one morning, he did a welfare check. P.J. recognized that Ms. Parker had OD'd and gave her Narcan, but it was too late. My partner and I got there within three minutes. So did the EMTs. She was pronounced at the scene. Dr. Siu concluded that she OD'd on fentanyl."

"Was anybody else there at the time?"

"A lot of people were around. We talked to everybody we could find. Most were reluctant to get involved."

"Did you identify any other potential suspects?"

"No."

It was the answer I expected. "Did you know Lenny?"

"I'd talked to him once or twice." He said that Lenny had been arrested a few times for shoplifting and public intoxication. "He never did any time."

"Was he selling drugs?"

"He was never arrested for it."

"You didn't answer my question."

"I don't know."

"Who would know?"

"I don't know."

I find that hard to believe. "Come on, A.C. The TL is a tight community."

"The TL has the City's highest concentration of drug dealers and homeless. You'll forgive me if I can't remember everybody by name."

"Understood. Did you know Annie Parker?"

"No."

"Did you know anything about her?"

"There are hundreds of runaways like her in the TL. Some of them end up doing sex work. Others get hooked on alcohol or drugs. Unfortunately, it frequently ends badly."

"We heard that she had a falling out with her pimp. His name was Marcus Strong."

"I know. He's dead."

"Do you know who stabbed him?"

"I can't comment on an ongoing investigation."

"I'm not asking you to name any names. I'm just trying to figure out if Strong might have given Annie some spiked pills."

"We have no evidence that he did."

"I've been told that Strong beat up Annie pretty badly a few weeks before she died. Any idea why?"

"I don't know. It usually comes down to money or control or both."

"I understand that Annie used to live at the El Camino Hotel on Larkin. Her neighbor was a woman named Patty Dawson, who also worked for Strong. Did you talk to her?"

"Briefly. She confirmed that she was also working for Strong, and that she and Parker had lived in the same hotel. She told us that Parker had a fight with Strong. He took her money, and she had to move out of the hotel."

"Any chance that she had something to do with Annie's death?"

"We found no evidence that she did."

"Did she think that Strong had anything to do with Parker's death?"

"She didn't know, and she didn't provide any evidence."

It was a more circumspect answer than I had anticipated. "I'd like to talk to Ms. Dawson."

"You'll have to find her first. She disappeared after Strong was killed."

It's almost impossible to disappear nowadays. "Couldn't you trace her phone?"

"We've tried. She must be using a burner."

"Credit or debit cards?"

"Nope." He glanced at his watch, suggesting that our conversation was coming to an end.

"Is there anybody I should talk to down at U.N. Plaza who knows the players?"

He frowned. "I'm afraid not, Mike."

"My trial starts Monday. If you were in my shoes, who would you talk to who knows what's going on down there?"

He hesitated. "There's a guy named Brian Holton who has lived on U.N. Plaza for a long time."

There's that name again.

Brown was still talking. "He grew up in the Excelsior and used to work at his father's auto body shop. Then he got into heroin and meth and went off the rails. When he's straight, he's a decent guy who keeps an eye on people in the neighborhood. When he's not, he's a train wreck."

"How often is he straight?"

"Not very."

"Is he dealing fentanyl?"

"Not as far as I know."

"You think he might know who is dealing on U.N. Plaza?"

"Probably."

"You got a phone number?"

"Afraid not."

"Where can I find him?"

"U.N. Plaza."

11

"IT WAS MORE THAN I COULD HANDLE"

A cold winter wind made my face raw as I was leaving Tenderloin Station.

Pete's name appeared on my phone. "Where are you?" he asked.

"Heading back to the office. You?"

"Home. I set up a couple of computers in the garage. It's a little cold, but it'll do for now. Did you get anything useful from A.C. Brown?"

"Not really." I ducked into the doorway of a closed sandwich shop and pressed the phone against my ear. "He said that I should try to find a guy named Brian Holton who knows who's who and what's what on U.N. Plaza. Ever met him?"

"Afraid not." He lowered his voice. "You aren't thinking of going down there, are you?"

"If I have to."

"Don't even think about going at night. Even during the daytime, it isn't a good idea."

"You got anybody working down in the TL?"

"At the moment, no."

"Do you think one of your usual operatives might be willing to help me?"

"Afraid not, Mick. I don't ask my people to do stuff that I'm not willing to do myself."

Good policy. "Can you make a few calls and see if anybody knows anything about Annie Parker?"

"Already started."

"Can you see if anybody has any info on who stabbed Marcus Strong?"

"I'll ask. Anything else, Mick?"

"Can you get me a photo of Brian Holton?"

"Let me see what I can do."

The P.D.'s Office was quiet at eight-forty-five the same night. I studied the prosecution's witness list and took a sip of the Diet Dr Pepper that I allowed myself only once a week—doctor's orders. The caffeine and chemicals were bad for my sleeping habits and stomach. It was a substantial change from the days where I would consume at least two cans a day.

Terrence "The Terminator" knocked on my open door. "You need anything, Mike?"

"I'm good, T."

"I'm going to head home."

"Thanks for staying late."

"No worries. You really going to trial on Monday?"

"Yes."

"You got anything?"

"Working on it, T."

He smiled. "You'll find something, Mike."

I was working on witness selection strategy at nine-fifteen the same night when my phone vibrated again. The display indicated that it was an unknown caller. I figured that somebody wanted to sell me an extended warranty for my car, but I decided to answer on the off chance that it might have been one of Pete's operatives in the Tenderloin.

"Michael Daley speaking."

The woman's voice sounded tired. "It's Perlita Garcia, Lenny's sister. I'm sorry it took so long to return your call."

"No worries. Thank you for getting back to me." I had left a message for her after I met with Nady. I didn't expect her to provide evidence to exonerate her brother, but she was Lenny's only family, so I felt an obligation to reach out. "I'm sorry for troubling you at home."

"I'm still at work, Mr. Daley."

"Mike."

"Perlita. I don't know what Lenny told you, but I'm a nurse at Seton Hospital in Daly City. You'll have to forgive me if I can't talk for long. We're getting overwhelmed with Coronavirus cases, and my break is almost over."

"Thank you for taking the time. It must be very stressful."

"It is. This virus is very serious."

The initial predictions that the virus would be no worse than the flu might be premature. "I wanted to let you know that Lenny's trial is starting on Monday."

"Thank you."

"Is there anybody else that I should contact?"

"No."

"I was hoping that you might be able to come to the trial for a bit to provide a little moral support. It would mean a lot to Lenny."

She let out a heavy sigh. "I'm sorry, Mr. Daley. I just can't do it."

I let her answer hang for a moment, and she felt inclined to fill the void.

"I don't know how much Lenny told you about me. I'm a single mother of a six-year-old daughter. I'm working double shifts because of the virus, and everybody here is exhausted. We've been told that it's likely to get much worse. Even if I could get some time off—which I can't—I'm not going to put myself, my daughter, and my colleagues at risk by going down to the Hall of Justice. If I'm going to get sick, I'm going to do it at home with my daughter or taking care of my patients." Her tone softened. "I'm sorry if this sounds harsh, but you caught me at a very difficult time."

"Understood. Lenny told me that you gave him a lot of support over the years."

"I tried. I paid for three trips to rehab. I was going through my divorce when he dropped out the third time. It was more than I could handle."

"I understand."

"Thank you, Mr. Daley."

She reminded me of my baby sister, Mary, who taught first grade in L.A. She got married to her high school sweetheart after she graduated from college. Things started great, then Danny starting drinking and cheating. When the drinking got out of hand, he became abusive. Mary paid for multiple trips to rehab, but Danny kept relapsing. After an acrimonious divorce, I had to get a restraining order to keep him away from Mary. When that didn't work, Pete and a couple of his best operatives went down to L.A. and "had a word" with him. I'm not sure what Pete told him, but Danny never bothered Mary again.

Her voice quivered. "Lenny is a good guy who got in over his head when he came back from Afghanistan. If he gave those pills to that young woman, he did it because he was trying to help her. If they contained fentanyl, I'm sure that he didn't know about it. Or it was an accident. After everything that he saw in the Army, he wouldn't hurt anybody."

I could feel a lump forming in my throat. "I'll give Lenny your best," I said.

"Thank you, Mr. Daley. I have to get back to my patients."

12

"WE NEED A PLAN"

Sylvia Fernandez marched into her cramped dining room and put a plate of chicken enchiladas in front of me. "How is Nady's mother?"

"In intensive care, but not on a ventilator."

She frowned. "I don't like it. Will they let Nady see her?"

"Only on Facetime."

"I don't like that, either. This virus is serious."

Rosie looked up from her phone. "They say it'll pass in a few weeks, Mama."

"That's what they said about the Spanish flu in 1918. My parents were teenagers when it happened. My father lost his brother. When all was said and done, three hundred thousand people died—and that's just the ones they recorded. There were probably a lot more."

"It may not be so bad, Mama."

"I hope you're right, Rosita."

Sylvia was born eighty-five years earlier in Monterrey, Mexico. My ex-mother-in-law was an older, stockier, and equally intense version of Rosie. At twenty-four, Sylvia and her late husband, Eduardo, a carpenter, made their way to San Francisco's Mission District along with Rosie's brother, Tony, who was six months old at the time. Rosie was born a couple of years later. Sylvia and Eduardo worked hard and saved for a down payment on the little house that cost twenty-four thousand dollars. Today, Sylvia could sell it to a tech entrepreneur for almost two million, but she's made it abundantly clear that she has no intention of ever doing so.

She looked at Rosie. "Are you sending everybody home?"

"Probably, Mama."

"For how long?"

"At least a couple of weeks. We'll see how it goes."

She pointed at me. "Does that include Michael?"

"Yes, except he's agreed to stop by the office from time to time to check the mail. Terrence has volunteered to help him."

"Do you think that's wise?"

"People commit crimes during pandemics. We can't shut the criminal justice system down entirely."

"Maybe the criminals will be afraid to go out because of the virus."

Rosie grinned. "Maybe."

Sylvia's serious expression didn't change. "I don't want Rolanda going to the office. It's too risky with a baby at home."

Sylvia's granddaughter, Rolanda, was the co-head of the Felony Division at the P.D.'s Office. Tony was her father. Rolanda had been on maternity leave for six months to take care of her daughter, Maria Sylvia Teresa Fernandez Epstein. Sylvia's great-granddaughter was a beauty who had inherited Sylvia's brains, stubbornness, and independent streak.

"I extended her maternity leave," Rosie said.

"For how long?"

"Indefinitely."

Sylvia finally smiled. "Good."

At ten-forty-five on Wednesday night, the aroma of Sylvia's homemade salsa and tortillas wafted in from the tiny kitchen in the two-bedroom, one-bath bungalow where the plaster walls were covered with photos of four generations of the Fernandez clan. Rosie, Tony, and I had joined Sylvia in the stucco house across the street from Garfield Square Park.

Sylvia took her seat at the head of the table and nodded at Tony, who was picking at his food. The one-time Marine was a savvy businessman who owned a successful fruit and vegetable stand a half-block north of St. Peter's Catholic Church, which Sylvia had attended for sixty years. Tony's wife, Maria, had died of cancer almost twenty years earlier. He had a long-term relationship with a woman who ran a boutique on the upscale strip of Valencia Street on the western end of the Mission. For the last six months, he had reveled in his new role as a grandfather.

"Is the City going to allow you to stay open?" Sylvia asked him.

"Yes, Mama. People have to eat."

"What about your staff?"

"We'll keep everybody on as long as we can. We may have to limit the number of customers in the store. We already get a lot of online orders. I'm going to set it up for a lot of pickups and deliveries."

"What about your suppliers?"

"Everything is holding up so far."

When the Mission started to gentrify two decades earlier, Tony added a selection of upscale organic produce. His old-time customers still bought the regular fruits and vegetables. The tech kids and venture capitalists were happy to pay a premium for the fancy stuff.

Sylvia turned back to me. "Rosita tells me that you're starting a murder trial on Monday."

"I'm covering for Nady on the Lenny Garcia case."

"The courts are still open?"

"For now."

"Can't you ask for a continuance?"

"Our client wants to proceed. He's been in jail for over a year."

"I understand that he gave a young woman some painkillers laced with fentanyl."

"He gave her some painkillers that he got from the V.A. He claims that somebody else gave her the tainted pills."

"You believe him?"

I never try to BS my ex-mother-in-law. "I don't know, Sylvia."

She eyed me. "You aren't planning to look for witnesses in the Tenderloin, are you?"

"Only if it's absolutely necessary."

She shot a glance at Rosie, then she turned back to me. "I want you to be extra careful, Michael. I don't want you to infect yourself, your kids, Rosita, Tony, Rolanda, or the baby." She waited a beat before she added, "Or, for that matter, me."

"I promise, Sylvia."

She gave me her "Don't even think about messing with me" stare, which Rosie had appropriated. "I mean it, Michael. Think about what your mother would have told you to do."

My mom, Margaret Dunleavy Daley, had been gone almost ten years, my dad twenty-four. They had grown up when the Mission was still filled with working-class Irish and Italian families. We lived in a two-bedroom apartment until I was seven, when we moved to a three-bedroom house two blocks from Big John's saloon. Around the same time, many of the Irish and Italian families moved out, and the Latino families (including Rosie's) moved in. The neighborhood was changing again as tech workers were squeezing out the Latino community. The only constant was St. Peter's.

Rosie finished her iced tea and looked at her mother. "Mama, we need a plan to deal with the virus."

"I already have one, Rosita. I'm staying home unless it's absolutely necessary. The only people allowed inside my house until further notice are you, Michael, Tony, Rolanda, and the baby. I'll order everything I need from Safeway and Amazon. Tony will keep me stocked with vegetables and fruit. Benny the Butcher will deliver meat." Her expression indicated that the topic was no longer open to discussion.

"What about doctor appointments?" Rosie asked.

Tony spoke up. "I've got them covered."

Rosie turned to her mom and softened her tone. "I don't want you to be lonely, Mama. I worry about you."

"I worry about you, too, honey." Sylvia held up a hand. "I talk to you and the kids mostly by phone and on Facetime anyway. I don't want to risk infecting anybody, and I don't want you to worry about infecting me. They'll probably get this under control in a few weeks. It isn't as if they're asking us to jump out of airplanes to land on Omaha Beach, Rosita. We've been through a lot worse than wearing masks and staying home and watching Netflix for a few weeks."

Sylvia always says that wisdom comes with age.

Rosie smiled. "What about your mahjongg game?"

"There will be no interruption, dear. Char has already set it up to play online. Marge's daughter found a new supplier on Valencia with free delivery."

Sylvia and a rotating cast of her neighbors had been playing mahjongg on Sunday nights since Rosie was in grammar school. Sylvia was the youngest of the group. Mercedes Crosskill was in her late eighties. Marge Gilbert and Flo Hoffenberg were both in their early nineties. Char Saper had recently turned ninety-five. A few years ago, at the suggestion of Ann-Helen Leff, a ninety-year-old hippie, great-grandmother, and lifelong rabble rouser, they switched the refreshments from sherry to marijuana. Sylvia likes to say that she's gotten more adaptable as she's gotten older.

I saw the twinkle in Rosie's eye as she lost yet another argument to her mother—the only person who ever bested her in debating. Rosie reached over and touched her mother's hand. "Sounds like you have everything under control, Mama."

"Thank you, Rosita. I knew that you would see it my way."

Rosie pushed out her chair and stood up. "I need to get home, Mama. I have to finish my contingency plan for putting the office on work-from-home status."

"We'll get through this, Rosita."

"Yes, we will, Mama."

Sylvia turned my way. "Good luck with your trial, Michael."

"Your mom was feisty tonight," I observed.

Rosie smiled as she took a sip of Cab Franc. "You expected anything less?"

At eleven-twenty the same night, we were sitting at the kitchen table in Rosie's post-Earthquake bungalow in Larkspur, a leafy suburb about ten miles north of the Golden

Gate Bridge. Rosie had rented the house after she and I split up, and I moved into an apartment a couple of blocks away behind the fire station. Since the Public Defender was required to have an "official" residence in San Francisco, Rosie also leased a studio apartment down the street from her mother's house. I spent most nights here with Rosie, but I kept my apartment when we needed a little space. On occasion, we met up at the studio for "staff meetings."

"You okay with her contingency plan?" I asked.

"It seems like a reasonable precaution." The light from the embers in the fireplace danced off her eyes. "Tony and I will check in on her every day. Hopefully, things will get back to normal pretty soon."

"Hopefully. Are you going to be okay?"

"Of course."

"Anything I can do to help?"

"Keep doing your job, Mike. Get an acquittal for Lenny Garcia. And for God's sake, don't you dare get sick."

"Seems like a good plan."

"It's the best we can do. For the moment, I'm simply trying to stay safe, sane, and solvent." She finished her wine. "You want to stay tonight?"

"Yes."

The house seemed bigger since Grace moved out and Tommy had gone off to college.

"Is there a 'but' coming?" she asked.

"I need to pick up some stuff at my apartment. And I have to be up at the crack of dawn."

"Are you planning to look for witnesses in the Tenderloin?"

"Yes."

She shook her head. "As your boss, I find your dedication to your job admirable. On a personal level, however, I find your decision unwise." She leaned forward and kissed me. "I want you to be extra careful, Mike."

"I will, Rosie."

I was lying in bed at two-thirty a.m. when my phone vibrated. I looked over and saw Pete's name on the display.

"You're up late," I said.

"I'm going to text you a photo of Brian Holton. My source says that you should be able to find him on U.N. Plaza most mornings."

"Thanks, Pete."

"You're welcome. Don't go down there at night."

"I won't."

"And don't do anything stupid that might get you killed."

13

"WHO'S ASKING?"

A burly City maintenance worker adjusted his gray jumpsuit highlighted by fluorescent orange stripes. "You might want to wait around the corner until I'm finished," he said.

"Thanks," I said. "I'll be fine."

A blast of cold wind hit my face and the aroma of urine permeated the area in front of the statue of Simón Bolivar on U.N. Plaza at seven-fifteen the next morning. Natives like me would describe the precipitation falling from the sky as a heavy mist. The tourists would call it fog. Everybody else would call it rain.

He put on an industrial-strength mask and activated his pressure washer. "You really should get out of the way unless you want to smell like urine for the rest of the day."

"Thanks." I gestured at the haphazard array of tents, sleeping bags, tarps, lean-tos, and lawn chairs lining the red-brick plaza between the back side of the Orpheum Theater and the Federal Building. "How often do you clean up here?"

"Every morning." He nodded at the majestic dome of City Hall, two blocks west on the opposite side of Civic Center Plaza. "If the Mayor is coming to the plaza, we'll wash it down again before she arrives." He rolled his eyes. "We could wash it ten times a day. It always looks like this when we get here in the morning."

"We appreciate your efforts."

"Thank you." He grabbed his equipment. "Haven't seen you before. You a cop?"

"Even worse: I'm a lawyer, and I'm looking for somebody." I pulled out my phone and showed him a photo of Brian Holton. "Ever seen this guy?"

He studied the picture. He pointed at the fountain adjacent to the perpetually broken escalator to the Civic Center BART Station. "He's usually over there."

I approached the slightly built man of indeterminate middle age sitting on a lawn chair in front of a tattered tent adjacent to the BART Station. "Are you Brian?"

He lowered his burner phone and played with the strings of his black Giants hoodie. "Who's asking?"

"Mike Daley. I'm with the Public Defender's Office. I'm representing Lenny Garcia."

He flashed a smile, exposing a set of perfectly aligned teeth stained with tobacco. "What happened to the young woman who was handling Lenny's case?"

"She was called away on a family emergency. We're starting Lenny's trial on Monday."

"You gonna get him off?"

"I'm not sure. I was hoping you might be able to help me."

He responded with a full-throated laugh that quickly transformed into a smoker's cough. "You think I killed Annie Parker?"

"No, but I think you might be able to help me find the person who did."

"The cops think Lenny did."

"Lenny tells me that they're wrong."

"If Lenny didn't give her the pills, who did?"

"That's what I'm trying to find out."

"And you think I'm going to give you the answer a year after Annie died?"

"Probably not." I kept my voice even. "I need your help, Brian. Lenny tells me that you know everybody in the neighborhood."

"It's a big neighborhood."

"I have to start somewhere. Let me buy you something to eat and ask you a few questions. If you can help me, great. If not, at least you'll have a decent breakfast."

He thought about it for a moment. "I'm in."

"How long have you been living in the plaza?" I asked.

Holton took a sip of black coffee from a white mug. "About five years."

Under normal circumstances, I would bring an investigator with me when I interviewed a witness in case I needed somebody to corroborate their story in court. Unfortunately, the circumstances were not normal, so I had to fly solo.

Holton's voice was businesslike as he explained that he had grown up in the Excelsior and gone to work at his father's auto body shop after he graduated from high school. "I'm dyslexic, so I had trouble in school. I was also more interested in partying than studying. I didn't like working for my dad, who was a hardass and an alcoholic who took out his frustrations on my mom." He said that he started drinking when he was in high school. That led to marijuana and then more potent drugs. "My dad dropped dead of a heart attack, and my mom drank to dull the pain. By then, I was doing coke and trying heroin. Then my mom died, and I discovered that my parents had left me with more debt than money. The landlord evicted me, and the creditors took everything. I had a couple of jobs that didn't work out. That's when I ended up over here."

"You still doing heroin?" I asked.

"I spend most of my money on bourbon. It goes down easier."

"I can help you get into a program."

"I've tried."

"I can help you find a place to live."

"I've tried that, too." He shrugged. "I'm not good at obeying rules."

We were sitting at a table next to the wall in the aptly named Local Diner, a nondescript coffee shop between two empty storefronts on Market Street. The southwest corner of the Tenderloin has been gentrifying in fits and starts for the last twenty-five years and remains in flux. We had walked past the Orpheum Theater where *Hamilton* was playing. The century-old low-rise buildings across the street were torn down to make way for upscale apartments and a Whole Foods. The Earthquake-era Whitcomb Hotel had been refurbished into an upscale boutique. The City had shut down the Burger King after the cops finally acknowledged something that most of us already knew: they were selling more drugs than Whoppers. A block west, a high-rise housing Dolby Sound sat across the street from the headquarters of Twitter.

I inhaled the sweet aroma of eggs, bacon, and coffee. Local Diner's neon sign boasted that it had the "best breakfast in town." While that may have been a slight exaggeration, the coffee shop where you ordered at the counter and sat at one of a dozen mismatched tables served hearty fare. It would never be featured on the Food Channel, but the eggs, omelets, pancakes, and waffles were cooked to order, and our server, Pamphillo, was friendly.

I took a bite of my hash browns. "How well did you know Lenny?"

"Not well." Holton looked out the window at Market Street. "I'd seen him around."

"You think he would have slipped Annie Parker some spiked pills?"

"I don't know." He sipped his coffee. "He seemed like an okay guy, but you never know."

"Was he selling fentanyl?"

"Not as far as I know."

I asked him if he knew Annie Parker.

"I talked to her a few times. She seemed like a nice kid going through a tough time." He devoured a piece of sourdough toast and confirmed that she had come to town from Modesto and hooked up with Marcus Strong.

"Did you know him?"

"I'd met him."

"I heard he was a bad guy."

"Really bad." He confirmed that Strong preyed on young women in the TL.

"Any idea who stabbed him?"

"Afraid not."

"You think he was the kind of guy who would have slipped her some spiked pills?"

"Wouldn't surprise me. He was definitely the kind of guy who would have beaten the crap out of her."

"Can you point me to anybody who knew him?"

"Everybody knew him. I tried to stay away from him."

"We heard that Annie was neighbors at the El Camino Hotel with a woman named Patty Dawson who was also one of Strong's women. Do you know her?"

"I met her once or twice."

"Any idea where we can find her?"

"Last I heard, she left town. I have no idea where she went."

"Who might know?"

"Not a clue."

Not helpful. I finished my eggs. "I appreciate your help, Brian. I understand that you told my colleague that you might be willing to testify at Lenny's trial."

"I don't have any relevant information."

"I need you to confirm that Strong was a bad guy."

"I need to think about it." The corner of his mouth turned up. "If you're willing to compensate me for my time, we might be able to work something out."

"Deal." I pulled out my wallet, took out five twenties, and slid them across the table along with my business card. "Here's an advance on your testimony. If there's anybody else who I should talk to, I would appreciate it if you let me know."

He pocketed the cash. "I will."

14

"SHE DOESN'T LIVE HERE ANYMORE"

The young woman with short black hair, black lipstick, and a gold nose ring looked up from her phone and glared at me from behind a Plexiglas shield. "Yes?"

"I'm trying to locate a former resident named Patty Dawson." I slid my business card through the slot under the Plexiglas. "My name is Michael Daley. I'm with the Public Defender's Office. I'm representing Lenny Garcia."

She looked me up and down. "She doesn't live here anymore."

"How long ago did she move out?"

"I don't remember."

"I understand that Ms. Dawson was friends with another former tenant: Annie Parker."

"Could be."

You know more than you're letting on. "Ms. Parker died of a fentanyl overdose on U.N. Plaza a little over a year ago."

"I'll take your word for it."

At nine-thirty the same morning, a Thursday, I was standing in the narrow hallway of the El Camino Hotel, a five-story post-Earthquake structure at the corner of Larkin and Turk, catty-corner to the Stalinesque Phillip Burton Federal Building and Courthouse, and two blocks north of Civic Center Plaza. If you looked closely, you could see the intricate masonry and brickwork indicating that the El Camino was once a nice hotel. A hundred years of deferred maintenance later, it provided modest accommodations in cramped rooms with bathrooms down the hall. As SROs go, it didn't look too bad.

I looked at the stairway where the banister had been ripped from a wall that hadn't been painted in decades. No light filtered through the steel plates reinforcing the heavy wooden door, and many of the old-fashioned light bulbs were not working. The aroma of Pine-Sol, cigarettes, and urine wafted through the cramped space with linoleum floors and no furniture.

I tried again. "It's important that I find Ms. Dawson. She has information that may be helpful to my client. I understand that she knew a man named Marcus Strong."

She looked up from her game of Candy Crush. "Never heard of him."

"Somebody stabbed him in the alley behind this hotel about six months ago."

The telltale hesitation. "Oh yeah. I don't know anything about it."

"Did you ever meet him?"

"I don't know. A lot of people pass through."

"Ms. Dawson worked for him. So did the young woman who died."

"Wouldn't surprise me. Marcus had a lot of girls working for him."

"So you did know him?"

"I knew who he was. Bad guy. Pimping. Stealing. Extortion."

"Drugs?"

"Probably."

I decided to level with her. "I have reason to believe that Strong gave some tainted pills to Ms. Parker. It was enough to kill her."

"Then why is your client charged with murder?"

"He gave her some clean pills earlier that night. I want to ask Ms. Dawson about it."

"Why would she talk to you?"

Good question. "To help us find the truth about what happened to her friend. And because it's the right thing to do."

"Ask the cops."

"I did. They can't find her." I inhaled the heavy air. "My client's trial starts Monday."

She thought about it for a moment. "Last I heard, she was working at the Mitchell Brothers."

The Mitchell Brothers O'Farrell Theatre was, in its own unique way, a Tenderloin institution. In 1969, two brothers named Jim and Artie Mitchell started showing X-rated movies in a converted Pontiac dealership at O'Farrell and Polk. Three weeks later, they were arrested for obscenity for the first time. After a circus-like trial, the jury deadlocked, and the boys were set free. The Mitchells also started producing porn films. They hired a wholesome nineteen-year-old model named Marilyn Chambers to star in their first feature, *Behind the Green Door*. According to legend, Chambers had once appeared on Ivory Snow detergent boxes. It cost the boys sixty grand to make the film. It went on to make fifty million.

Flush with cash and facing a competitive film market, the Mitchells pivoted and turned the O'Farrell into a state-of-the-art club with strippers, private rooms, and lap dancers. The brothers were arrested more than two hundred times, but they always managed to skate free with assistance from their attorney Michael Kennedy. On the club's thirtieth anniversary, Marilyn Chambers returned for a celebratory performance that Mayor Willie Brown dubbed, "Marilyn Chambers Day." The Mitchells' longtime friend, gonzo journalist Hunter S. Thompson, called the Theatre the "Carnegie Hall of public sex."

The fun and games came to a tragic end in 1991 when Jim fatally shot Artie. Michael Kennedy defended Jim on the murder charge and convinced the jury to convict on the lesser charge of voluntary manslaughter. The Theatre remained open while Jim did six years at San Quentin.

"Is Patty Dawson still working at the Theatre?" I asked.

"I don't know."

Pete answered my call on the first ring. "Where are you, Mick?"

"The Tenderloin."

"At least you didn't go at night."

"I'm being careful." A brisk wind made my eyes water as I walked through the homeless encampment in front of the El Camino. I told Pete about my conversations with Holton and the desk clerk. "Do you know anybody at the Mitchell Brothers?"

"Ask for Bruno." He chuckled. "Be sure to tell him that you're my brother."

15

"I HAVEN'T SEEN HER"

My head ached at ten-fifteen on Thursday morning as I trudged down Polk and crossed O'Farrell, where I paused to admire the faded fantasy mural on the exterior wall of the Mitchell Brothers O'Farrell Theatre. I've always thought that it was incongruous for a strip club to be decorated with a painting of flying fish, turtles, and whales with a silhouette of San Francisco Bay in the background. Not surprisingly, the whimsical aquatic scene was tagged with graffiti.

I turned and headed east on O'Farrell. There was a new high-rise apartment complex on the north side of the street that seemed out of place—an example of the sporadic attempts at gentrification. I wondered how many people paid north of two grand a month to live in a studio apartment with an unobstructed view of the Mitchell Brothers. The south side of O'Farrell looked much the same as it did a century earlier, although the businesses had changed. In addition to the Theatre, the two- and three-story buildings housed a smoke shop, a knockoff jewelry store, a Vietnamese community center, and a converted vaudeville house called the Great American Music Hall, which was once a regular stop for the Grateful Dead and continued to host mainstream acts. In between were several SROs.

I pulled up my collar and made my way around a half-dozen homeless people. I walked under the marquee bearing photos of four scantily clad women above a caption reading "O'Farrell Theatre: Where the Wild Girls Are."

I tried the handle of the heavy door protected by steel bars. To my surprise it was unlocked. I entered the musty lobby which resembled a fifties movie house. The walls were covered with velvet drapes that needed a cleaning. There was a ticket window to my left, a bar to my right. Three doorways led into the Theatre. A discreet sign noted the entrance to the "private areas." The linoleum floor was sticky. The aroma of cleaning solvent overwhelmed the faint smell of cigarettes from a generation ago.

As my eyes were adjusting to the darkness, a young woman sporting workout clothes and carrying a gym bag bearing the Nike logo walked out of the seating area and gave me a half smile. "They take deliveries in the back at the loading dock."

"I'm not a deliveryman."

"Sorry. We're closed. The first show starts at two."

"I'm not here for the show. I'm looking for somebody."

She flashed a practiced smile. "We're all looking for somebody, hon."

Yes, we are. And it's been a long time since somebody called me "hon." "I need to speak to Bruno."

"I'm not sure that he's here."

"Could you please find out, Ms.—,"

"Cindy," she said. She didn't offer a last name. "May I tell him what this is regarding?"

I handed her a card and played it straight. "My name is Michael Daley. I'm a Public Defender representing a man named Lenny Garcia whose trial starts on Monday. I'm looking for a woman named Patty Dawson. I understand that she works here."

"She used to. I haven't seen her in about six months."

"Did you know her well?"

"I met her a couple of times. She didn't work here very long."

"Do you know why she left?"

"You'll have to ask Bruno."

"Do you have any idea where I might find her?"

"You'll have to ask Bruno."

Got it. "Would you mind telling him that I'm here?"

"Uh, sure."

"Would you also please tell him that I got his name from Pete Daley?"

A look of recognition. "How do you know Pete?"

"He's my brother."

This time her smile was genuine. "Tell him that Cindy says hi."

"I will." I wondered how many of her co-workers were on a first-name basis with my brother.

She picked up her bag. "Wait here, hon. I'll see if Bruno is around."

The stocky African-American man sat across from me at one of the round tables in the empty auditorium that would be filled with lights, music, and nudity a few hours later. With his spiked hair, James Harden beard, and muscular arms the size of my thighs, Bruno King looked like he could have gone toe-to-toe with Terrence "The Terminator."

He spoke to me in a high-pitched voice. "Haven't seen your brother lately."

"I didn't realize that he was a regular."

"He doesn't come for the dancing anymore. He comes for information." A smile appeared through the beard. "When he was younger, he used to stay for the shows."

The Mitchell Brothers was more depressing in the daytime than at night. The lights were on, the tables and chairs were pushed against the walls, and a custodian was mopping the floor. A technician tested the microphones, and a stagehand adjusted the lighting. The heavy air smelled of sweat and mildew.

King chuckled. "Pete spent more time here when he was a cop. He wasn't the only one."

Depending on who was sitting in the Mayor's Office, the police were sometimes encouraged to make life difficult for strip clubs. Mayor Dianne Feinstein was especially hard on what she referred to as "adult entertainment venues." My dad had performed similar duties a half-century earlier. It was hardly a newsflash that some of San Francisco's Finest also frequented the clubs while they were off duty.

"Pete is married and has a teenage daughter," I told him. "They live in Marin County where it's harder to get into trouble."

"Sounds like he should come down here more often."

"Maybe so." I asked him how long he'd worked at the Mitchell Brothers.

"Almost thirty years. Jim and Artie hired me to work security at the door. Then I tended bar. Eventually, I became a part-time DJ. Nowadays, I'm the daytime manager." He held up a hand. "I play guitar for a couple of bands, but we've never made any real money. This is a steady gig that pays the bills."

"How's business?" I asked.

"Lousy, and it's going to get worse. It isn't like the days when Jim and Artie opened this place. People can see whatever they want on their phones for free. The neighborhood's gotten worse, and everybody is nervous about the China virus." He told me that he had grown up in the Bayview, was divorced, and had a seventeen-year-old daughter who lived with his ex-wife in South City.

I asked him if his daughter knew that he worked at the Mitchell Brothers.

"Of course."

"How does she feel about it?"

"Not great." He shrugged. "You got kids?"

"A twenty-five-year-old daughter and a twenty-year-old son."

"Then you understand that my job is only one of my many deficiencies."

I smiled. "Nobody gets through the teenage years unscathed, Bruno."

He let out a hearty laugh before his expression turned serious. "You didn't come here to give me parenting advice."

"I'm representing a man named Lenny Garcia. His trial starts Monday."

"I read about it." He said that he'd never met Lenny.

"I'm looking for a woman who used to work here. Her name is Patty Dawson. She knew the decedent. She may have some information that might be useful for Lenny's case."

He frowned. "Patty was a nice kid and a good hostess. The customers liked her."

"How long did she work here?"

"A couple of weeks. Then she stopped showing up." He held up a hand. "Many of our employees have worked here for years, but others come and go pretty quickly."

"Do you know anything about her?"

"She grew up in Salinas. She got into drugs when she was in high school and came to the City to get away from an abusive father. She ended up doing sex work to pay her bills. She had a room in a hotel on Larkin. Then she had a falling out with her pimp, and she needed a job. I liked her, so I decided to give her a chance." He shrugged. "And then she stopped coming to work."

"She was living in the same building as the decedent in my case. They had the same pimp: Marcus Strong."

He raised an eyebrow. "I've heard the name. Somebody stabbed him last year."

"Was he the kind of guy who gave fentanyl to his girls?"

"Wouldn't surprise me."

"Do you have any idea where I can find her?"

"Afraid not." He said that he didn't have a phone number or contact information.

"Any suggestions about where I should look?"

"She may be living on the street. Start here and work your way out block by block."

"My trial starts Monday."

"Maybe you should have Pete make the rounds here in the neighborhood."

"He's staying home until the virus passes."

"Realistically, it may be a better use of your time to focus on other parts of your case."

Probably true. "Is there anybody I can talk to who has info on homeless people? Maybe one of the ambassadors that the City hires for outreach?"

He thought about it for a moment. "There's a guy at City Hall named Kyle Adams who runs the City's outreach activities. He supervises the programs run by Urban Alchemy and has developed a database of contact information for some of the homeless."

"How do you know him?"

"He works with the business community here in the TL. He's putting together some pilot programs to deal with the homeless." He winked. "And he's a customer."

I was reasonably sure that he wasn't the only person at City Hall who patronized the Mitchell Brothers. "I'd love to talk to him."

King took out his phone, punched his speed dial, and pressed it to his ear. "Kyle, it's Bruno. Fine, thanks. I need a favor. A lawyer friend of mine is looking for somebody who may be in your database. I would appreciate it if you would help him."

He listened attentively for a moment, nodding, and repeating, "uh-huh" several times. He concluded by saying, "Thanks very much, Kyle."

He ended the call and looked at me. "He'll see you at eleven-forty-five. Room ten in the basement of City Hall."

"Thanks, Bruno."

"You're welcome, Mike." He stood up. "Give my best to Pete."

16

"IT'S COMPLICATED"

The clean-cut young man sitting behind a gunmetal gray desk in a windowless office in the basement of City Hall stood up, gave me a firm handshake, and greeted me with an enthusiastic, "Kyle Adams."

"Mike Daley. I'm with the P.D.'s Office. Thanks for seeing me."

"You're welcome." He adjusted the collar of his powder blue oxford cloth shirt and absent-mindedly stroked his salt-and-pepper hair, which he wore in a manicured buzzcut. "Always happy to do a favor for Bruno."

I decided to lay it on a little thicker. "He spoke very highly of you."

"Good to hear." He flashed a practiced smile showing perfect white teeth. "He's been a respected businessman in our community for years. We try to keep our constituents happy."

Smooth. "I've seen you on TV." *A small lie. On my way here, I googled him.*

"A couple of years ago, the Mayor hired me to address homeless issues."

"You're the City's 'Homeless Czar'?"

"My boss is the 'Homeless Czar.' I'm the 'Outreach Czar.' I coordinate our programs with Urban Alchemy and our other partners to offer services to our unhoused community and mitigate the impacts of our homeless constituencies."

"I appreciate your efforts. We need guys like you."

"We're all public servants trying to do our jobs."

Except I try to conduct my public service without the false modesty. I looked around the spartan office between the boiler room and the men's restroom. Its mismatched furniture, peeling paint, and water-stained ceiling contrasted with the marble hallways and the majestic rotunda upstairs. "Reminds me of the old P.D.'s Office at the Hall of Justice."

"Space is at a premium here in City Hall, and it would be bad optics if those of us dealing with our unhoused neighbors worked in opulent quarters, wouldn't it?"

Very smooth. "Yes."

In response to my question about his background, he said that he grew up in Piedmont, an affluent enclave whose founders decided to secede from Oakland a century ago. "I got my undergrad degree in English and a master's in urban planning from Berkeley."

I told him that I was also a Cal alum. "Go, Bears."

"Go, Bears." He said that he had worked in the planning departments in Denver and Los Angeles after he graduated from Cal. "I always wanted to come back to the Bay Area. My father knew some people involved in Mayor Ward's campaign, so I volunteered. After the election, she offered me this job."

It came as no surprise that he had political connections and his family had money. "Do you want to run for office someday?"

"Not in the immediate future."

Good answer. "You have a tough job dealing with the homeless."

"It's complicated."

That it is. Every mayor in my lifetime has tried to address the issue with mostly unsatisfactory results. One tried a compassionate approach which led to the establishment of a huge tent camp on Civic Center Plaza. When people got tired of seeing the tents across the street from City Hall, he was voted out and replaced by a former police chief, who cleared out the plaza and moved the homeless to smaller encampments in other parts of town. A subsequent mayor took a "care-not-cash" approach with mixed results. The problem has been exacerbated by the lack of resources for mental health treatments and the proliferation of heroin, crystal meth, and, more recently, fentanyl.

I wanted to keep him talking. "What's the game plan?"

"We have a multipronged approach."

Every administration in my lifetime has had a "multipronged approach."

He sat up straighter. "First, we've created a database of the unhoused. Second, we've contracted with entities like Urban Alchemy to do welfare checks and offer services. Third, we've set up transition centers and provided living quarters for as many people as we can. Fourth, we work with the police and the D.A.'s Office to deal with crime. Fifth, we partner with drug and mental health agencies to get people the services they need."

Makes sense. "Do you have enough beds?"

"Not even close. It's a huge problem that can't be solved without a substantial influx of resources. There's also the unfortunate reality that many of the people we're trying to help are unwilling to accept our services."

"How do you solve it?"

His tone was realistic. "We'll never solve it completely, but we try to mitigate the negative effects by offering housing and services. For example, we are planning to open a walk-in center on U.N. Plaza where people will be able to get help with housing, medical issues, employment, and alcohol and drug treatment."

I give you credit for trying. "Keep fighting the good fight."

"We will." He glanced at his phone and decided that it was time to turn to business. "Bruno said that you're looking for somebody."

"I am. I'm representing a man named Lenny Garcia, who is accused of giving a young woman some pills spiked with fentanyl."

"I'm familiar with the case. It's a terrible tragedy."

"Yes, it is. Do you have a listing for Lenny?"

"Let me check." He typed a few strokes on his laptop. "He's in our database. We made contact three times at U.N. Plaza and once next to the main library, but he turned down our offers of assistance." He reported that Lenny showed signs of alcohol and drug use as well as anger management issues. "He was getting painkillers from the V.A."

"He was addicted to Oxy."

He nodded. "That's a tough one. Where did he get the spiked pills?"

"He didn't. He gave a couple of his V.A. pills to a woman named Annie Parker. She got the tainted pills from somebody else."

"I'll take your word for it."

"Do you have any idea where she may have gotten them?"

"As you undoubtedly know, a lot of people are selling, buying, and distributing fentanyl in the TL. There are a lot of fake pills in circulation. We rely on the police and the D.A. to enforce our drug laws." Recognizing that his tone had sounded a bit harsh, he quickly added, "Of course, we encourage them to do so in a humane and meaningful way."

Of course. I asked him if he had a listing for Annie Parker.

He input her name and turned the computer around so that I could see it. "One of our ambassadors approached her once near U.N. Plaza. She was in distress which may have reflected mental illness or drug use. She declined services."

"I'm looking for a former neighbor of hers named Patty Dawson. Early twenties. Used to live at the El Camino Hotel on Larkin. Ms. Dawson also worked for a man named Marcus Strong, who was killed a few months ago."

"I'm familiar with Mr. Strong."

"Do you have any idea who killed him?"

"Afraid not."

"The clerk at the El Camino told me that Ms. Dawson left no phone number or forwarding address. Her last known employer was the Mitchell Brothers. Bruno told me that she worked there for only a couple of weeks and disappeared. He hasn't heard from her since."

He stared at his laptop. "One of our ambassadors talked to Ms. Dawson about four months ago. She came in for lunch at St. Boniface."

St. Boniface is the magnificent Catholic Church in the heart of the Tenderloin that serves the disenfranchised and the destitute.

He was still looking at his computer. "That was the only contact. No phone number. No address. The ambassador thought that she was using crystal meth. He offered her services, but she declined. She was living on the street near St. Boniface at the time."

"Any idea where I might find her?"

"Afraid not."

"Can you give me the name of the ambassador?"

He squinted at his laptop. "Dennis McCarthy. Solid guy. Army vet who came back from Afghanistan with PTSD and a drinking problem. He did some time at Soledad for possession. We helped him get off the streets and into a shelter. Now he has his own apartment."

"Any idea where I might find him?"

"He still volunteers at the dining room at St. Boniface."

I was walking down the steps of City Hall when I heard the familiar smoker's hack behind me. "Michael Daley," the voice rasped. "What brings you to City Hall on this fine day?"

I turned around and looked into the bloodshot eyes of Jerry Edwards, the *Chronicle*'s award-winning political columnist. He remained pugnacious after three acrimonious divorces and periodic trips to rehab for a decades-long battle with alcohol. Rosie and I had been on the receiving end of his barbs on several occasions. Though I respected his tenacity, it was painful to engage with somebody who relished verbal combat.

"Good to see you, Jerry," I lied.

"Same here, Mike." The stubble on his leathery face and his faded trench coat gave him the appearance of one of the homeless people on U.N. Plaza. "What brings you to City Hall?"

"Working on the Lenny Garcia case."

He pulled out his leather-bound notebook. "The guy who gave the fentanyl-spiked pills to the homeless girl?"

"That's the accusation. Andy Erickson still has to prove it."

"I heard that they found your client's prints on the pill bottle."

"It was his bottle," I said. "He got the pills from the V.A."

"Who gave her the tainted pills?"

"That's what I'm trying to find out." I pointed at the homeless encampment on the opposite side of Civic Center Plaza. "There are lots of possibilities."

He responded with a laugh that turned into a smoker's hack. "No kidding, Mike. Things have gotten out of hand. Maybe they'll finally nail somebody who was distributing poison."

"It wasn't my client."

"Says your client."

"I'm looking for a woman named Patty Dawson. I think she may be living on the street."

"You think you're going to find her here at City Hall?"

"I was talking to a guy named Kyle Adams. You know him?"

"I've met him. Nice kid with connections. Now he's part of the homeless industrial complex. I have no doubt that he means well, but he's in over his head."

"He seems to have some good ideas."

"Every new administration says that they're going to fix the problem."

"Maybe it will be different this time."

"Maybe. People are getting pissed off. You can't have people selling fentanyl and shooting up on the streets. We're becoming a national laughingstock."

"You got any connections in the TL?"

"I have connections everywhere, but I don't go down there anymore. Too dangerous."

"Isn't it your job to work in dangerous areas?"

"I'm sixty-five, Mike. I'd like to make it to sixty-six. You gonna get an acquittal?"

"This is where I give you the standard line that my client is looking forward to his day in court and I'm very confident that we'll get an acquittal."

He put away his notebook. "Off the record?"

"It's like every other case, Jerry. I like our chances of getting at least one juror to reasonable doubt, but you never know what's going to happen in court."

"Good luck, Mike."

"Thanks, Jerry."

17

"IT'S BEEN A COUPLE OF MONTHS"

The man with the leathery skin wore a net over his shoulder-length gray hair. He handed me a plastic tray and pointed at the overflowing buffet table. "What would you like?"

"Information," I said. "My name is Michael Daley. I'm an attorney with the Public Defender's Office."

Dennis McCarthy smiled. "You're the priest?"

"Ex-priest. How did you know?"

"People talk. I heard that you've taken good care of Terrence 'The Terminator.'"

"He's an excellent employee." I put the tray down. "I'm representing Lenny Garcia."

"Never met him."

"He's going on trial for murder on Monday."

"I don't know anything about it."

"Kyle Adams gave me your name. He said that you might be able to help me locate a potential witness in Lenny's case. Her name is Patty Dawson."

The smile disappeared. "I get off in ten minutes."

"I'll wait."

I took a seat at a nearby table as McCarthy finished his shift in the social-hall-turned-dining-room in the basement of St. Boniface, the Catholic Church on Golden Gate Avenue in the middle of the TL. The parish dates back to the Gold Rush days when it served San Francisco's German community. The Romanesque Revival building was a reconstruction of the majestic church that burned down after the Great Earthquake. The German community had dispersed decades earlier, and

St. Boniface became a place of comfort for the downtrodden. It gained notoriety when it partnered with a nonprofit called the Grubbio Project, which administered a controversial program allowing the homeless to sleep in the sanctuary in what they called "sacred sleep."

I looked around at the stragglers sitting at the long tables in a room that smelled of bologna sandwiches, potato chips, and coffee. The mosaic of humanity included a teenage mother comforting her crying infant, a man with glazed eyes who was staring at his phone, a senior citizen wearing once-fashionable clothing who pushed her walker toward the door, a man with wild hair trying to persuade one of the volunteers that he needed a drink, and an earnest young priest comforting an overwhelmed mother accompanied by two preschoolers. It reminded me of my days as a junior priest at St. Anne's in the Sunset, although our homeless flock was smaller. I wondered if everybody would find shelter and warmth on a rainy afternoon.

At two o'clock, the supervisor announced that the dining room was closed. McCarthy removed his apron and hairnet, grabbed a cup of coffee, and took a seat across from me.

"Can I buy you lunch?" I asked.

"I'm good."

"How long have you been volunteering here?"

"About a year." He said that he had returned to the TL after he was released from Soledad Prison. He didn't elaborate.

"You live nearby?"

"On Turk. The City got me into a program to get my meth issue under control. Then they helped me find a room. It isn't the Fairmont, but it's better than sleeping on the street." He took a sip of watery coffee. "What can I do for you?"

"I'm looking for a woman named Patty Dawson who may have some information for Lenny's trial." I pointed at his Urban Alchemy windbreaker. "Kyle Adams told me that you're an ambassador. He said that you met Ms. Dawson."

"I meet a lot of people. It's been a few months since I saw her."

"Any idea where I might find her?"

"She was living on the street when I met her. She said that she might have a new place in the Mission, but I don't know if it worked out." He looked at the contacts on his phone. "I don't have an address, and her burner phone was disconnected."

"Did she mention where in the Mission?"

"Near St. Peter's."

It was a start. "Is there anybody else that I can talk to?"

"I don't know."

"We've been told that she was working for a guy named Marcus Strong."

He recognized the name. "Bad guy."

"Any idea who stabbed him?"

"Afraid not. Strong pissed off a lot of people. Be careful if you start asking around. They're the kind of people who stab first and ask questions later."

Got it. "Strong was also pimping a woman named Annie Parker who was Ms. Dawson's neighbor at the El Camino Hotel. My client is accused of slipping Ms. Parker some fentanyl-laced pills. She OD'd."

He eyed me. "Did your client give her the pills?"

"He claims that he gave her some Oxy pills that he got from the V.A."

His expression turned skeptical. "You think Patty gave her the pills?"

"Probably not. Realistically, I'm hoping that Ms. Dawson might be able to tell me where Annie Parker was getting her pills."

"Good luck with that."

"You think Strong might have given her the pills?"

"Beats me."

"You said he was a bad guy. Bad guys distribute bad drugs."

"True." He shrugged. "Strong was one of many bad guys who did."

"You know anybody who was selling stuff at U.N. Plaza?"

"Dozens of people. It's one-stop shopping."

"Anybody I should talk to?"

"A guy named Brian Holton has been there for a long time. He knows everybody."

"I already talked to him. He sent me to the hotel where Patty used to live. Any chance that Holton is moving fentanyl?"

"Wouldn't surprise me, but I don't know for sure."

"Anybody else?"

He thought about it for a moment. "Have you talked to Joe D?"

"Joe D?"

"Joe Davis. People call him 'Go-To' Joe."

"Why?"

"Because if you need anything, Joe knows where you can find it."

"He sells drugs?"

"Supposedly not anymore, but I don't know for sure. He used to do deliveries for one of the bigger suppliers. Joe got pinched by an undercover cop. His lawyer negotiated a deal for probation in exchange for some helpful testimony and a promise that Joe would keep his nose clean."

"I'm surprised that the supplier didn't come after him."

"The supplier is no longer in business. In fact, he's no longer alive."

"Was his supplier Marcus Strong?"

"I don't know. There are many dealers here in the TL."

"Do you know where I can find 'Go-To' Joe?"

"Last I heard, he was working security at a liquor store at Turk and Jones."

At three-fifteen the same afternoon, a cold wind made my face numb as I made my way around four men sitting on milk crates in front of T and L Liquors on the ground floor of an SRO at Turk and Jones, catty-corner to a City-sponsored tent encampment. The pizza place next door had gone out of business. The two-story parking structure down the street was tagged with graffiti. There was a line outside the Vietnamese restaurant down the block.

I walked under the faded sign of the liquor store and pushed open the door, which was covered with plywood. I noticed the surveillance cameras inside and out. I walked through the metal detector and looked at the lotto numbers on the scoreboard above the Plexiglas-protected counter. I thought about buying a couple of Quick Picks and retiring to Hawaii. I saw an imposing man with broad shoulders and a beard with no mustache. He was wearing a Warriors windbreaker. Even though he was indoors, his eyes were covered by aviator-style sunglasses.

"Are you Joe?" I asked him.

"Maybe. Who's asking?"

"My name is Michael Daley. I'm an attorney with the Public Defender's Office. I'm representing Lenny Garcia. I need to ask you some questions."

He glanced at the gruff man behind the counter, then he turned back to me. "I'm working."

"We can talk later. What time do you get off?"

Another look at the owner. I wasn't sure if "Go-To" Joe was packing, but I was certain that his boss was.

"What's this about?" he asked.

"I was hoping that you might be able to help me locate a potential witness."

No response.

I looked over at the man behind the counter, who glared at me as if to say, "You gonna buy something or not?"

"Five Quick Picks, please," I said.

He turned to the Lotto machine.

I decided that it was probably premature to start driving to Sacramento to collect my winnings. I looked at Joe. "Let me buy you dinner. And if one of my lotto numbers hits, I'll split the winnings with you."

His stoic expression transformed into a wry grin. "Meet me here at nine."

18

"SHE SEEMED LIKE A NICE KID"

At nine-thirty on Thursday night, I handed "Go-To" Joe Davis a takeout box holding a chicken kabsah dinner with rice and pita that I had picked up at Yemen Kitchen a couple of doors down the street. "I hope you're hungry," I said.

"I am." Davis was wearing a worn Nike T-shirt and a pair of faded Levi's. He placed the box on the table in the corner of his single room on the third floor of the Padre Apartments, a refurbished twenties-era building next door to the Tenderloin Police Station. It was a half-block from the liquor store where he worked, and across the street from Power Exchange, a BDSM club. "Thanks for picking this up."

"Thanks for seeing me." I held up a hand. "I saw some people downstairs wearing masks. Do you want me to put one on?"

"Then you won't be able to eat."

True. "You aren't worried about the virus?"

"A little. The manager asked everybody to wear a mask in the lobby."

I looked around the tidy room big enough for a twin bed, a three-drawer dresser, a table, and two chairs. The window looked at the wall of the building next door. The bathroom was down the hall. "This is pretty nice."

He took a bite of his chicken. "Not bad."

"How long have you lived here?"

"Almost a year. It's better than living on the street."

He explained that he had lived on and off the street for the past six years. He was a native of Vallejo; his parents had split up when he was a baby; and he was raised by his grandmother in the projects at Hunters Point. "I got in with a rough crowd in high school. We drank a lot and did some weed. When my grandma died, I got a job doing security at a couple of bars down here. I picked up some extra dollars by delivering weed and harder stuff. Then I started sampling the products, and I got hooked on crack."

"That's a tough habit to break."

"I found out the hard way." He said that he was making more money delivering drugs than working security. "I needed the money to support my habit."

"And you got busted?"

"Several times." He confirmed Dennis McCarthy's story that he had provided information to the police in exchange for a suspended sentence after his most recent arrest. "They helped me get into rehab, find a job, and get this room." He took a sip of water. "I have to stay clean if I want to stay alive."

"You aren't afraid that the guy you told the cops about will come after you?"

"He's dead."

Got it.

He glanced at his phone. "Why did you want to talk to me?"

"I'm representing Lenny Garcia. You know him?"

"I met him a few times."

I didn't feel compelled to ask him if it was personal or business. "His trial starts Monday. He's accused of giving a woman named Annie Parker some pills tainted with fentanyl. She OD'd."

"I don't know anything about it."

"Did you ever meet Ms. Parker?"

He waited a beat. "I don't think so."

"You know anybody who was distributing fake pills at U.N. Plaza?"

"Dozens of people."

"Can you narrow it down a bit?"

"Afraid not."

I showed him Patty Dawson's picture. "I'm trying to find her. She used to live in the same hotel as Ms. Parker."

He studied the photo. "She used to live in the neighborhood. She seemed like a nice kid."

"Was she a customer of yours?"

"Maybe once or twice. You think she killed Annie Parker?"

"I have no evidence that she did. I'm hoping that she may know who was supplying Ms. Parker with Oxy and other drugs. She and Ms. Parker both worked for a man named Marcus Strong, a pimp and a drug dealer."

He corrected me. "A *dead* pimp and *dead* drug dealer."

"You think he might have given Ms. Parker some tainted pills?"

"Wouldn't surprise me, but I have no idea how you're going to prove it."

Neither do I. "That's why I need to find Ms. Dawson."

He chuckled. "You want her to say that Strong gave Parker some dirty pills?"

"Yes."

"And it'll be her word against the dead guy's, right?"

"That's the idea."

"Good luck with that."

"Thank you." I waited a beat. "Have you seen her lately? She was working at the Mitchell Brothers for a while."

"Afraid not."

"Any idea where I should start looking?"

"She said that she might be moving down to the Mission near St. Peter's."

"Who else should I talk to?"

He thought about it for a moment. "There's a guy named Brian Holton who spends most of his time over at U.N. Plaza. He seems to know everybody."

"I've met him. He denied giving Ms. Parker any pills."

"Of course, he did."

"You think he was lying?"

"Yes."

"What makes you think so?"

"Because he was giving pills to everybody in the neighborhood."

19

"I WAS IN THE NEIGHBORHOOD"

Sergeant A.C. Brown flashed a sardonic grin from his seat on the opposite side of a metal table in a consultation room in the bowels of Tenderloin Station. "You wanted to see me?"

"I was in the neighborhood."

He glanced at his watch. "It's ten-thirty p.m. Let me give you a little friendly advice. Hanging out by yourself in the TL at night is not good for your health."

Good advice. "Thank you. I promise to go straight back to my office."

"I'll give you a ride."

"I appreciate that."

"Why are you here?"

"I'm still looking for Patty Dawson."

"I have no new information."

"I just spent a few minutes with Joe Davis." I pointed to my left. "He lives in the building next door."

"I know Joe."

"It seems that everybody in the neighborhood knows 'Go-To' Joe."

"He's kept his nose clean since his last arrest. He has a job and an apartment. We'll take a few small victories where we can."

"Is he still dealing?"

"Not as far as I know."

"But you don't know for sure?"

"I don't know anything for sure, Mike. For the record, I have no personal knowledge of any illegal activities by Mr. Davis." He stood up. "The offer of a ride still stands."

I remained seated. "Joe said that Brian Holton is dealing over at U.N. Plaza."

"I have no personal knowledge that he is. If you have information and would like to file a report, I would be happy to take it."

"Come on, A.C."

"You know how the process works. If you think that Holton committed a crime, you can file a report, and I'll investigate."

"Lenny's trial starts on Monday."

"If you have information pertaining to Mr. Holton that is relevant to your client's case, I suggest that you talk to the D.A.'s Office."

I tried not to let my frustration show. It was, after all, a perfectly legitimate response. "Joe told me that we might be able to find Patty Dawson in the Mission."

"I'll take your word for it. We tried to find her, but we didn't have any luck."

"Do you have an address for her?"

"Afraid not, Mike." He took a deep breath. "I know that you're doing your job, but you're looking for a needle in a haystack on an insanely short time frame. If I were in your shoes, I would go back to the office and work on your trial presentation."

He's right. "Thanks, A.C."

"Get some sleep, Mike." He stood up again. "I'll give you a ride back to the office."

I was at my desk at eleven-fifteen when my phone vibrated, and the name of Rosie's brother, Tony, appeared on the display. "Any luck tracking down Patty Dawson?" I asked.

"I'm afraid not. You might talk to Gil. He knows everybody."

"I will." Father Guillermo Lopez was the charismatic priest at St. Peter's. "I'll talk to him in the morning."

"You need his number?"

"I'll go see him in person. I have a few sins to confess to."

It was almost midnight as I was driving north on the Golden Gate Bridge through a heavy mist. Traffic was light, and I was transfixed by the swishing of my wipers.

Nady's name appeared on my phone. As always, she got straight to business. "How are trial preparations coming along?"

"As well as can be expected. How's your mother?"

"Out of intensive care, but not out of the woods."

"That's good."

"In the grand scheme of things, it is."

I could barely see the Alcatraz beacon which was obscured by fog. My throat was scratchy as I turned up the heat in my Prius. "Any idea when she might be able to go home?"

"Too soon to tell." She said that she hadn't been able to see her mother in person. "At least I can see her on Facetime."

"Thank goodness for modern technology."

"Indeed." She waited a beat. "Any luck finding Patty Dawson?"

"Not yet," I said. I described my conversations with Bruno King, Kyle Adams, Dennis McCarthy, and "Go-To" Joe. "I'm going to talk to a couple of my contacts in the Mission in the morning, but I'm not wildly optimistic that I'll be able to find her."

"Even if you do, I'm not sure that she'll give you anything that will help."

This was Nady's polite way of saying that I was tilting at windmills. "Any other suggestions?"

"You can try to put the blame on Brian Holton. At least you know that he was in the vicinity of Annie's tent on the night that she died."

"I have no way of proving that he gave her the pills."

"You just need to convince one juror that he might have done it."

True. "I'm also going to try to blame Marcus Strong."

She chuckled. "Blame it on the dead guy, eh?"

"A very bad dead guy," I said. "And he can't defend himself."

"You think it's enough to get an acquittal?"

"I don't know. More realistically, I might be able to convince one juror to vote to acquit and get the jury to hang."

"Then you'll have the privilege of doing it all over again."

"Hopefully, you'll be home by then."

"Hopefully," she said. "You going home?"

"I'm going to see Rosie."

20

"WE NEED TO BE SMART"

"You warm enough?" Rosie asked.

I pulled up the collar on my down jacket. "Fine."

At twelve-twenty a.m., I was sitting next to the propane heater on Rosie's back porch. In an abundance of caution, we had agreed that I wouldn't go inside since I had made my rounds in the Tenderloin. I thought it was perhaps an overreaction, but case numbers were rising, and Tommy was talking about coming home for the weekend.

Rosie took a sip of Cab Franc and adjusted the hood of her faded Cal sweatshirt. Her black eyes gleamed from the porchlight. "Did your trip to the Tenderloin provide anything that you can use?"

"Not yet."

"Trial starts in three days."

"I'm well aware of that, Rosie."

"Any leads on Patty Dawson?"

"Nothing solid. She may be living in the Mission. Your brother came up empty. Pete is calling in some favors. I'm going to talk to Gil Lopez later this morning. He knows everybody in the Mission."

She eyed me skeptically. "What if you find her?"

"Maybe she can tell us who was supplying Annie Parker with Oxy."

"What are the odds that she'll know?"

"About the same as the odds that I'll be able to find her."

She took another sip of wine and chuckled. "I trust that you have a Plan B?"

"Lenny hasn't reconsidered the possibility of a continuance, so we'll go to trial on Monday with the evidence that we have."

"Anything new from Erickson?"

"Nothing."

"Any chance of a revised plea deal?"

"Seems unlikely. We're supposed to meet with Judge Powell later today to talk about final witness lists and motions. We'll see if Erickson offers anything."

She shook her head. "I'll be surprised if he does."

"So will I." I finished my wine and put the goblet on the table. "I'm not feeling wildly confident, Rosie."

"You're doing everything that you can, Mike." She flashed her stunning smile. "No pressure, but I'm expecting you to perform yet another miracle."

"I may need one."

"You'll find something, Mike. You always do."

I'm not so sure. "When do you think we'll be able to go back to the office?"

"Two weeks." She reconsidered her answer. "Maybe three. The doctors are telling us that these types of viruses run their course pretty quickly."

"I hope they're right." I glanced inside the house. "You still want me to stay at the apartment for the time being?"

"Yes." She read my pained expression. "We need to be smart, Mike. It's going to be really hard to keep the P.D.'s Office operational if we both get sick."

"Agreed."

"You'll keep me posted?"

"I'll Facetime you if anything comes up."

At one-forty-five a.m., I was staring at the ceiling of my cramped bedroom in my apartment behind the Larkspur fire station. The platform bed was elevated by cinder blocks. The nightstand was an IKEA special.

I reached over and scratched the head of the pearl white cat sleeping soundly beside me. "Looks like it's going to be just the two of us for a while, Wilma."

Her right ear wiggled, but her eyes remained closed. Wilma used to live in the apartment next door. When my neighbors had twin boys, she started coming over to my place for peace and quiet. It turned out that the twins were allergic to cats, so my neighbors asked me to adopt Wilma, who was delighted to have a place to herself and a human to make sure that the kibble dish was full, and her box was clean.

I was startled by my vibrating phone. Wilma's right eye opened halfway. It took an instant for my eyes to adjust to the darkness. Pete's name appeared on the display.

"You up, Mick?" he asked.

"Yes. So is Wilma. What's up, Pete?"

"I may have something for you. I'll get back to you as soon as I can."

21

"BLESS ME, FATHER"

"Bless me, Father, for I have sinned," I said.

The familiar voice responded from the other side of the confessional. "How long has it been since your last confession, Mike?"

"A couple of weeks, Gil."

"I'm going to have to ding you for poor attendance."

"Did you consider the possibility that I haven't done anything sinful during that time?"

Father Guillermo Lopez chuckled. "No."

At eight o'clock on Friday morning, I was sitting in a musty confessional in the back of St. Peter's Catholic Church on Alabama Street, around the corner from the apartments where my parents had grown up, and a short walk from Rosie's mother's house. The modest church had anchored the Mission for more than a century.

I could see the outline of Gil's Roman nose and prematurely gray goatee. At thirty-six, he was one of the younger priests at the church where Rosie and I had been baptized and later married. Gil had attended St. Peter's Elementary School, St. Ignatius High, and USF before heading to the seminary. Smart, savvy, charismatic, and intensely political, he was primed to lead the community deep into the Twenty-first Century.

His voice was patient. "What have you got for me?"

"I had impure thoughts about someone who is not my wife."

"Did you act upon them?"

"Yes."

"With Rosie?"

"Yes."

He feigned exasperation. "We've been through this, Mike. You and Rosie never got an annulment from the Church. As a result, in the eyes of our Lord, you're still married, so it isn't a sin if you continue to sleep together."

True.

"Anything else?" he asked.

I thought back to the days when I went to catechism class on Wednesday afternoons. When I hadn't done anything else especially sinful during the week, Pete and I would swear at each other, so we'd have something to confess. "I have made a few untrue statements."

"In other words, you lied?"

"I did."

"To whom?"

How much time do you have? "I don't recall."

"Is that because you told so many lies that you can't remember all of them?"

"I'm a lawyer, Gil."

"I thought that perjury was illegal."

"Only if you lie under oath."

"So you're okay with lying as long as you don't end up in jail?"

"It's part of my job, Gil."

"You of all people should know that God doesn't look at it that way."

I grinned. "That's why I'm here to see you."

"Maybe it's better that you aren't a priest anymore." He pushed out a melodramatic sigh and imposed a modest penance.

The air was tinged with smoke from votive candles as we walked down the aisle of the unassuming church that was dedicated on July 4, 1886, and rebuilt twice after it was destroyed by fire. It was constructed of painted redwood in an era of Victorian-style designs. The interior is an architectural style known as Carpenter Gothic, full of gewgaws and elaborate fretwork. The ceilings are painted to resemble Gothic stone tracery in a manner called trompe l'oeil. There was talk of tearing it down after it was damaged by a third fire in 1997, but the community rallied, and the Archdiocese came up with millions. Gil's church looks better than it did when I was a kid. The stained-glass window above the altar had been painstakingly restored, and the smaller ones along the walls were remade from scratch. A new organ sat in the loft behind us.

I looked at the ceiling and silently recited the words of Isaiah inscribed on the highest arch: "I have loved, O Lord, the beauty of thy house and the place where thy glory dwelleth." St. Peter's would never match the grandeur of St. Mary's or the majesty of Sts. Peter and Paul, but it embodied its parish's working-class roots. Although I was now a member of St. Patrick's Parish in Larkspur, St. Peter's would always be my home.

I dutifully recited my Hail Marys, then Gil and I made our way through the labyrinth of hallways to the three-story rectory at the corner of Twenty-fourth and Bryant, down the block from the forties-era grammar school that I attended until we moved to the Sunset. We took seats in the dining room that reminded me of St. Anne's, where I spent three years as a junior priest: an oak table surrounded by a dozen wooden chairs; a credenza with stacked white plates; a Mr. Coffee machine. A simple wooden cross hung above the door. The only hint of the new millennium was a laptop on a table next to a bookcase filled with religious texts.

"Are you worried about the virus?" I asked.

"Yes."

"I didn't see anybody wearing masks in church."

"That's likely to change."

"Are you going to stay open?"

"I hope so." He took a sip of watery Folgers. "We have the capacity to broadcast mass online if we have to. I don't like it, but you do what you have to do. I'm more concerned about the children and their parents as well as our seniors. The young people who work for tech firms will be fine, but many of our other parishioners have limited means. If we have to shut down school even for a few days, it's going to be a tremendous burden. Some of our parishioners have caught the virus and are in the hospital. People are scared, Mike."

"It'll pass, Gil."

"I hope so." His expression turned thoughtful. "This is where we priests are supposed to say that the situation is in our Lord's hands. In this case, I hope that He is giving solid guidance to the doctors, nurses, and scientists." He placed his coffee cup onto its saucer. "Why did you come to see me, Mike?"

"I was hoping that I could enlist your help on a case that's going to trial on Monday. I'm looking for a young woman named Patty Dawson." I showed him a photo. "I've been told that she may have been living nearby." I explained her connection to Annie Parker.

A look of recognition crossed his face. "I've met her. She's a nice young woman who had a difficult childhood and developed substance issues. She got into a fight with her pimp, ran out of money, and ended up on the street. She was living in a tent city near Civic Center when she stopped by the church. We gave her food, clothes, and a phone. We got her into a shelter on South Van Ness for a few days, but she left. Our people tried to get her a spot in a program, but she disappeared before we could get her hooked up."

"When was the last time that you saw her?"

"A couple of months ago. I don't know if she's still in the neighborhood."

"Is there anybody I can talk to?"

He thought about it for a moment. "She told me that her mother had hired a private investigator to look for her. The investigator made contact. She was very upset about it."

"Did she give you the name of the investigator?"

"Afraid not, Mike."

I was driving north on Mission Street toward the office when my phone vibrated, and Pete's name appeared on the display. "Did Gil have anything on Patty Dawson?" he asked.

"He met her a couple of times." I summarized my conversation with Gil. "Her family hired a P.I. to find her. She got spooked when the P.I. approached her."

"I know."

Huh? "How?"

"I made a few calls, Mick."

"I need to talk to the P.I."

"How soon can you get to North Beach?"

"Twenty minutes."

"INDEED I AM"

A cool breeze whipped through Washington Square Park in North Beach as I sat down on a bench next to a diminutive nonagenarian. "Good to see you, Nick," I said. "You okay?"

"Indeed I am." A surgical mask covered his face, and a stylish fedora sat on top of his toupee. He spoke in a melodious voice. "How the hell are you, Mike?"

"Fine."

"Good to hear."

Still energetic and wildly successful at ninety-five, Nick "The Dick" Hanson had opened the Hanson Investigative Agency seventy-five years earlier in a single room above the Condor Club on Broadway. The son of Russian immigrants whose father ran a magic shop next door to the Tosca Café and across the street from City Lights Bookstore, Nick played baseball with Joe DiMaggio on the North Beach playground. During the Great Depression, he helped his father make ends meet by sweeping up at the Valente Marini Perata Funeral Home on Green Street, handing out towels at the Italian Athletic Club, and bilking tourists at three-card monte.

At five feet tall and a wiry hundred and thirty pounds, Nick still ran the Bay to Breakers every year and worked out at the upscale Bay Club below his Earthquake-era mansion down the street from Coit Tower. His agency had evolved into a high-tech operation employing dozens of his children, grandchildren, and great-grandchildren. A savvy businessman and astute investor, Nick had accumulated a portfolio of apartment buildings in North Beach rumored to be worth a cool fifty million. In his spare time, he wrote mystery novels that were thinly veiled embellishments of his more colorful cases. Danny DeVito played Nick in a long-running Netflix series.

The wind whipped through the mature trees in the park bordered by Columbus Avenue and Union, Stockton, and Filbert Streets. I looked up at the majestic double steeples of Sts. Peter and Paul, the magnificent Catholic church which originally served the Italian community. Nowadays, masses are celebrated in English, Italian, Cantonese, and Latin. Nick was in attendance when Joe DiMaggio married Dorothy Arnold in the church in 1939. There are photos in front of Sts. Peter and Paul of Joltin' Joe and Marilyn Monroe on their wedding day, but they actually got married at City Hall. Joe and Marilyn weren't allowed to marry in the church because Joe obtained a civil divorce from Dorothy, but not an annulment from the Church. The Yankee Clipper's funeral was held at Sts. Peter and Paul on March 11, 1999. It was officiated by Father Armand Oliveri, a DiMaggio family friend who was born in Italy and moved to North Beach in 1929. He was still going strong at ninety-nine.

"You warm enough?" I asked.

"Indeed I am." He pulled up the collar of his Burberry overcoat. "The fresh air feels good."

"We could grab a bite inside."

"My kids and grandkids won't let me eat inside a restaurant, and they won't allow me to have visitors in my house."

"They're just being careful, Nick."

"I know. I didn't make it to ninety-five by taking unnecessary chances."

"You working?" I asked. Over the years, Nick had tried to retire a dozen times.

"A little," he said, "and only from home. I'd rather be out in the field."

And having three-hour lunches at Fior d'Italia and Caffe Sport and drinking copious amounts of wine at Gino and Carlo's. "Soon," I said.

"I hope so." He adjusted his mask. "Your brother okay?"

"Fine, thanks." Pete worked for Nick for a short time before he decided that he preferred to be on his own. "He's doing everything from home, too."

"Give him my best." He lowered his voice. "I'm sorry about Big John. He was a fine gentleman."

"Thank you."

For a half-century, Nick had made regular pilgrimages to Dunleavy's to drink Guinness and play liar's dice with his pal, Herb Caen, the *Chronicle*'s celebrated gossip columnist. According to legend, Nick provided Caen with many of his exclusive scoops. Nick started that legend himself.

He added, "I'm sorry that I couldn't make it to the memorial. I understand that you spoke very nicely."

"Thanks, Nick."

I spent the next fifteen minutes listening to Nick expound upon growth plans for his agency, his real estate portfolio, his great-grandchildren's college choices, and the marketing plan for his latest novel. He reported that this would be the final year of his Netflix series unless Danny DeVito decided to re-up for an encore, which Nick viewed as unlikely.

"We've had a good run," he said. "Hopefully, my fictional counterpart will be entertaining people for many years to come."

"I have no doubt," I said.

A ray of sunlight poked through the clouds as a young woman wearing a mask and carrying a white paper bag approached us from the Columbus Avenue side of the park.

Nick lowered his mask and smiled. "You've met my great-granddaughter, Nicki."

I nodded. "Nice to see you again, Nicki."

"Same here, Mr. Daley."

"Mike."

"Mike." She turned back to Nick. "Put your mask back on, Grandpa."

"Yes, ma'am."

"Do you have enough food up at the house?"

"Indeed I do."

Nicki was a fourth-generation member of Nick's firm. She had graduated at the top of her class at Lowell High School, earned a computer science degree at UC-San Diego, and a master's in data analytics at UCLA. She was the head of the agency's cybersecurity group. Married. No kids. Lived around the corner on Greenwich. Her facial features were vaguely similar to her great-grandfather's, but she was six inches taller than he was, and her short black hair had a magenta streak. She was every bit as relentless as Nick.

She handed us sandwiches. "A Meatball panini for you, Grandpa. Prosciutto panini for you, Mike." She told Nick that she had also gotten him a double order of meat lasagna and two helpings of tiramisu. "For later."

"Thanks, honey. Was it crowded at Mario's?"

"Always."

Mario's Bohemian Cigar Store Café is a café and bar in a triangular 1909-vintage building. Nowadays, there are no cigars, and tourists are mixed in among the regulars. If you're lucky enough to get a seat next to the window, you get an unobstructed view of Washington Square. The service is more friendly than fast, the sandwiches are hearty, and the espresso drinks are almost as good as Café Trieste.

We took off our masks, opened the wrappers, and devoured our lunches. When Nick finished his meatball sandwich, he finally decided that it was time to turn to business.

"Pete told me that you picked up Lenny Garcia's case," he said to me. "You going to be able to get an acquittal?"

"I think we've got a pretty good chance."

"I heard that your client gave the decedent some tainted pills."

"Lenny gave her some of his own Oxy pills that he got from the V.A. He believes that somebody else gave her some fake pills loaded with fentanyl."

Nick contorted his rubbery face into a skeptical expression. "Uh-huh."

I filled in Nick and Nicki on the details. They listened attentively as they ate tiramisu and drank Italian sodas.

Finally, Nicki finished her dessert, put the empty paper cup down on the bench, and looked at me. "This is all very interesting, and it's nice to have lunch with you and Grandpa, but I don't understand why we're here."

"I'm looking for a woman named Patty Dawson who knew the decedent. She lived in the same SRO in the Tenderloin and worked for the same pimp. She may have some useful information. Pete told me that Ms. Dawson's mother hired you to look for her daughter."

"She did." She glanced at her great-grandfather. "I handled the investigation."

"Did you find her?"

"Yes." She shrugged. "Let's just say that the reunion with her mother didn't go well. The mother tried to convince Ms. Dawson to go into rehab, but she wasn't willing to do so. She told her mother that she never wanted to see her again."

"How long ago was this?"

"About six months. I haven't had any contact with Ms. Dawson or her mother since then."

"Was Ms. Dawson working at the time?"

"She had just left her job at the Mitchell Brothers."

"Where did you find her?"

"She had a room in a basement of an SRO in the Mission." She gave me the address. "I have no idea if she's still there."

23

"YOU HAVE TO EAT"

At two-fifteen the same afternoon, I was back in the Mission, where I knocked on the metal gate leading into a gangway between the Roosevelt Tamale Parlor and the St. Francis Fountain on Twenty-fourth Street, two blocks from St. Peter's.

No answer.

I shook the gate and it sprang open. I let myself inside and walked down the urine-soaked path between two Earthquake-era buildings. Tech professionals were buying up and remodeling the old houses in the western end of the Mission above Dolores Park, but gentrification hadn't found its way to this alley. The address that Nicki Hanson had provided matched the number on the door of a two-story stucco building. I figured that it was unlikely that I would find Patty Dawson in the unit behind the front door, so I knocked on the door leading to the basement.

No answer.

I knocked again.

Still no answer.

I spoke up in a non-threatening voice. "Ms. Dawson? My name is Michael Daley. I'm with the Public Defender's Office. I'd like to ask you a few questions about Annie Parker."

I heard a noise inside, but there was no answer at the door. Finally, I heard the deadbolt click, and the door opened about four inches—until the chain tightened. I saw brown eyes looking at me through the gap."

"Patty Dawson?" I asked.

A male voice responded. "She doesn't live here anymore."

Crap. "How long ago did she move?"

"A couple of months ago."

"Do you know where I can find her?"

"I saw her a couple of weeks ago in the plaza at the Twenty-fourth Street BART Station. I don't know if she's still there."

The afternoon sun provided a welcome respite from the cold as I made my way past the JCDecaux public toilet and walked by the street vendors selling their wares in a carnival-like atmosphere on the plaza above the underground BART Station on the corner of Twenty-fourth and Mission. The aroma of carne asada from the Taqueria San Jose next door combined with the smell of Big Macs from the McDonald's across the street. Musicians played rap music. A drumline banged on over-sized white buckets. The food offerings included burritos, sandwiches, churros, ice cream, sodas, and even organic vegan treats. You could buy CDs, electronics, and phone cards from neighborhood entrepreneurs, and handmade crafts from local artists. The ever-present contingent of homeless were scattered among the tables. Drugs were not as readily available as they were at the Sixteenth Street BART station, but there was a good selection.

I went from table to table and showed Patty Dawson's photo to the vendors. A couple of people recognized her, but nobody had seen her for a few weeks. Finally, a street preacher told me that he had seen her most recently in the plaza across Twenty-fourth between Taqueria El Farolito and El Taco Loco. I put a twenty into his contribution jar and made my way across the street where I saw a young woman sitting on a cement planter next to a shopping cart holding her belongings. She was wearing a soiled down jacket and faded yoga pants. Her shoulder-length brown hair was pulled into a ponytail. Her complexion was ruddy, her cheeks red from the wind.

"Are you Patty?" I asked.

She looked up from her burner phone. "If you're looking for a date, I'm not interested."

"My name is Michael Daley. I'm a lawyer with the Public Defender's Office. I'm representing a man named Lenny Garcia. I'm looking for information about Annie Parker."

A look of recognition crossed her face. "Annie was a good person."

"So I understand." I handed her my card. "Let me buy you lunch."

She accepted the card. "I don't know anything about what happened to Annie."

"You have to eat, right? Give me ten minutes. If you can't help me, no worries."

She thought about it again. "What's in it for me?"

"A hot meal. Some good company. And the possibility that you can help me find out what really happened to your friend."

"How did you know that she was my friend?"

"I talked to some people at the El Camino." I needed to offer something. "What can I do to make your life a little easier?"

"I need a place to live and a job."

"Our office has access to services."

"I've heard that one before."

"I'm the second-in-command at the P.D.'s Office. I don't make promises that I can't keep, and I'll pay you for your time." I reached into my pocket and pulled out five twenties.

She palmed the bills. "I guess it couldn't hurt to get a bite to eat."

24

"IF YOU HELP ME, I'LL HELP YOU"

"Where are you staying?" I asked.

Patty Dawson took a bite of a carne asada burrito and washed it down with a Diet Coke. "Here and there."

"Inside or out?" I asked.

"Depends on the night."

"When was the last time that you slept with a roof over your head?"

"A couple of weeks ago."

"My office can help you find a place to live."

Her voice filled with skepticism. "Sure."

We were sitting at a table in El Farolito, a narrow taqueria next to the plaza where I had found Dawson. The restaurant didn't look like much—an assembly-line counter fronting an industrial grill and a couple of refrigerators. A half dozen mismatched tables lined the wall opposite the counter, and there was a patio in the back. While it lacked ambiance, the carne asada super burrito was an almost-perfect combination of steak, rice, beans, salsa, and avocado slices in lieu of guacamole. The food was on par with longtime Mission stalwarts like Pancho Villa, La Cumbre, La Taqueria, El Faro, and Taqueria San Jose. It was cash only, and there was usually a line until closing time at one-forty-five a.m.

"Where are you sleeping tonight?" I asked.

"Not sure."

"If I get you a room, will you take it?"

"Will you pay for it?"

"Yes."

"Prove it."

I took out my phone, dialed Terrence's direct line, and asked him to book a room at a hotel where we housed witnesses under a program that Rosie and I had initiated. He promised to get back to me right away.

I looked across the table. "We have a deal with the Golden Gate Hotel near the Hall of Justice. It isn't the Ritz, but it's clean and safe. I'll take you there when we're finished eating."

She nodded in appreciation.

I finished my burrito and balled the foil wrapping in my fist. "You from the City?"

"Salinas." She said that she was twenty-two. Her mother was a waitress who had three kids with two different men when she was still in her teens. "I never met my biological father. My first stepfather beat my mother. Then he started beating me. My mother was in and out of rehab. I left home when I was eighteen."

"I understand that your mother hired a private investigator to find you."

"She did." Her eyes turned down. "I told my mother that I didn't want to see her until she got herself straightened out."

How sad.

I listened intently as she filled in the details of a difficult existence. She made her way to San Francisco in hopes of finding a job and an apartment. She quickly fell in with a tough crowd and met Marcus Strong, who wooed her with attention, money, and drugs. It didn't take long before she was a low-paid sex worker living in an SRO in the TL.

She took a deep breath. "Marcus gave me meth. I got addicted."

"Did he hit you?"

"Yes."

"Did he hit Annie Parker?"

"Yes. He gave her drugs, too. He was a total control freak who used us to make money." She described how Strong manipulated young women into a form of indentured servitude.

I kept my voice even. "I take it that you aren't heartbroken that Strong is no longer with us?"

"That would be an understatement."

"Any idea who stabbed him?"

"No." She added, "A lot of people didn't like him."

"How did you end up over here in the Mission?"

"I ran out of money after Marcus died, so I got a job at the Mitchell Brothers. I didn't like it, and I needed to get out of the TL. An acquaintance let me stay with her for a couple of months, then she moved out of town. I spent my money on meth, so I ended up on the street."

"And here you are."

Her voice was melancholy. "And here I am."

"How long did you live in the same hotel as Annie Parker?"

"We were neighbors at the El Camino for a few months."

"Did you like her?"

"She was fine. I didn't know her very well."

"She was also working for Strong?"

"Yes."

"The police have reason to believe that she engaged in sex on the night that she died."

"She did that many nights."

"Was she working for Strong around the time that she died?"

"She said that Marcus wanted her to come back to work for him."

"Do you know if any of her customers were supplying her with Oxy?"

"It wouldn't surprise me. She was always looking for pain meds for her shoulder. She got them mostly from Marcus."

"Did she ever get meds from people on the street?"

"On occasion."

"Do you have any idea who supplied the pills?"

"She used to do business sometimes with a guy named Joe Davis who had good prices. They call him 'Go-To' Joe."

"I've met him. Anybody else?"

"I think she may have gotten some stuff from a guy named Brian Holton."

"I talked to him, too. He told me that he's clean."

She shook her head. "He isn't who he says he is. I've seen him sell stuff: drugs, booze, cigarettes, phones, iPads, MUNI cards."

Interesting. "Any chance he sold some tainted pills to Annie?"

"I wouldn't be surprised, but I have no way of proving it."

Didn't think so. I took a sip of my strawberry aguas frescas and leaned forward. "I need you to testify at a trial next week."

"No."

"Please?"

"No."

"I will make sure that you have a place to stay until the trial. I will arrange for your meals and transportation to and from the Hall of Justice. I need your help, Patty."

She considered her options. "What do you want me to say?"

"That Strong was a bad guy who gave drugs to Annie Parker." I recognized the look of fear in her eyes. "He can't hurt you."

"He had friends."

"They have no reason to hurt you. Strong can't do anything to them. And I need you to testify that Brian Holton and Joe Davis were selling drugs on U.N. Plaza."

"Absolutely not. They're still alive and dangerous."

True. I glanced around the packed restaurant. "Will you testify about Strong?"

She took a deep breath. "Maybe."

"If you help me, I'll help you."

"I've heard that before."

"I'm the co-head of the felony division of the Public Defender's Office. My ex-wife is the Public Defender. We have access to people and programs that others don't. Please, Patty."

"I need to think about it for a few days."

It didn't seem like an ideal time to threaten her with a legal summons. "Of course."

"Can I still stay at the hotel tonight?"

"Absolutely."

"THE CIRCUMSTANCES ARE NOT IDEAL"

The Honorable Gordon J. Powell IV leaned back in his leather chair, straightened the perfect Windsor knot in his Haws and Curtis paisley tie made of high-end silk, rested his hands on his mahogany desk, and spoke in a voice bearing the inflection of a Boston Brahmin, even though he was a fifth-generation native of San Francisco. "Gentlemen," he said.

Erickson and I answered simultaneously in a deferential tone. "Your Honor."

The judge's pale face transformed into a practiced cherubic smile. "It's nice to see you."

Andy sucked up first. "Same here, Your Honor."

I gave him my best phony smile. "Yes, Your Honor."

Now in his seventies, Gordy Powell was the heir to a mining and logging fortune. An alum of the tony Drew High School, Harvard, and Stanford Law, he became the head of the antitrust group at one of the white-shoe law firms downtown. A well-connected Republican in a liberal city, he was appointed to the bench by Arnold Schwarzenegger—California's last Republican governor. Judge Powell was smart, conscientious, and thorough. He expected the attorneys before him to be prepared and concise, and he ran his courtroom with the efficiency of a Swiss railroad.

I took a moment to look around his custom-furnished chambers. His bookcases were filled with musty court reporters that he hadn't opened in years. The wall above his desk displayed civic citations, pictures of the judge with San Francisco dignitaries, and framed diplomas from Harvard and Stanford. On the credenza, there was an enlarged color photo of the judge along with his wife (the chair of the symphony board), three sons (two lawyers and a doctor), and seven grandchildren.

He looked my way. "Mr. Daley, I understand that Ms. Nikonova was called away to deal with a family health emergency."

"Yes, Your Honor. Her mother has contracted the Coronavirus. She's in the hospital in Los Angeles."

He moved his reading glasses to the top of his round head. "I'm sorry to hear that. Please give Ms. Nikonova and her mother my best wishes for a full and speedy recovery."

His concern was genuine. "Thank you, Your Honor."

"Have you discussed the possibility of a continuance with your client?"

"Yes, Your Honor. He would like to proceed on Monday."

He scowled. "Despite the fact that I have granted two extensions already, given the current circumstances, this court would be willing to entertain another one."

"Thank you, Your Honor. My client wishes to proceed."

"Very well." His small eyes narrowed. "I trust that counsel of your esteemed stature and decades of experience would not file an appeal claiming that you did not have adequate time to prepare for trial?"

"Absolutely not, Your Honor." *Well, maybe.*

"Good." His eyes shifted to Erickson. "I trust that you will also be ready to go on Monday?"

"Yes, Your Honor."

"Any chance that you and Mr. Daley might be able to come to a resolution of this matter before we empanel a jury?"

"There is no proposal on the table at this time."

"Perhaps you could get together and give the wheel another turn?"

"We will, Your Honor."

"Thank you. I want to remind you that we resolved all pre-trial motions last week. The defense request to exclude the pill bottle was denied. The Chief Medical Examiner's report is admissible, and Dr. Siu will be allowed to testify as to her conclusions. The prosecution and defense experts on fentanyl poisoning and DNA evidence may testify. So may the defense expert on Ms. Parker's heart condition. The gag order on all parties remains in place. The proceedings will not be televised." He looked up. "Any other open issues?"

"No, Your Honor," I said.

"Good." He turned to Erickson. "Any additions to your witness list?"

"No, Your Honor."

"How long will your presentation last?"

"We are hoping that jury selection will be fast. Our presentation will take just a few days. The facts are not in dispute."

The facts are always in dispute, but I won't gain anything by correcting him in chambers.

The judge turned my way. "Any additions to your witness list?"

"Several," I said. "The first is a woman named Patty Dawson, who was the decedent's friend and former neighbor."

Erickson feigned irritation. "It's too late, Your Honor. We agreed to exchange final witness lists last week."

"We just located her," I said. "She has critical information about people who were supplying illegal drugs to the decedent."

The judge held up a hand. "I'll allow the addition, Mr. Daley, but I'm going to give Mr. Erickson some leeway if you do, in fact, call upon her to testify."

"Understood. In addition, we plan to call two individuals who lived in the vicinity of U.N. Plaza. The first is Brian Holton, who has lived on the plaza for several years. The second is Joseph Davis, who has substantial knowledge of drug dealing activities in the vicinity."

Erickson tensed. "We object, Your Honor."

The judge listened as Erickson and I did the customary dance when the defense wants to introduce new witnesses at the last minute. I argued that the probative value of their testimony would outweigh Erickson's claim that he had insufficient time to question them. Judge Powell ruled in my favor. He said that it was in the interests of justice, but, in reality, it was an attempt to mitigate a claim on appeal that he had excluded important witnesses.

We discussed the questionnaires that we would distribute to potential jurors, the details of the *voir dire* process, the number of challenges each side would get, and how long our daily court sessions would last. Erickson reconfirmed that he planned to proceed on the charge of first-degree murder. He had no intention of adding a so-called "special circumstance," which would trigger the possibility of the death penalty.

"Anything else?" the judge asked.

"Your Honor," I said, "have you given any additional thought as to whether you will be instructing the jury as to the lesser charge of manslaughter?"

"I haven't decided, Mr. Daley."

In a first-degree murder case, the judge is required to instruct the jury that it may find the defendant guilty of the lesser charge of second-degree. The judge also has the option, but not the obligation, to instruct the jury that it may find the defendant guilty of voluntary or involuntary manslaughter. Obviously, a manslaughter conviction is preferable to a murder conviction. On the other hand, it makes it easier for the jury to compromise and convict on the lesser charge.

"When are you planning to decide?" I asked.

"After both parties have concluded their presentations."

This was expected. Most judges wait to make this call until after both sides have presented their cases.

The judge folded his arms. "Gentlemen, given the Coronavirus, I need to set some ground rules. The circumstances are not ideal for trial. As a result, I plan to implement the following procedures in the interest of safety.

"First, spectators will not be permitted to sit in the gallery except for three media representatives chosen by lottery. My staff will arrange for a closed-circuit feed to an adjacent courtroom where others may watch.

"Second, potential jurors will be seated in the gallery during the *voir dire*, and they will be asked to leave at least one seat between them. When we have selected our jury, I will have them sit in the gallery with appropriate spacing.

"Third, everyone in court must wear a face covering. Attorneys, witnesses, and I may remove our masks when we speak.

"Fourth, we will be operating with limited on-site staff, so I ask you to be patient given the unusual nature of our situation."

It isn't as if we have any choice. "Yes, Your Honor," I said.

Erickson nodded. "Of course, Your Honor."

"Thank you, gentlemen. We'll see you at ten o'clock sharp on Monday morning."

26

"WILL SHE TESTIFY?"

Terrence "The Terminator" was the only person in the P.D.'s Office when I returned on Friday evening. He looked up from his computer and asked, "How did it go with Judge Powell?"

I unbuttoned my coat. "About what I expected. Trial starts Monday. I got Patty Dawson settled in at the Golden Gate Hotel for a few days. Thanks for setting it up so quickly."

"You're welcome." He stopped typing. "Did she provide any useful information?"

"She confirmed that Marcus Strong was a bad guy who was supplying Annie Parker with Oxy and other drugs."

"It doesn't prove that Strong gave her the pills that killed her."

"True. She also told me that Brian Holton and 'Go-To' Joe Davis were dealing drugs in the TL."

"That doesn't prove that either of them gave Annie Parker the spiked Oxy pills, either."

"Also true. On the other hand, it may give us some options."

"Will she testify?"

"Probably yes about Strong. Probably not about Davis and Holton."

He shrugged. "Can't blame her. Fingering a couple of drug dealers could be dangerous. Will the jury believe her?"

"Hard to say."

He leaned back in his chair. "Doesn't sound like a slam-dunk acquittal."

"Our best case may be a hung jury. Have you heard from Nady?"

"Her mother is doing a little better."

It was nice to get a little good news. "And Rosie?"

"She's at the Mayor's Office." He scanned the empty corridor. "Effective in fifteen minutes, this office is closed until further notice, and everybody will work remotely."

"You're still here."

"I got special dispensation to come in and check the mail and deal with emergencies."

"You okay with that?"

"Seems unlikely that I'll catch the virus when I'm the only one here."

"You have to get to work. This isn't an ideal time to be taking MUNI."

"I'll drive to and from my apartment. Rosie gave me a key card to park downstairs." He grinned. "I could get used to having my own parking space."

An hour later, Rosie appeared in my doorway wearing a surgical mask. "Terrence told me that you're going to trial on Monday. You ready?"

"Of course." *What else could I say?* I looked up from the fifth draft of my opening statement. "You okay?"

"Fine. I brought you a mask."

"Thanks. Do they work?"

"I don't know. I'm operating under the assumption that it can't hurt."

Probably true. "How long are we going to be working from home?"

"Hard to say. Hopefully, not much longer than a week or two."

"Trials?"

"Still moving forward, but galleries will be empty except for jurors, who will be spaced apart and required to wear masks. Procedures for witnesses, lawyers, and judges will be decided at each judge's discretion."

I told her about our meeting with Judge Powell.

She shrugged. "Sounds like he's being appropriately cautious. The judges have been instructed to honor all requests for continuances. If things get worse, it's possible that they'll do a blanket extension of all pending trials." She eyed me. "Any chance you can persuade Lenny to ask for a delay?"

"I'll ask him again in the morning. Chances are slim. You hear from the kids?"

"Grace and Chuck are fine. Pixar told everybody to work from home, so they're camped out at the condo until further notice. Tommy texted me that Cal is likely to start teaching classes online in the next couple of weeks, and they may ask everybody to clear out of the dorms."

"Maybe he should come home for a while. It's not an ideal way to spend your freshman year, but it's better than being sick."

"True. I'm heading home soon. Do you want a ride?"

"I have my car."

"Don't stay too late."

"I won't."

"You going straight home?"

"I need to stop in the TL to talk to Brian Holton."

27

"WHAT'S IN IT FOR ME?"

Pedestrian traffic was light, and the smell of urine filled the air as I made my way through U.N. Plaza at seven-fifteen on Friday night. The daytime vendors had departed. The pre-theater crowd was starting to assemble among the security guards under the marquee of the Orpheum.

I found Holton sitting on a lawn chair under a leafless tree in the cement-encircled planted area adjacent to the broken escalator of the Civic Center BART Station.

"I brought you dinner," I said.

He looked up from his phone. "Thank you."

I handed him a brown bag containing chicken, beef, and lamb gyros from Gyro King, a longtime neighborhood favorite near the main library. "I wasn't sure what you liked best, so I got you some choices. Got a sec to talk?"

"Okay." He took a bite of the lamb gyro. "To what do I owe the honor of your company again?"

"Lenny Garcia's trial starts Monday. I need you to testify that Marcus Strong was a bad guy." *And it may give me the opportunity to accuse you of giving Annie Parker some tainted pills.*

"What's in it for me?"

"I'll buy you another nice dinner."

"You're going to have to do a little better."

"I'll pay for cab fare. You can come to the office and pick out some going-to-court clothes that you can keep. And you'll have the satisfaction of knowing that you performed your civic duty."

He rolled his eyes. "You're going to have to come up with a little more."

"I can get you a room at the Golden Gate Hotel so you'll have a place to stay until you testify."

"Room service?"

"No, but I can provide a gift card for meals."

"I'll pass. When would I have to testify?"

"Probably middle of next week."

"And all I have to do is testify for an hour?"

"Yes. I just need you to show up and tell the truth." *And throw Strong under the bus.*

"What makes you think I'll show up?"

"I trust you, Brian." *That's a whopper.*

Holton flashed a knowing smile. "Five hundred dollars for one hour of my time."

"I can get you a hundred for your time and incidental costs."

He finished his gyro. "I think we can work something out."

I was driving north on Van Ness Avenue when my phone vibrated. The display indicated that I had a text from Andy Erickson. I stopped at the red light at Broadway.

The message read, "Please come see me ASAP, tonight if possible. Important. Prefer to discuss in person."

28

"LAST CHANCE"

Erickson was wearing a mask as he sat behind his desk, eyes somber, tone serious. "Thank you for coming over so late. We've been scrambling to get our people set up to work from home."

"So have we," I said.

The D.A.'s Office was quiet at nine-thirty on Friday night. The lights were on in a couple of the offices down the hallway, where Erickson's colleagues were loading files onto their laptops.

He took off his wire-framed glasses, wiped them with a cloth, and put them back on. "My glasses fog up when I wear the mask."

"We'll adapt." In response to his inquiry about Nady's mother, I told him that she was doing a little better. *Time for business.* "Why did you want to see me, Andy?"

"I take it that you weren't able to persuade your client to ask for a continuance?"

"I'm afraid not. Three more people at San Bruno Jail tested positive today." I touched my mask. "Even if everybody starts wearing these, it's unclear whether they'll stop the spread. Lenny is terrified that he's going to catch the virus. He wants to go to trial right away."

"Can't blame him, I suppose."

"You didn't ask me to come over at this hour to convince me to ask for an extension."

"I didn't." He templed his fingers in front of his face. "I have a proposition for you."

I waited.

"DeSean has authorized me to make a final offer. Your client will plead guilty to voluntary manslaughter. No enhancements."

We're making progress. First-degree murder carries a minimum sentence of twenty-five years, second-degree fifteen. The maximum sentence for vol man is eleven years, but the minimum can be as low as three.

"It's a good deal, Mike," he insisted.

Yes, it is. "Recommended sentence?"

"Higher end of the scale. We'll recommend ten."

"I won't be able to sell it to my client."

"I might be able to go as low as eight."

"Five."

"Seven."

We're entering the realm of possibility.

He held up a hand. "Your client gave the decedent a bottle of tainted pills. His name was on the label, and his prints were on the bottle."

"He gave her some real Oxy pills that he got from the V.A."

"You're going to argue that a handful of fentanyl-spiked pills somehow managed to find their way into the very same bottle?"

"I don't have to prove that somebody else gave her the pills. I just need to convince one juror that there is reasonable doubt that Lenny did."

"Be reasonable, Mike."

"Be realistic, Andy."

"What would it take for you to convince your client to accept a deal?"

"I can try to sell him on involuntary man with a minimal sentence."

"How minimal?"

"No more than three years."

"I can't do it, Mike."

"Sure you can, Andy."

"That isn't justice."

"Sure it is. Your best chance at a conviction is telling the jury that Lenny accidentally gave Annie Parker some tainted pills. You'll never make vol man, and you certainly won't make murder."

He took off his mask. "Last chance. The offer is voluntary manslaughter with a recommended sentence of seven years. He'll get credit for the year that he's already served. You have a legal obligation to take it to your client. It will remain open until five p.m. on Sunday."

29

"THAT ISN'T GOING TO WORK FOR ME"

Lenny's answer was succinct. "No."

"It's a good deal," I said. "We won't get anything better."

"That isn't going to work for me."

"With credit for time served and good behavior, you'll be out of here in six years. You'll still be a young man."

"And an admitted killer. No deal, Mike."

"I'll let the D.A. know."

Lenny was agitated as he sat on the opposite side of the table in the drab consultation room in County Jail #5 in San Bruno the following morning, a Saturday. He was trying to process the reality that we were starting trial in two days. In addition to discussing legal strategies, I needed to manage his expectations and emotions.

"You okay?" I asked.

"Terrific."

His orange jumpsuit was stained with perspiration. "You're sweating."

"It's hot in here."

No, it isn't. "Did they give you a mask?"

"No."

"I'll make sure that you get one. Do you have any symptoms?"

"I'm fine, Mike."

He looked as if he'd lost weight. "Are you eating and sleeping?"

"Some."

I took a deep breath of the stale air that smelled of Clorox. "I found Patty Dawson. She seems willing to testify about Marcus Strong."

His expression brightened. "That's good, right?"

Hopefully. "Yes."

"Does she know who gave Annie the pills?"

"No."

His optimism disappeared. "What is she going to say?"

"That Strong was a bad guy who was beating Annie and giving her drugs. She'll confirm that drug dealing was rampant on U.N. Plaza."

"Will she name other names?"

I sighed. "Not yet. She told me that Joe Davis was selling drugs on U.N. Plaza. So was Brian Holton. She isn't willing to testify about them—yet."

"Not good enough."

"It's the best that I can do for now. I'll put Davis and Holton on the stand and go after them."

"You expect them to confess?"

Doubtful. "If I can muddy the waters enough, I can get at least one juror to reasonable doubt, and we'll get a hung jury. Best case, I'll convince all twelve jurors to acquit, and you can go home."

"Or back to U.N. Plaza."

"We'll find you a place to live, Lenny."

He remained skeptical. "Bottom line, you don't have any hard evidence that somebody else gave Annie the tainted pills, do you?"

No. "There were prints and traces of DNA on the bottle and DNA on Annie's panties that didn't match yours."

"Have you been able to match them to somebody else?"

"No."

"You aren't making me feel more confident."

"The evidence is what it is, Lenny. We'll start our defense with testimony from a medical expert who will say that Annie had an existing heart condition that could have caused her death."

"The Chief Medical Examiner is going to say that she OD'd."
True. "Our expert is very good."

"From what I've heard, the M.E. is good, too."

She is. "We don't need to prove that she's wrong. We only need to create enough doubt to get one juror to reasonable doubt. Patty Dawson will testify that Strong was beating Annie and giving her drugs. Then I'll put Davis and Holton on the stand and accuse them of giving Annie the spiked pills."

"You think any of this will work?"

"Hard to say. Juries are unpredictable. I think it's our best shot."

"Do you want me to testify?"

"Probably not, but I need you to be ready just in case."

"Why can't I get up and tell the truth?"

"Because a smart prosecutor like Erickson will twist your words." I had walked Lenny through a practice cross-exam earlier in the week. It had gone pretty well, but not great.

He frowned. "What's going to happen on Monday?"

I told him that he would be driven from the jail to the Hall of Justice, where I would meet him. I would bring him a suit and tie. I asked him to be clean-shaven. I reminded him that trial work is theater, and appearances are critical. "Everybody will be watching you. I want you to be respectful and engaged. People will pay close attention to your facial expressions, so I want you to remain subdued. I need you to look the judge, the jurors, and the witnesses in the eye. Judge Powell is a stickler for decorum, so it is absolutely critical that you avoid any disruptions or make any remarks. Got it?"

He nodded.

I explained that we would spend the first few days of the trial doing jury selection, which was a critical but repetitive process. "We'll do opening statements after we've picked the jury. The D.A. gets to present his case first. Then it will be our turn. Erickson told the judge that his case will be short—just a day or two. Our defense will be brief, too. The whole process could wrap up by the end of the week."

His Adam's apple bobbed as he took it in. Finally, he asked, "How do you think this is really going to go, Mike?"

Hard to say. "I can get the jury to reasonable doubt. Anybody I should call before trial?"

"Maybe you could check in with my sister. I don't think she'll come to the trial, but I want her to know that she still means a lot to me."

30

"MY BROTHER IS A GOOD GUY"

Rain pounded my windshield as I sat in my car about a mile down the mountain from County Jail #5. There is no cell reception in the parking lot of the jail, so I had to drive down the hill until I saw bars on my phone. I checked my e-mails, exchanged texts with Rosie, swallowed two Advils, and placed a call to Lenny's sister.

"Perlita Garcia."

"It's Mike Daley."

A hesitation. "Uh, hi."

"Did I catch you at a bad time?"

"I'm at work, Mr. Daley. I can't talk for long."

"I know that you're insanely busy, so I'll be brief. I wanted to let you know that Lenny's trial is starting on Monday at ten a.m. It would mean a lot to him if you could stop by for a short time to give him a little moral support."

She took a deep breath. "I don't think that's going to be possible."

"I understand." I waited a beat. "Lenny wanted me to tell you that he is very grateful for everything that you've done for him and that you still mean a lot to him."

"Thank you." A pause. "Anything else?"

"I think that's it. I'll let you get back to work."

"Thank you." I was about to end the call when she spoke up again. "Mr. Daley?"

"Yes?"

"How is Lenny doing?"

"He's holding up okay in the circumstances. He's worried about getting the virus—especially in light of his, uh, living arrangements."

"Is he eating?"

"I think so. I just saw him. It looked like he's lost a little weight." In the background, I could hear her name announced on the hospital's paging system. "Sounds like you need to go."

"I do." She lowered her voice. "My brother is a good guy, Mr. Daley. He's been through a lot and has had some bad luck." Her voice cracked. "Lenny isn't a murderer."

Pedestrian traffic was light on Turk Street as I caught up with a masked Joe Davis as he walked toward his apartment building at eleven-forty on Saturday morning.

"Got a sec?" I asked him.

He kept walking. "Now what?"

I held up a bag with a couple of turkey sandwiches, coleslaw, chocolate chip cookies, and drinks. "I bought you lunch."

"I already ate. What do you want?"

"I found Patty Dawson. I came to thank you."

"You're welcome." He opened the door to his building and took the bag from me. "Thanks for the food."

I followed him inside the lobby. "I need your help."

He lowered his mask. "I told you everything last time."

"Lenny's trial starts on Monday. I need you to testify that Marcus Strong was a bad guy." *And a few other things that I don't want to talk about now.*

"I don't have time."

"I'll talk to your boss and get you time off work."

"That's a bad idea."

"I'll pay you for your time."

This got his attention. "How much?"

"A hundred dollars an hour—including time for travel and cab fare."

He paused to consider his options. "When do you need me?"

"Later this week. Probably Thursday or Friday."

"How will I know when to come in?"

I handed him a prepaid burner phone. "I'll call you on this phone a day or two in advance. It has a hundred dollars of time on it. You can keep it."

"How long do you think it will take?"

"Figure an hour each way and about twenty minutes in court."

"Cash in advance."

I pulled out my wallet and handed him five twenties. "Here you go."

He stuffed the bills into his pocket and gave me a wry grin. "What makes you think I'm actually going to show up?"

I returned his smile. "I trust you."

31

"WE'RE GOING TO DO TAKEOUT FOR A WHILE"

Joey set a pint of Guinness in front of me on the weathered bar. "To your health, Mike."

"And to yours, Joey."

We were the only people inside Dunleavy's at nine-thirty on Saturday night. A hand-lettered sign on the door noted that the watering hole would not be seating customers indoors tonight. Joey reported that business had been slow. The cold weather and pouring rain had left the patio empty. Joey turned up the lights. The jukebox played Fleetwood Mac's "Don't Stop Believing." I looked at the enlarged photo of Big John above the bar. It made me melancholy.

"You want some fish and chips to take home?" he asked.

"No, thanks, Joe. I got plenty of food. You gonna shut down?"

His voice turned emphatic. "Dunleavy's doesn't close. We're going to do takeout for a while."

"You need help?" I asked.

"I'll be fine, Mike. Besides, you have a full plate. Are you still starting trial on Monday?"

"Yes."

"Can you get Lenny off?"

"We have some good arguments."

"Doesn't sound like you're wildly optimistic."

"We'll see how it goes."

"Jerry Edwards wrote in the *Chronicle* that you have no chance."

"He's a better writer than a lawyer."

"He gets it right most of the time."

"That's why we go through the exercise of doing the trials."

Joey smiled. "You're a good lawyer, Mike. You'll figure something out."

We turned to the TV and watched the highlights from the Warriors' game. It was nice to think about something other than Lenny's trial and the virus. Then the backdoor swung open, and Pete let himself inside using the key that Big John had given him decades earlier. He hung up his bomber jacket on one of the hooks next to the door, shook the rain out of his hair, and walked over to the bar, where he took the stool next to mine. He nodded at Joey, who put a cup of black coffee on the bar in front of him.

"You hungry?" Joey asked. "I could make you something."

"I'm fine."

"I didn't think Donna was letting you leave the house."

"I got special dispensation to see my favorite brother and my favorite cousin. I promised that I would wear a mask and sit at least ten feet away from both of you."

Pete was unmasked and sitting a couple of feet from us.

"You want me to put on a mask?" Joey asked.

"Nah. I won't be here for long."

I gave my brother a knowing smile. "Is Donna still making you sleep in the garage?"

"For now."

"It must be cold."

"I've been on stakeouts where it's been a lot colder. We're an adaptable species, Mick." He took a sip of coffee. "You get anything new on Lenny's case?"

"I found Patty Dawson."

"That's good."

"She didn't provide anything terribly useful."

"That's bad."

He listened attentively as I summarized my conversions with Dawson, "Go-To" Joe, and Holton. I told him that Lenny had rejected Erickson's plea offer. I described my conversation with Lenny's sister.

He took it in and responded with a scowl. "Doesn't sound like you have a winner, Mick."

"We'll see. Was your DNA person able to run tests on the samples that I gave you for Holton and Davis?"

"Yes."

I had surreptitiously pocketed Holton's coffee mug when I took him out for breakfast. I got a sample from "Go-To" Joe when I brought him dinner. Neither would be admissible in court, but if we got a match, I would figure out a way to get another sample and introduce it at trial.

"No luck." Pete handed me a printout. "The samples that you provided did not match the DNA from the unidentified prints on the pill bottle or the semen on Annie Parker's clothes. Looks like you're back to square one, Mick."

"I knew it was a long shot. Was your person able to match the samples to anybody else?"

"Afraid not, Mick. She's standing by if we need her to do another DNA test."

"Thanks, Pete. I'll let you know."

He eyed me. "Do you think you have any realistic chance of getting an acquittal?"

"It's going to be a heavy lift, Pete."

32

"WHAT'S THE NARRATIVE?"

"The Terminator" knocked on the open door to my office. "You need anything, Mike?"

I looked up from my laptop. "I'm good, T."

Terrence and I were the only people in the P.D.'s Office at eight-fifteen the following night. It was always quiet on Sundays, but there were usually a few stragglers preparing for court appearances on Monday morning. The silence was a bit unnerving.

"Anything new?" he asked.

"Afraid not."

"Okay if I head home?"

"Sure." I held up a hand. "You feeling okay, T?"

"Fine, Mike. You?"

"Fine."

"Good. I'll be here early tomorrow if anything comes up."

"Thanks."

I looked on as the hulking former boxer returned to his desk, put on his oversized parka, and headed out the door.

An hour later, I was staring at my laptop when Nady's name appeared on my phone.

"How's your mom?" I asked.

"A little better." She sounded tired. "Still in the hospital, but out of intensive care."

"Good. Have you seen her?"

"Not in person." She said that it was too soon to determine when her mother might be able to go home.

My phone notified me that another person was joining our conversation. The co-head of the Felony Division and Rosie's niece, Rolanda, was added to the call. The mother of a six-month-old daughter, Rolanda sounded more exhausted than Nady. My great-niece, Maria Sylvia Teresa Fernandez Epstein, was an energetic beauty who didn't sleep much. Rolanda and her husband, Zach, had learned the first lesson of parenthood: nothing prepares you for the exhaustion.

"You and Zach getting any sleep?" I asked.

"Maybe someday." She said that she was extending her maternity leave for another three months. "Zach's law firm told everybody to work from home for a few weeks. It's going to be a little crowded here." She turned to the matters at hand. "You still going to trial tomorrow?"

"Yes."

"Have you finished your closing argument?"

"Working on it now."

You might think that on the night before trial, I would be focused on my opening, which I had completed a few days ago. One of the first things I learned from Rosie when I was a baby P.D. was that when you're preparing your case, you should also write your closing and work backward to the beginning. It forces you to focus on the story that you want to emphasize during the trial, which impacts how you plan to present the evidence.

"What's the narrative?" Rolanda asked.

"Our medical expert will testify that Annie Parker had a pre-existing heart condition that likely caused her death."

"You think it will fly?"

"Dr. Kramer is very good."

"I trust there's more?"

"If necessary, I'll go with a SODDI defense."

"SODDI" is defense-lawyer speak for "Some other dude did it." It means that I'm going to try to foist the blame on somebody else, even if the connections are tenuous.

Rolanda's voice turned skeptical. "You'll look desperate."

Yes, I will. "I'm working with limited evidence, time, and options. Patty Dawson will testify that Annie's pimp, Marcus Strong, was an abusive guy who gave Annie drugs to control her. There's a good chance that he gave her some fentanyl-laced pills that were pressed to look like OxyContin."

"Proof?"

"Innuendo. If it looks like the jury isn't convinced, I'll put 'Go-To' Joe Davis and Brian Holton on the stand and suggest that they were both dealing drugs in the TL."

"Can you connect them to Annie Parker?"

"They knew her."

"But do you have any evidence that either of them provided her with pills?"

"Uh, no."

Rolanda went silent.

Nady spoke up again. "Are you going to admit that Lenny gave Annie the pill bottle?"

"Yes. It won't be credible to suggest otherwise."

"So you're going to argue that he gave her some real Oxy pills, and somebody else gave her the dirty ones?"

"Coincidentally, it's the truth."

"According to our client." Nady waited a beat. "Does that mean you're going to put Lenny on the stand?"

"If I have to."

"Erickson will take him apart."

"It will humanize him in front of the jury."

"Maybe. Did you use a jury consultant?"

"No. I didn't have the time or resources to do a deep-dive into juror attributes. I'm going to look for people who might be sympathetic to the homeless."

"Good luck finding them in San Francisco."

True.

Nady chuckled. "So you're going to wing it?"

"It's hardly the first time."

"You have good instincts, Mike."

"I'm going to need them."

33

"YOU'LL COME UP WITH SOMETHING"

Sylvia Fernandez's jet-black eyes stared at me from the little box in the Skype screen on my laptop. "Is your case going forward in the morning?"

"Yes."

"Jerry Edwards said that Lenny Garcia is likely to be convicted."

"He's wrong."

My ex-mother-in-law gave me a knowing smile. "He's usually right."

"Not this time." *We'll see.*

At ten-twenty on Sunday night, Sylvia, Rosie, and I were having a check-in on Skype. Sylvia was sitting in her usual spot in her dining room, Rosie was in her office at home, and I was at the table in the kitchen of my apartment. It was a cumbersome setup, but grainy images were better than nothing.

Rosie leaned in closer and spoke to her mother. "Did you get the package that I sent?"

"Yes, Rosita. I appreciate fancy steaks and chops, but I need you to stop sending food. Tony brought over eggs, butter, and vegetables. I don't have any room in my freezer."

Rosie smiled. "Did you and the ladies play mahjongg tonight?"

"Yes, dear. We're playing online. It's a little tricky at first, but we're getting the hang of it. Ann-Helen won again. I think she's been practicing with her daughters."

Rosie's grin broadened. "She's always been a shark. Did you have the usual refreshments?"

"Of course. The young woman from the dispensary left the stuff on my front porch. She has excellent taste in edibles. I'll ask her to bring some for you next time."

"Thank you."

I should get in touch with Sylvia's supplier.

Sylvia assured us that she had everything that she needed—as if she would ever acknowledge that she needed anything. She would never admit that she was slowing down after two hip replacements and a knee replacement.

Finally, her expression turned serious, and her voice became somber as she spoke to me. "Do you really think you can get an acquittal for Lenny Garcia?"

"Hard to say. We have some good arguments, but we don't have any obvious exculpatory evidence."

"You'll come up with something, Michael." She turned to Rosie. "I saw that they're talking about transitioning to online classes at Cal. Is Tommy coming home?"

"Not yet, Mama."

"And Grace?"

"She and Chuck are working from home."

"You don't think we'll have to postpone the wedding, do you?"

"Not a chance, Mama. The virus will go away in a few weeks, and for sure by summer."

"I hope you're right, dear." She looked my way. "Good luck with your trial, Michael."

"Thanks, Sylvia."

Rosie looked at me from the box on Skype. "You okay?"

My head feels like somebody hit me with a two-by-four.

"Fine. You?"

"Not bad."

I asked her if she was planning to go in to the office in the morning.

"I'm going to work from home. I'm trying to set an example." Her voice remained businesslike. "We have to adapt, Mike."

A gentle rain tapped the ceiling of my apartment at ten-thirty on Sunday night. Wilma the cat was sleeping on the sofa. An untouched Cobb salad in a carry-out container was next to my laptop. I can never eat on the night before trial.

"You good to go in the morning?" she asked.

I have no choice. "Yes."

"I'm sorry that you have to fly solo."

"It's like the good old days when we were baby P.D.'s. We never had the resources for an army of lawyers."

"We usually had somebody sitting second chair on murder trials. You got enough to get an acquittal?"

"Realistically, the best case is probably a hung jury."

She smiled. "It would be nice to add an acquittal to our statistics."

"Our stats may take a hit this time."

I gave her the shorthand version of my trial strategy. During jury selection, I would look for people who were smart enough to understand the nuances of our case, but open-minded enough to give Lenny a chance. The conventional wisdom says that defense attorneys should search for jurors who are susceptible to persuasion. In other words, people who aren't too bright. In this case, I wanted people who were smart enough to question the prosecution's case.

Rosie agreed. "This may be a rare instance where you should look for some college-educated people, and maybe even a lawyer or two."

"They won't be hard to find in a San Francisco jury pool." I told her that the prosecution's case would be short. "The City Ambassador who discovered the body, the first officer at the scene, the Medical Examiner, an evidence tech or two, and then Ken Lee will tie their case together."

"And your narrative?"

"It has two parts. First, our medical expert will say that Annie Parker died of a heart condition. If it looks like the jury is buying it, I may stop there."

Her expression turned skeptical. "And if not?"

"I'll put Patty Dawson on the stand to testify that Marcus Strong was abusing Parker and giving her drugs. I'll try to convince the jury that there is a good chance that Strong gave her the tainted pills. If it looks like that won't be enough, I'll put Joe Davis and Brian Holton on the stand and try to persuade the jury that they may have given Parker the tainted pills."

"Any evidence?"

"They were in the neighborhood and were known to distribute drugs."

She eyed me. "Any *real* evidence?"

"No. It would be nice if we can prove that one of them had sex with Parker on the night that she died, but the DNA didn't match up. Neither did the smudged prints on the pill bottle."

"How did you get DNA so fast?"

"Pete has a contact."

"Figures. Any chance he might be able to find something to help at the trial?"

"He's trying, but I can't ask him to go down to the TL this week."

"Understood."

We sat in silence while Wilma stretched, yawned, and went back to sleep.

Rosie spoke up again. "This doesn't sound wildly promising, Mike."

"You know how it goes with trials. You plan everything out in advance. Then something changes and it turns into improvisational theater."

"You'll come up with something, Mike. You always do. Have you gotten outside?"

"A few trips down to the TL to look for witnesses."

"Is your heart okay?"

"Fine."

"You should go for a walk in the morning. It'll be good to clear your head."

"Maybe I will if the rain stops."

"Zvi will be at the steps rain or shine."

"True."

Our friend, neighbor, and hero, Zvi Danenberg, was a brilliant and relentlessly upbeat ninety-seven-year-old retired science teacher who walked up and down the one hundred and thirty-nine steps connecting Magnolia Avenue in downtown Larkspur with the houses on the adjacent hill. He used to do it every day, but he slowed down to twice a week after he celebrated his ninety-fifth birthday, and his doctors advised him to preserve what was left of his overworked knees. I joined him from time to time in my never-ending quest to improve my conditioning. In his spare time, Zvi maintained a carefully curated collection of classical records that he had accumulated over eight decades. I was honored when he invited me to view the room in his house that he devoted to his albums.

"I'll pass along your regards to Zvi," I said.

"Give him my best."

"I will." I looked at Rosie—beautiful Rosie.

"What?" she asked.

"We aren't going to be able to do our usual pre-trial ritual."

"That wouldn't be prudent in the circumstances."

"Is there such a thing as 'Skype sex'?"

She chuckled. "I don't think so, Mike."

"You'll make it up to me if I get an acquittal?"

Her eyes gleamed. "I'll make it up to you no matter what."

34

"THE FACTS ARE NOT IN DISPUTE"

At nine-ten on a drizzly Monday morning, I lugged my laptop, trial bag, and exhibits up the front steps of the Hall and past the handful of reporters on Bryant Street who were keeping warm by shouting questions.

"Mr. Daley? Does your client plan to cut a deal?"

"Mr. Daley? Did your client give the victim the pills that killed her?"

"Mr. Daley? Is it true that your client has contracted the Coronavirus?"

I stopped, turned around, faced the cameras, removed my mask, and recited the platitude that every defense attorney says before the start of every trial. "I am pleased to have the opportunity to defend my client in court. I am confident that he will be exonerated."

I saw Mayor Nicole Ward walking up the steps accompanied by Andy Erickson, Kyle Adams, and the mayor's customary entourage of handlers, hangers-on, and sycophants. Her Honor and I had been on opposite sides of several cases during her tenure as D.A. The photogenic law-and-order zealot and cable news wannabe was a mediocre lawyer, but a world-class politician. Even in liberal San Francisco, she was heavily favored to win a second term.

She removed her mask, located the nearest camera, flashed a thousand-watt politician's smile, and spoke to the gaggle of microphones. "We are here to support Andrew Erickson of our District Attorney's Office who is about to begin the prosecution of Leonard Garcia, who killed a young woman named Annie Parker by giving her pills tainted with fentanyl.

The rampant distribution of illegal drugs is a tragedy for our city, and it needs to stop—especially in the Tenderloin. We commend Mr. Erickson for filing a murder charge. We believe this sends an important message to the drug dealers in our community that they will be punished."

She touted her alleged success as a prosecutor and mayor at ridding San Francisco's streets of drugs. In reality, things had gotten so much worse on her watch that she had declared a state of emergency in the TL. For those of us who had lived here for our entire lives and seen parts of our city overwhelmed by drug dealing and homelessness, her words rang hollow.

Ward was still talking. "I would like to ask Mr. Erickson to say a few words."

Erickson knew that she was using him as a prop. "I have no comment at this time."

Ward pointed at Adams. "I would also like to ask our dedicated head of homeless outreach, Kyle Adams, to provide a comment."

Adams feigned reluctance as he marched to the microphones. "Annie Parker died tragically of a fentanyl overdose. We will try to ease the pain of her family and friends by bringing her killer to justice."

As Adams and Ward played to the cameras, I slipped inside the Hall.

Two deputies escorted Lenny into court, where he sat down at the defense table next to me. Freshly shaved and wearing the charcoal suit and striped tie that I had picked out for him, he was anxious.

I whispered, "Stay calm and look the judge and the jurors in the eye."

"Right."

I turned around and pointed at his sister, who was sitting in the back row of the almost-empty gallery. She pulled down her mask and said, "Good luck, Lenny."

He mouthed, "Thanks for coming."

Erickson was sitting at the prosecution table along with Inspector Lee. As the lead homicide inspector, Lee was the only witness allowed in court before his testimony. In a display of institutional support, DeSean Harper sat behind them in the gallery. Jerry Edwards was two rows behind Harper, scribbling in his notebook. A reporter from Channel Two was the only other media representative. The usual ragtag assortment of courtroom junkies, retirees, law students, and homeless people were relegated to a courtroom down the hall, where the proceedings were being shown on a closed-circuit feed. To his credit, Judge Powell never allowed his trials to be broadcast.

I felt a rush of adrenaline as the bailiff recited the call to order. "All rise."

Here we go.

A standing fan pushed around the heavy air. While I didn't like wearing a mask, there was an unanticipated upside: I could not smell the mildew that permeated the courtroom.

Judge Powell emerged from his chambers, surveyed his domain, and lumbered to his tall leather chair. He turned on his computer, put on his reading glasses, glanced at his docket, and removed the glasses. "Please be seated."

Nowadays, most judges don't use their gavels.

He turned on his microphone and addressed the bailiff in a commanding voice. "We are on the record. Please call our case."

"The People versus Leonard Garcia."

"Counsel will state their names for the record."

"Andrew Erickson for the People."

"Michael Daley for the defense."

"Given the current medical emergency, I must ask everybody in my courtroom to wear a face covering unless they are speaking. I would also request that you maintain an appropriate distance when possible. In addition, we will be seating our potential jurors and, later, our selected jurors in the gallery with spacing to reduce the risk of exposure. Does anyone have any questions about these policies?"

Silence.

"Let's pick a jury."

Under Judge Powell's skillful and relentless supervision, we selected twelve jurors and four alternates by the close of business on Tuesday. At ten o'clock on Wednesday morning, those who hadn't come up with a convincing sob story sat in every other seat in the gallery, feigning nonchalance, eyes revealing nervousness. Jerry Edwards and a sketch artist were the only non-jurors in the gallery. Perlita had watched the first twenty minutes of jury selection and hadn't returned.

Most trial attorneys (including yours truly) believe that cases are won and lost during jury selection. The legal issues in our case weren't complicated, so I tried to pick people who were likely to pay attention and were susceptible to persuasion. I wouldn't know if I had chosen wisely until the trial was over.

Our lineup included eight women, six of whom were college graduates, and four of whom were people of color. We had five mothers (two single), three fathers, two African-Americans, two Latinas, and one Filipino. Three worked for tech firms, two worked for the City, one was a supervisor at PG&E, one was a lawyer with an insurance defense firm, and two were retirees. I had a hunch that the woman who worked at PG&E would take a leadership role.

Judge Powell thanked the jurors for their service and invited them to notify the bailiff if they had concerns. Then he read the standard instructions. "Do not talk about this case to anyone or among yourselves until deliberations begin. Do not do any research on your own or as a group. You may take notes, but do not use a dictionary or other reference materials, investigate the facts or law, conduct any experiments, or visit the scene of the events to be described at this trial. Do not look at anything involving this case in the press, on TV, or online."

He added the now-standard admonition that was unnecessary when I started as a Deputy Public Defender almost three decades ago. "Do not post anything on Facebook, Twitter, Instagram, Snapchat, WhatsApp, or other social media. If you tweet or text about this case, it will cost you."

A couple of the stone-faced jurors nodded.

The judge looked at Erickson. "Do you wish to make an opening statement?"

He wasn't required to do so, but I had never seen a prosecutor turn down the invitation.

"Yes, Your Honor." He stood up, buttoned his charcoal jacket, strode to the lectern, placed his laptop in front of him, removed his mask, and spoke directly to the jury. "My name is Andrew Erickson. I am the Chief Assistant to the District Attorney. I am grateful for your service, and I appreciate your time and attention."

Lenny tensed.

Erickson activated the flat-screen TV and showed a high school graduation photo of a smiling Annie Parker. "Annie Parker was a vibrant young woman who was a wonderful daughter, a gifted dancer, a treasured confidante, and a cherished friend. She was only nineteen when she died of an overdose of fentanyl provided by the defendant." He pushed out a melodramatic sigh. "It is an unspeakable tragedy." He pointed at Lenny. "The facts are not in dispute. We will demonstrate beyond a reasonable doubt that the defendant gave Annie some pills tainted with fentanyl in January of last year."

Erickson was following the conventional playbook. The first thing they teach every Assistant D.A. is to point at the defendant. The second is always to refer to the decedent by name to humanize her. The third is never to mention the defendant's name to dehumanize him. They don't teach this stuff at law school, but they should.

He lowered his arm. "Annie's family and friends are devastated. We cannot bring her back, but we can bring her murderer to justice."

It is generally considered bad form to interrupt during an opening, but I wanted the jury to know that I was paying attention, so I interjected in a respectful tone. "Objection to the term 'murderer.' My client is innocent until proven otherwise."

"Sustained. The jury will disregard the use of the term 'murderer.'"

Sure they will—especially since you just repeated it.

Erickson pretended to ignore me. "I ask you to listen carefully, weigh the evidence, and find justice for Annie." He moved closer to the jury. "Annie loved people. The sad irony is that Annie knew the defendant and tried to help him. Yet he reciprocated by giving her a deadly substance. There is no doubt that the defendant gave her drugs—he admitted it, and his name and fingerprints were on a pill bottle found in Annie's tent. It contained six pills laced with fentanyl. The defense will probably argue that the defendant gave Annie legitimate prescription drugs. They will suggest that somebody else put tainted pills in the very same bottle. We will hear from a fingerprint expert that the defendant's prints were on that bottle. We will hear from the Medical Examiner that Annie died of a fentanyl overdose. We know that the pills were tainted because there were more pills in the bottle. We know that the defendant was angry at Annie because we will hear from a witness who broke up a heated argument between them the night before Annie died."

I stood up and spoke respectfully. "Objection. Mr. Erickson's opening has transitioned from a statement into argument, which isn't allowed during openings."

"Sustained. Please, Mr. Erickson."

Erickson shot a disdainful glance my way, then he faced the jury. "Mr. Daley is going to try to convince you that somebody other than the defendant gave Annie the tainted pills. He's also likely to suggest that Annie died of a medical condition unrelated to the poison that the defendant gave her. Or maybe he'll say that it was a misunderstanding or an accident. Mr. Daley is a fine lawyer who is simply doing his job—to distract you. That's why I am asking you to evaluate the evidence carefully."

I stood up again. "I must object again, Your Honor. More argument."

The judge cocked his head slightly as he looked at Erickson. "Sustained."

Erickson got the message. He spent the next ten minutes walking the jurors through a description of the crime scene, the discovery of the pill bottle, and the Medical Examiner's analysis of cause of death. The jurors were locked in.

Lenny leaned over and whispered, "Can you stop this?"

No. "It'll be our turn shortly."

Erickson returned to the lectern. "During this trial, you are going to hear a lot about 'reasonable doubt.' It's a key legal concept. But common sense is every bit as critical. It is your job to evaluate the evidence, deliberate carefully, and, most important, use your common sense. I am confident that you will do so. And I promise to provide more than enough evidence for you to find the defendant guilty."

He returned to the prosecution table and sat down.

Judge Powell looked at me. "Opening statement, Mr. Daley?"

"Yes, Your Honor."

I could have deferred until after Erickson had completed his case, but I wanted to connect with the jurors right away.

I walked to the lectern and placed a single piece of paper in front of me. The jurors were in the gallery behind me, so I turned sideways so that the judge and the jurors could see my face. "My name is Michael Daley. I am the co-head of the Felony Division of the Public Defender's Office. Lenny Garcia has been wrongly accused of a crime that he did not commit. It's your job to correct this error and see that justice is served."

I moved closer to the jurors. "Lenny is a San Francisco native, a decorated military veteran, a beloved brother, and a trusted friend. After he returned from multiple deployments in combat zones overseas, he developed alcohol and drug issues. Unable to keep his job, he ended up living on U.N. Plaza in gut-wrenching circumstances. Multiple treatments for his addictions were unsuccessful, and his life spiraled into homelessness. Lenny doesn't want me to make excuses for him, but I want you to understand why he was living on the street."

I made eye contact with the jurors in the first row. "Lenny is tough. Lenny is kind. Lenny is resilient. Lenny was injured in combat for which he was prescribed a painkiller called OxyContin, which most of you have heard of. He got his prescriptions from the V.A. On a cold night last January, Lenny's neighbor, Annie Parker, was in terrible pain because of an injury suffered in an auto accident years earlier. Lenny was scheduled to go to the V.A. to pick up a refill of his Oxy pills the following day, so he gave Annie the bottle containing his last three Oxy pills. He was trying to help her. That's the kind of guy that Lenny is."

The jurors were listening, but I couldn't tell if they were buying into what I was selling.

"The Chief Medical Examiner concluded that Annie died of a fentanyl overdose. However, she also noted that Annie had a serious pre-existing heart condition that could have caused her to go into cardiac arrest at any time. Our medical expert will testify that Annie may have died of that heart condition. While we have made great strides in medical science, well-respected doctors often disagree about complicated cases. This is one of them.

"At some point that same night, Annie engaged in sex with a man other than Lenny. We know this because the Medical Examiner found traces of semen on her clothing. DNA testing showed that the semen did not match Lenny's. It is very possible that the man that she slept with provided her with the tainted pills. A friend of Annie's will also testify that several other individuals in the area provided drugs to Annie. One of those individuals was a man named Marcus Strong, who was Annie's pimp. Strong was physically abusive to Annie and maintained control over her finances. He also provided her with illegal drugs. I believe that it is likely that Mr. Strong or one of the other individuals provided her with the tainted pills."

The juror who issued marriage licenses at City Hall was paying attention.

"In addition, we will present evidence that at least one fingerprint on the bottle did not match Lenny's or Annie's. That print has never been identified. There is a substantial chance that the person whose print was on the bottle provided Annie with the tainted pills."

I lowered my voice. "Annie Parker's death is a great tragedy. Frankly, so was her life. She had a difficult childhood. She came to San Francisco to escape abusive relatives. She became a sex worker. She took drugs. She was homeless."

Erickson made his presence felt. "Objection. Annie Parker is not on trial."

I replied before Judge Powell could answer. "It is a matter of record that the decedent had issues involving prostitution and drugs. We will provide evidence that several of the people from whom she acquired drugs were in the vicinity on the night that she died."

"The objection is overruled. You may continue, Mr. Daley."

"Mr. Erickson and I agree that Ms. Parker's death is a tragedy. On the other hand, it would also compound the tragedy to convict an innocent man of a crime that he did not commit."

"Objection," Erickson said. "Argumentative."

Judge Powell addressed the jury. "An opening statement should not be treated as fact. It merely constitutes a road map of what the anticipated evidence will show."

As if they're going to forget what they had just heard.

I flashed a caustic grin at Erickson, nodded at the judge, and picked up where I had left off. "Mr. Erickson asked you to use common sense. So will I. Bottom line: Mr. Erickson cannot prove his case beyond a reasonable doubt. As a result, you cannot convict Lenny of murder."

There was no reaction from the jurors as I walked back to the defense table.

The judge spoke to Erickson. "Please call your first witness."

"The People call Mr. P.J. Jenkins."

It was a logical starting point. Jenkins had found Annie's body.

35

"A ROUTINE WELFARE CHECK"

Erickson stood at the lectern. "Please state your name and occupation for the record."

"Paul James Jenkins. My friends call me P.J. I am a City Ambassador employed by a nonprofit organization called Urban Alchemy."

"What does a 'City Ambassador' do?"

"My colleagues and I do outreach in the Tenderloin. We discourage people from blocking sidewalks and using drugs. We direct people to locations where they can find services, housing, and treatment."

"How long have you worked for Urban Alchemy?"

"A little over a year."

Erickson asked Jenkins if he liked his job.

"Yes, I do. It's my way of giving back to the community."

At three-hundred pounds, the soft-spoken Jenkins was a hulk with a ZZ Top beard and tattoos covering every visible inch of skin.

"What did you do before you were hired by Urban Alchemy?" Erickson asked.

"I was in jail for a couple of years for drug possession. I was also a drummer in a band, and I was a security guard at a club in the Tenderloin."

"You're no longer playing music?"

"I got stabbed breaking up a fight at the club. The damage to the nerves in my right arm was so bad that I couldn't play anymore. I got addicted to painkillers and then heroin. The City helped me get into a program, and I've been clean for almost two years."

Good for you.

Erickson's voice was sincere. "Congratulations, Mr. Jenkins."

"Thank you."

The juror who worked for the City nodded.

"Where do you live?" Erickson asked.

"In a City-subsidized apartment on Turk Street."

The judge granted Erickson's request to approach the box. "Were you working for Urban Alchemy on the morning of Monday, January twenty-first, of last year?"

"Yes." He said that he got to work at nine a.m.

"Could you please describe what you did when you arrived?"

"We start every day by meeting with our supervisors. My partner and I were assigned to four blocks around U.N. Plaza." Jenkins said that the ambassadors are encouraged to patrol the same blocks to get to know the residents. "Ideally, we build trust."

"You made your rounds on U.N. Plaza that morning?"

"Yes."

"Had you ever met a young woman named Annie Parker?"

"We spoke on several occasions. She grew up in the Central Valley in an abusive family. She came to the City and became a sex worker. She had a bad shoulder and was addicted to prescription painkillers. She was also using other drugs—mostly crystal meth, I believe."

"Did you try to help her?"

"Absolutely. I offered her information about treatment programs and housing options, but she declined our services. It's a shame."

"Did you see her on the morning of January twenty-first of last year?"

"I did." He quickly corrected himself. "Well, when I saw her, she was, uh, deceased."

Erickson had put the first points on the board. In a murder trial, you need a decedent.

Erickson moved a little closer to Jenkins. "What time did you find her?"

"Around ten-fifteen a.m."

"Could you please describe the circumstances?"

"Sure." Jenkins took a deep breath. "When I walked by Annie's tent, I asked a couple of people if they had seen her that morning, but nobody had. One person said that he saw her come home the previous night and she appeared upset. I asked him if he knew why, but he said that he didn't. I walked up to her tent and called out to her, but she didn't answer. I tried a second time, but there was still no answer. My partner and I decided to do a routine welfare check."

Erickson darted a glance at the jurors spread out in the gallery, then he turned back to Jenkins. "What happened next?"

"I opened her tent and looked inside. Annie was lying on her back. Her eyes were open, and her face was blue. It looked like she wasn't breathing." He took a moment to compose himself. "I told my partner to call nine-one-one, and then I tried to perform first aid."

"Street ambassadors are allowed to do that?"

"I'm not an EMT, but we have some emergency training. It looked like she had overdosed, so I administered Narcan."

Narcan is a widely-used nasal spray that's effective in reversing overdoses.

"What made you think that she had OD'd?"

"I've been trained to recognize the signs." He lowered his voice. "I've overdosed a few times, so I have a pretty good idea of what I'm looking for."

"Did the Narcan work?"

"No." Jenkins said that the EMTs arrived within minutes, but they were unable to revive Annie.

Erickson lowered his voice. "Ms. Parker died at the scene?"

"Objection," I said. "This is outside the scope of Mr. Jenkins's expertise."

"Withdrawn." Erickson already had what he needed from Jenkins. A later witness would confirm that Annie Parker had been pronounced at the scene. "No further questions."

The judge looked my way. "Cross-exam, Mr. Daley?"

"Just a few questions, Your Honor." I stood, buttoned my suit jacket, removed my mask, and walked to a spot about three feet in front of the box, careful to position myself so that Jenkins and the jurors could see me. "You thought Ms. Parker had died of an overdose?"

"Yes."

"But you have no medical training, right?"

"Right."

"So you would acknowledge that it's possible that you may have been wrong and Ms. Parker died of other causes?"

"I suppose."

"Was my client present when you found Ms. Parker?"

"No."

"I take it that means that you didn't see my client give her any drugs?"

"Correct."

"So you don't know if he did so, do you?"

"No."

"And it's possible that somebody other than my client gave her drugs, isn't it?"

"I suppose."

"There are a lot of drug dealers in the Tenderloin, aren't there?"

"Unfortunately, yes."

"It is therefore possible that any number of people in the neighborhood could have given her tainted pills, isn't it?"

"Objection. Speculation."

"Sustained."

I had made my point. "No further questions, Your Honor."

"Redirect, Mr. Erickson?"

"No, Your Honor."

"Please call your next witness."

"The People call Sergeant A.C. Brown."

It was a logical next step in Erickson's case. Jenkins had found the body. Brown was the first officer at the scene.

36

"WE RESPONDED IMMEDIATELY"

Sergeant A.C. Brown sat in the box, uniform pressed, star polished, arms folded. He had poured himself a cup of water, but he wouldn't touch it. Strong witnesses never drink water because it makes them look nervous.

He spoke deliberately. "I have been a sworn officer since 1986. I have held the rank of sergeant for twenty-four years." Erickson led him through a crisp summary of his C.V. Brown confirmed that he started his career at Mission Station and then worked at Bayview. "I moved to Tenderloin Station in 1991 to help form a new task force."

Erickson spoke from the lectern. "What was the purpose of that unit?"

"To disrupt drug trafficking. In the early years, it was mostly crack and heroin. More recently, crystal meth. Nowadays, fentanyl. Lots of fentanyl."

Judge Powell's courtroom was silent at eleven-forty on Wednesday morning. A few of the jurors were starting to fidget. It was a reminder that trial work is theater, and the jurors are your audience. You need to keep them engaged and entertained.

Erickson's tone was conversational. "Were you on duty on the morning of Monday, January twenty-first, of last year?"

"Yes." Brown said that he and his partner began their shift at Tenderloin Station at six a.m. "It was the Martin Luther King holiday, so we hoped it would be relatively quiet." He said that he handled paperwork for the first couple of hours. Then he attended a meeting with the station's captain and lieutenants. "At approximately nine-forty a.m., my partner and

I drove to Civic Center Plaza to assist two officers who had broken up an altercation. By the time we arrived, the matter had been de-escalated, and the participants had dispersed with a warning."

"Where were you at approximately ten-fifteen a.m.?"

"Still at Civic Center Plaza."

"Could you please tell us what happened next?"

"We received a call from nine-one-one dispatch that an Urban Alchemy City Ambassador had discovered an unconscious woman in a tent in the homeless encampment at U.N. Plaza. We responded immediately and requested police backup and a medical unit. We were told that EMTs had already been dispatched. We drove the two blocks to U.N. Plaza, where we arrived at ten-eighteen a.m."

Erickson activated the flatscreen, which displayed an aerial view of U.N. Plaza from Civic Center Plaza to Market Street. He entered the photo into evidence. I didn't object.

In response to Erickson's request, Brown left the box and pointed at Parker's tent. "An Ambassador named P.J. Jenkins directed us to Ms. Parker's body."

"Move to strike," I said. "Sergeant Brown is not qualified to determine whether Ms. Parker was deceased at the time."

The judge looked at Brown. "Could you please clarify your answer?"

"Yes, Your Honor. Mr. Jenkins led my partner and myself to this tent where we found a woman later identified as the victim, Annie Parker. She was unconscious and, as far as I could tell, she wasn't breathing. Mr. Jenkins informed us that he had administered Narcan to Ms. Parker. He also attempted CPR, but his efforts had been unsuccessful. My partner and I also administered CPR until the EMTs arrived approximately two minutes later. Unfortunately, Ms. Parker never regained consciousness. She was pronounced dead at the scene by the EMTs who were in real-time contact with an emergency room physician at San Francisco General."

It was textbook testimony from a veteran cop.

Erickson walked Brown through concise descriptions of how Brown and his partner secured the scene and organized a search for witnesses. "You interviewed Mr. Jenkins?"

"I took his preliminary statement. Inspector Lee followed up with a more detailed interview. Mr. Jenkins suspected that Ms. Parker had overdosed."

"Did he have any information as to how Ms. Parker obtained the drugs that killed her?"

"No."

"Did he suspect foul play?"

"He didn't know."

Erickson moved to the front of the box. "Did you suspect foul play?"

"We couldn't rule it out."

"What did you do when Inspector Lee arrived?"

"I briefed him and escorted him inside the victim's tent."

Erickson walked over to the cart and picked up a sealed evidence bag containing a plastic pill bottle about two inches long and about an inch in diameter. He introduced it into evidence and handed it to Brown.

"Did you find this bottle in Ms. Parker's tent?"

"Yes. Next to the mattress where we found her body."

"Can you tell us where this pill bottle came from?"

"The label is from the pharmacy at the San Francisco V.A. Medical Center at 4150 Clement Street in the Richmond."

"Does it include the name of the patient?"

Brown looked at Lenny. "The defendant, Leonard Garcia."

I could have objected to the introduction of the bottle on the grounds that there wasn't sufficient proof that it belonged to Lenny, but the jury wouldn't have bought it.

"Does the label indicate the nature of the prescription?" Erickson asked.

"OxyContin pills. In the course of conducting our inventory, we found six pills in the bottle. It was later determined that those pills contained substantial amounts of an illegal drug called fentanyl."

I could have objected on the grounds that the chemical composition of the pills was beyond Brown's area of expertise, but Erickson would soon call another witness to confirm that the pills were, in fact, laced with fentanyl. Most important, Erickson had another building block—the pills were the murder weapon.

"No further questions," he said.

"Cross-exam, Mr. Daley?"

"Yes, Your Honor." I removed my mask, walked to the lectern, and spoke to Brown. "Ms. Parker wasn't moving when Mr. Jenkins took you inside her tent?"

"Correct."

The judge granted my request for permission to approach Brown. "You said that you thought that she had overdosed?"

"It looked that way to me."

"Do you have any medical training?"

"Just first aid."

"You would agree that it wasn't within your expertise to determine cause of death?"

"Of course, Mr. Daley."

"Likewise, Mr. Jenkins had no medical training?"

"Right."

"So his guess that Ms. Parker had OD'd was also based on conjecture, wasn't it?"

"I would call it informed observation."

That's fair. "But he wasn't qualified to make that determination, was he?"

"No. A determination of cause of death is the responsibility of the Medical Examiner."

Who Erickson will call shortly.

I walked over to the evidence cart and picked up the pill bottle, which I handed to Brown. "You confirmed that the V.A. had issued a prescription for OxyContin to Lenny?"

"I did." He confirmed that he found six pills in the bottle.

"Those pills were laced with fentanyl?"

"Correct."

"Is it your contention that the V.A. issued pills laced with fentanyl?"

"No, I believe that the V.A. gave your client a legitimate prescription for OxyContin, and your client then put tainted pills in the same bottle and gave it to Ms. Parker."

"Did you question the pharmacist at the V.A. about it?"

"Yes. Obviously, she denied that she had provided pills spiked with fentanyl."

"You took her word for it?"

"I had no reason to disbelieve her."

"But you don't know for sure, do you?"

"No."

"Did you see my client put tainted pills in the bottle?"

"No."

"Did you find any witnesses who saw my client put tainted pills in the bottle?"

"No."

"Did you consider the possibility that somebody other than my client gave Ms. Parker some tainted pills?"

"It seemed highly unlikely."

"But not impossible."

Erickson stood up and started to object on the grounds that my question was asking for speculation, but he changed his mind. He probably decided that Brown could hold his own.

Brown waved me off with a terse, "Anything's possible, Mr. Daley."

"Bottom line, you have no direct knowledge of how the tainted pills got inside that bottle, do you?"

"No, Mr. Daley."

It was all that I could do for now. "No further questions, Your Honor."

Erickson declined redirect.

Judge Powell looked up at the clock. "I'm going to recess for lunch. Who will be your next witness, Mr. Erickson?"

"The People will call the Chief Medical Examiner of San Francisco."

37

"FENTANYL OVERDOSE"

Dr. Siu was wearing a starched white lab coat as she sat in the box, makeup perfect, manner professorial. "I have been the Chief Medical Examiner of the City and County of San Francisco for seven years. Before that, I was a full professor and Chair of the Ph.D. program in anatomic pathology at UCSF."

Impressive.

Erickson started to lead her through her resume, but I interrupted when she got to her *summa cum laude* degree at Princeton. "We will stipulate that Dr. Siu is a recognized authority in her field."

The judge was pleased. "Thank you, Mr. Daley."

Erickson introduced the autopsy report into evidence and presented it to Siu. "You performed the autopsy of Ms. Annie Parker on January twenty-second of last year?"

"I did." She confirmed that she had produced the report in her hands.

"You were able to determine the cause of death?"

"I was." Siu glanced at her report but didn't open it. "The toxicology report was clear. Ms. Parker died of a fentanyl overdose." She spoke directly to the jurors. "Fentanyl is a Schedule II controlled substance similar to morphine, but it's about fifty times more potent. Under the supervision of a medical professional, it has valid therapeutic uses. However, even if it is prescribed by a doctor, users should be monitored for potential misuse or abuse.

"Illicit fentanyl is primarily manufactured in foreign clandestine labs and smuggled into the U.S., often through

Mexico. It is sold on the illegal drug market. It is frequently mixed in with other illicit drugs to increase their potency, sometimes sold as powders and nasal sprays, and increasingly pressed into pills made to look like legitimate prescription opioids. Because there is no official oversight or quality control, these counterfeit pills often contain lethal doses."

Erickson's voice was somber. "What are the risks?"

"Because of its potency and low cost, drug dealers have been mixing fentanyl with prescription medications and illegal drugs including heroin, methamphetamine, and cocaine, increasing the likelihood of a fatal interaction. Two milligrams of fentanyl can be lethal depending on a person's body size, tolerance, and past usage. Forty-two percent of pills tested for fentanyl contained at least two milligrams, which is considered a potentially lethal dose. Drug traffickers typically distribute fentanyl by the kilogram. One kilogram has the potential to kill 500,000 people, which is more than half the population of San Francisco."

I darted a look at the gallery, where the jurors were listening intently.

Erickson's voice remained even. "How much fentanyl did you find in Ms. Parker's bloodstream?"

"More than enough to kill her."

He held up the pill bottle. "Did you also test one or more of the remaining pills in this bottle found next to her body?"

"I did. They were fake pills pressed to look like real OxyContin pills, but they contained no OxyContin. The counterfeit pills contained approximately six milligrams of fentanyl. That's about three times what is considered a potentially lethal dose."

"Any chance of survival?"

"There's always a chance, Mr. Erickson. However, it came as no surprise that Ms. Parker died of an overdose given the dosage. Fentanyl is particularly dangerous for those who have not taken it before."

"I understand that Ms. Parker had a heart condition."

"She had an irregular heartbeat. However, in my medical judgment, it is highly unlikely that she died as a result of it."

"No further questions."

Erickson had another building block: cause of death.

"Cross-exam, Mr. Daley?"

"Yes, Your Honor." I walked to the front of the box. "There were six pills in the bottle found next to Ms. Parker's body?"

"Correct."

"Did you find my client's fingerprints on any of those pills?"

"The pills are small, so it would have been impossible to lift fingerprints from them."

"What about my client's DNA?"

"It would have been almost impossible to find DNA on such a small sample."

"So, you have no direct connection between those pills and my client, do you?"

"Your client's name and fingerprints were on the bottle."

"The bottle didn't kill Ms. Parker."

"True, but the fentanyl did."

"But you would agree that while my client's prints were on the outside of the bottle, you have no direct evidence that he put the tainted pills inside the bottle, do you?"

A shrug. "No."

"Did you consider the possibility that somebody at the V.A. gave Lenny Garcia some tainted pills?"

"I believe that the pharmacy gave your client legitimate OxyContin pills. At some point, he finished the real pills and gave Ms. Parker a bottle with tainted pills."

"But you have no physical evidence that he did."

"I do not, although I believe that your speculation that somebody else filled the bottle with tainted pills is unlikely."

"But that's just speculation on your part, isn't it?"

"Objection," Erickson said. "Calls for speculation."

Yes, it does.

Judge Powell held up a hand. "Overruled."

Siu turned and spoke to the judge. "I know the doctor at the V.A. who prescribed the OxyContin, and I know the pharmacist who filled the prescription. They are competent and professional. It is highly unlikely that they gave the defendant a bottle of tainted pills. It seems far more likely that he consumed the real pills and refilled the bottle with fake pills tainted with fentanyl."

I feigned skepticism. "But you don't know for sure, do you?"

"No, Mr. Daley."

"Your report notes that Ms. Parker had an irregular heartbeat or arrhythmia known as a ventricular tachycardia, right?"

Siu nodded. "Right."

"Could you describe the symptoms?"

"Shortness of breath, weakness, dizziness, lightheadedness, fainting or near fainting, and chest pain or discomfort."

"It can also cause a dramatic drop in blood pressure without warning and a collapse, right? And in such cases, the person's breathing and pulse can stop, right?"

"In extreme cases."

"Which would cause the person to die."

"If first aid is not available."

"Ms. Parker was living by herself in a tent on U.N. Plaza. If she had suffered such an episode, it is highly unlikely that there would have been somebody around to help her, right?"

"Objection," Erickson said. "This is outside Dr. Siu's scope of knowledge and asks for speculation."

"Sustained."

Once more. "Dr. Siu, in your capacity as a medical expert, if Ms. Parker had suffered from a serious ventricular tachycardia, it's possible that she could have died within moments, isn't it?"

"I found no evidence that she did."

"But it's possible, right?"

Her tone was grudging. "Right."

"No further questions."

38

"I WAS ABLE TO DE-ESCALATE"

A few minutes later, Officer Christa Carter was sworn in, took her seat in the box, and declined Erickson's offer of water.

Erickson spoke to her from the lectern. "How long have you been a police officer?"

"Eighteen years." She said that she had graduated with honors from Balboa High and UC-Davis. She was second in her class at the Academy and was the only female in SFPD history to record the highest score on the physical test. "I've spent my career at Tenderloin Station."

Carter's hair was pulled back into a ponytail, hands folded in her lap. At six-two with the broad shoulders of an all-conference swimmer, the native of the Excelsior was third-generation SFPD. Her grandfather had been a classmate of my dad at the Academy and rose to the rank of assistant chief. Her father had recently retired as a lieutenant at Taraval Station. I've always referred to SFPD as the "Daley Family Business." For the Carters, it was even more so.

Erickson pointed at Lenny. "Did you encounter the defendant on the evening of January twentieth of last year?"

"Yes. He was outside his tent on U.N. Plaza."

"Could you please describe the circumstances?"

"Of course." Carter nodded at the juror who worked at City Hall, then turned back to Erickson. "My partner and I had just finished dealing with an incident involving the sale of stolen merchandise behind the Orpheum Theater. We were returning to our police unit when we observed a disturbance." She pointed at Lenny. "The defendant was yelling at a young woman whom we later identified as the victim, Annie Parker."

"Can you describe the defendant's demeanor?"

Another look at Lenny. "He was very agitated and angry."

Lenny leaned over and whispered, "She's exaggerating. It wasn't a big deal."

Sounds like maybe it was.

"Did the defendant threaten Ms. Parker?" Erickson asked.

"Yes."

"Do you know what they were arguing about?"

"He accused Ms. Parker of taking his phone. He believed that it wasn't the first time that she had stolen from him. He told her that if he ever caught her trying to steal from him again, he'd beat the crap out of her."

"How did Ms. Parker respond?"

"She was terrified."

"Did you place the defendant under arrest?"

"No, but I gave him a warning. I was able to de-escalate the situation by using tactics that I learned in my SFPD training. After he calmed down, my partner and I found his phone among his personal belongings. The defendant grudgingly apologized to Ms. Parker. I instructed the defendant and Ms. Parker to stay away from each other."

"Did you think the defendant was going to harm Ms. Parker?"

"Objection," I said. "Calls for speculation."

"Your Honor," Erickson said, "I am not asking Officer Carter to read the defendant's mind. I am simply asking her to describe her impressions of his demeanor."

"Overruled."

Crap.

Carter measured her words. "I thought it was a possibility."

Erickson had accomplished what he wanted: he had given the jury a plausible motive.

"No further questions," he said.

"Cross-exam, Mr. Daley?"

"Yes, Your Honor." I moved to the front of the box. "You didn't arrest Lenny, did you?"

"No."

"If you thought he was such a threat, why didn't you place him under arrest?"

"I was able to calm him down. In my judgment, I didn't think that there would be a physical altercation with Ms. Parker."

"You didn't detain him, either?"

"No."

"If you were so worried that he was going to attack her, why didn't you at least haul him into the station for a few hours?"

"Because he had calmed down."

"So in your judgment, he wasn't a threat?"

"Not at that moment."

"Did you check his record?"

"Yes. The defendant has been arrested on several occasions for shoplifting and possession of controlled substances."

"But he's never been arrested for hitting anybody, right?"

"Not to my knowledge."

"And he apologized to Ms. Parker?"

"Yes."

"So you must have concluded that he wasn't going to hurt her, right?"

"I didn't think Ms. Parker was in immediate danger."

"It doesn't sound like a motive for murder, does it?"

"Objection."

"Sustained."

"No further questions."

39

"THE DEFENDANT'S FINGERPRINTS WERE ON THE BOTTLE"

Erickson's next witness sat in the box, manner professional, expression stoic. "My name is Lieutenant Kathleen Jacobsen. I have been an evidence technician for the San Francisco Police Department for thirty-six years."

Erickson addressed her from the lectern. "It's good to see you again, Lieutenant."

"Thank you, Mr. Erickson. It's good to see you, too."

I immediately stipulated to her expertise. Jacobsen was a no-nonsense professional in her mid-sixties who was SFPD's most respected evidence expert. Her badge was displayed in the breast pocket of the jacket of her gray pantsuit. Her makeup was subtle, her salt-and-pepper hair styled in a low-maintenance layered cut. The daughter of an IBM engineer, she had grown up in Atherton and spent her summers at the pool at the Burlingame Country Club. She turned down a tennis scholarship from Stanford to play water polo and study criminal justice at USC, where she graduated summa cum laude. She earned a master's from Cal in forensic science and then joined SFPD. One of the first lesbians to work her way up the ranks, she had a stellar reputation on forensic evidentiary matters, with specialties in fingerprints and blood spatter. Her wife, Jill, was a retired San Francisco firefighter.

Erickson's voice was businesslike. "On January twenty-first of last year, were you called to the scene of a potential homicide at U.N. Plaza?"

"Yes. The decedent was a young woman named Annie Parker." She said that she arrived at ten-forty-seven a.m.

"Who else was there?"

She pointed at the prosecution table. "Inspector Kenneth Lee had taken charge. The first officer at the scene was Sergeant A.C. Brown. They had secured the scene in accordance with standard police procedure. They provided a briefing to myself and my team."

Erickson turned on the flatscreen and showed a photo of Annie Parker's tent. He asked Jacobsen to describe the scene.

She walked over to the TV. "It was a complex scene because it was in the middle of a homeless encampment in a public place. The decedent's body was inside this tent, so the immediate vicinity was quite tight."

Erickson introduced a photo of the interior of the tent. "Could you please describe what you found inside?"

"The victim's body had been taken outside by the EMTs, so there was an empty mattress. Some of her belongings were found over here. Things were in a bit of disarray because the police and EMTs had come inside and administered first aid. She was pronounced at the scene."

Erickson pointed at a yellow evidence marker next to the mattress. "Could you please tell us what marker number seven represents?"

"A pill bottle."

Erickson walked over to the evidence cart, picked up the bottle, and handed it to Jacobsen. "Is this it?"

"Yes." Jacobsen confirmed that it had a label from the V.A. Hospital with an OxyContin prescription for Lenny. "It also contained six pills which were laced with a fatal amount of fentanyl."

I spoke up in an even tone. "Move to strike. With respect, Lieutenant Jacobsen's expertise is in evidence collection and analysis, not chemical compounds."

Judge Powell's response was half-hearted. "The jury will disregard Lieutenant Jacobsen's statement that the pills contained a lethal dose of fentanyl."

Sure they will. In reality, it didn't matter. Dr. Siu had already testified that the pills were spiked, and the dosage was fatal.

Erickson pointed at the bottle. "Did you find any fingerprints on this bottle?"

"Yes."

Erickson led her through a rehearsed direct exam in which she compared enlarged photos of the prints on the bottle with the prints taken when Lenny was booked. A moment later, Erickson lobbed the inevitable softball. "What did you conclude?"

"The defendant's fingerprints were on the bottle."

He nodded at the jurors. "No further questions."

"Cross-exam, Mr. Daley?"

"Yes, Your Honor." I moved to the front of the box. "Did you find any prints on the bottle other than my client's?"

"The victim's."

"Anybody else's?"

"There was a partial print that we could not identify, and there was a smudged print that was too distorted to allow us to find a match."

"You couldn't match the partial to Lenny Garcia, could you?"

"No."

"So somebody else must have handled this bottle, right?"

"It's possible."

"And it's possible that the partial and the smudged prints were made by different people, which means that two people other than my client may have handled this bottle?"

"It's possible."

"And it's possible that the person or persons whose prints you could not identify may have given Annie Parker the tainted pills, right?"

"Objection. Calls for speculation."

"Overruled."

I didn't think Judge Powell would give me that one.

She took a deep breath. "It's possible, Mr. Daley."

Sometimes it's better to stop when you're ahead. "No further questions."

The wiry man with the pale complexion, widow's peak, rimless spectacles, and dour demeanor hunched forward in the box. "My name is George Romero. I am a supervising lab technician in the Forensic Services Division of SFPD's Criminalistics Laboratory. I have held that position for eighteen years."

Erickson was standing in front of the box. "What did you do before that?"

"I was an assistant lab technician for twelve years."

"What is your area of expertise?"

"DNA evidence."

Romero was a dreary but competent little man who had spent three decades working in a windowless bunker in the basement of the Hall of Justice. The native of Bernal Heights had a chemistry degree from State, a meticulous manner, and an inquisitive mind. He wasn't charismatic or particularly engaging, but he had a knack for explaining complex scientific concepts in easy-to-understand soundbites. He was the D.A.'s go-to guy on DNA evidence.

Erickson led him through his C.V. Then he held up the pill bottle as if it was the Holy Grail. "You're familiar with this bottle, Mr. Romero?"

"Yes. It was found at the scene of the murder of a young woman named Annie Parker."

Come on. "Move to strike the term 'murder,'" I said.

Judge Powell rolled his eyes. "The jury will disregard."

Erickson pretended that he hadn't heard the exchange. "Mr. Romero, did you analyze this bottle for DNA?"

"Yes."

Erickson led Romero through a concise explanation of the nature and scope of the tests that he had performed. Romero's well-rehearsed presentation included just enough technical jargon to lend an air of gravitas but was accessible enough to keep the jurors' interest. Most important, it was mercifully short.

Erickson asked Romero if he had obtained a DNA sample from Annie Parker.

"Yes. We had samples of her hair, fingernails, and skin from her autopsy."

"Did you find Ms. Parker's DNA on this bottle?"

Romero waited a moment in a ham-handed attempt to build suspense. "I did."

This came as no surprise.

Erickson nodded triumphantly. "The police also obtained a sample of the defendant's DNA, didn't they?"

"Yes. They found a comb in his tent with a strand of his hair."

Erickson feigned surprise. "You can get a good DNA sample from a single strand?"

"If you know what you're doing."

"Did you have an opportunity to analyze the DNA?"

"I did."

Erickson teed it up for him. "Were you able to determine whether the DNA from the hair matched the DNA that you found on the pill bottle?"

"Yes. The DNA on the bottle matched the DNA of the hair. I therefore concluded that the defendant handled the bottle."

"No further questions."

"Cross-exam, Mr. Daley?"

"Yes, Your Honor." I walked to the front of the box and handed him the pill bottle. "Mr. Romero, there were six pills inside the bottle, right?"

"Right. They were tainted with fentanyl."

"Did you test those pills for DNA?"

"Objection," Erickson said. "Mr. Daley is raising an issue not addressed on direct exam."

It was a legitimate objection. Technically, I was not allowed to question Romero about subjects that weren't addressed during direct. I could, however, raise those issues if I called Romero during the defense case.

Here goes. "Your Honor, Mr. Erickson asked Mr. Romero to discuss matters relating to DNA tests on evidence collected at the scene of Ms. Parker's death. He opened the door. I should be allowed to explore the extent and scope of Mr. Romero's investigation."

Erickson fired back. "Mr. Daley can address these issues during the defense case."

The judge opted for expediency. "I'm going to overrule the objection and give you a little leeway, Mr. Daley. If you start straying too far from the matters at hand, I will rule that you'll need to address those issues during your case."

Fine. "Thank you, Your Honor." I turned back to Romero. "Did you find any DNA on the pills?"

"No."

"Were you able to determine when my client's DNA found its way to this pill bottle?"

"No."

"Did you find any DNA other than that of Ms. Parker or Mr. Garcia on this pill bottle?"

Romero's thin lips turned down. "Traces."

"Which did not match either Ms. Parker or Mr. Garcia, did they?"

"It was a very small sample."

"Which means that the answer to my question is that those traces did not match, right?"

"That's technically true."

That's good enough. "You tested other items in Ms. Parker's tent for DNA, didn't you?"

"Yes."

"And you didn't find my client's DNA on any other objects, did you?"

"No."

"You also tested Ms. Parker's clothing, didn't you?"

"Yes."

"You discovered some dried semen on her panties, didn't you?"

"Objection," Erickson said. "Mr. Daley is once again asking about matters that were not addressed on direct."

I held up a hand. "I'll get to the point right away, Your Honor, and I promise that this will be my last line of questioning for now." *Well, maybe.*

"Overruled."

Romero scowled. "It is true that we found traces of semen on Ms. Parker's panties."

"You conducted DNA tests on those panties?"

"I did."

"And the DNA in the semen didn't match the DNA of my client, did it?"

"No."

Good. "Did you run the DNA through the local, state, and federal DNA databases, including the national criminal database commonly known as 'CODIS'?"

"Yes. We found no matches."

"So you found DNA on Ms. Parker's panties from an unknown person?"

"Yes."

"And she had sex with that person, didn't she?"

"It looks that way."

"Did you consider the possibility that the unknown person gave Ms. Parker tainted pills?"

"Objection. Calls for speculation."

Yes it does.

"Sustained."

I had made my point. "No further questions, Your Honor."

"Redirect, Mr. Erickson?"

"No, Your Honor. The People call Inspector Kenneth Lee."

40

"YOU TOOK THEIR WORD FOR IT?"

A confident Inspector Ken Lee stood next to the flatscreen and used a Cross pen to point at an enlarged photo of Annie Parker's tent on U.N. Plaza. "A City Ambassador named P.J. Jenkins found Ms. Parker's body in this tent at approximately ten-fifteen a.m. on January twenty-first of last year. The EMTs arrived within minutes and attempted CPR, but they could not revive her. She was pronounced dead at the scene."

Erickson nodded. "Thank you, Inspector."

Judge Powell's stuffy courtroom was filled with an intense silence at three-forty on Thursday afternoon. A couple of jurors fidgeted with their masks. Jerry Edwards took notes. Lenny sat next to me, eyes forward, fists clenched. I could see perspiration on his forehead above his mask. His sister had not returned.

Lenny slid a note in front of me. "Is Lee the last witness?"

"Probably," I whispered. I figured that Lee would tie Erickson's case together just in time for the judge to recess for the day.

"You'll go after him?" he asked.

"Yes." I held up a hand to suggest that this wasn't a good time for conversation.

Lee returned to the box and described his arrival at U.N. Plaza. He assured us that he had secured the scene and collected evidence in accordance with SFPD's best practices. He confirmed that there had been no lapses in chain of custody. He said that he had taken statements from people in the immediate vicinity.

Erickson stood at the lectern. "Did you interview the defendant?"

"Yes. At first, he refused to cooperate. When I returned to see him after we found his name and fingerprints on the pill bottle, he reconsidered and said that he had seen the victim at approximately seven-thirty p.m. on January twentieth. He admitted that he had given her a bottle containing OxyContin pills."

Erickson held up the pill bottle. "This bottle?"

"Yes. As indicated in previous testimony, the defendant's fingerprints and DNA were on the bottle. It contained six fake Oxy pills laced with fentanyl."

"Did he say why he gave her the pills?"

"Ms. Parker was having shoulder pain. He claimed that he was trying to help her."

"Seems he didn't."

"Objection," I said. "There wasn't a question there."

"Withdrawn." Erickson feigned annoyance. "Did the defendant say anything else?"

"He claimed that he had given the victim pills that were not tainted."

"Seriously?"

"Objection."

"Withdrawn." Erickson was still looking at Lee. "Did the defendant offer any explanation as to how the tainted pills got into the bottle?"

"He said that Ms. Parker must have obtained them from somebody else."

"Did you find his explanation credible?"

"No."

Erickson took the bottle from Lee and returned it to the evidence cart. He went back to the lectern and fed Lee another softball. "Inspector, can you offer any explanation as to why the defendant gave Ms. Parker the tainted pills?"

"Officer Christa Carter of Tenderloin Station reported that she had broken up an altercation between the defendant and Ms. Parker the night before she died. I believe that the defendant was still angry at Ms. Parker."

"Inspector, could you please summarize your conclusion as to what happened on U.N. Plaza on January twenty-first of last year?"

"Of course, Mr. Erickson." Lee spoke with authority. "The defendant and Ms. Parker lived in adjacent tents on U.N. Plaza. The defendant and Ms. Parker got into a heated argument on the night before she died, and the defendant threatened Ms. Parker. The defendant gave Ms. Parker a bottle containing pills laced with fentanyl. The label had the defendant's name on it. The defendant's fingerprints and DNA were on the bottle. Ms. Parker consumed one or more pills laced with fentanyl. She was not a regular user, which made the fentanyl more dangerous. She suffered an overdose and died on the following morning."

"You believe that the defendant caused Ms. Parker's death?"

"Absolutely. But for the fact that the defendant gave Ms. Parker the tainted pills, she would be alive today."

"No further questions."

"Cross-exam, Mr. Daley?"

"Yes, Your Honor." I walked over to the evidence cart, picked up the pill bottle, and handed it to Lee. "The label indicates that this was a prescription for OxyContin for Lenny Garcia, doesn't it?"

"Yes."

"Who wrote the prescription?"

"A doctor at the V.A."

"Where was the prescription filled?"

"The V.A."

"The V.A.," I repeated. "Did you interview the doctor who wrote the prescription?"

"I did. He confirmed that he had written it. I also confirmed that the pharmacy at the V.A. had filled the prescription."

"Did you arrest the doctor?"

"No."

"The pharmacist?"

"Of course not."

"You've indicated that this bottle was filled with tainted pills."

"It was."

"How do you know that the pharmacy at the V.A. didn't give Lenny some tainted pills?"

"We had no evidence that they did, and we have had no reports of any such issues with prescriptions written by the V.A."

"In other words, you took their word for it?"

"Yes."

"Is it therefore your contention that the V.A. gave my client a bottle of clean OxyContin pills, and my client substituted tainted pills?"

"Correct."

"And it's my contention that you haven't provided any proof."

"Objection," Erickson said. "Argumentative."

"Sustained."

I gave the jurors a look of feigned disbelief. Then I turned back to Lee and spent the next twenty minutes challenging his supervision of the scene, handling of the evidence, and less-than-enthusiastic search for witnesses. On cross, I had to stick to issues addressed on direct, so I couldn't accuse him of ignoring other potential suspects until I presented our defense.

Finally, I walked up to the front of the box. "My client told you that he gave Ms. Parker some of his own Oxy pills to help her with her shoulder pain?"

"Yes. He admitted it."

"He didn't admit that the pills were tainted, did he?"

"No."

"And you don't have any physical evidence that my client put tainted pills in the bottle?"

"I think it's painfully obvious."

"I don't."

"Objection."

"Withdrawn. No further questions." We would have a longer discussion of this issue during the defense case.

"Redirect, Mr. Erickson?"

"No, Your Honor. We have no further witnesses. The prosecution rests."

The judge looked my way. "I take it that you wish to make a motion, Mr. Daley?"

"Yes, Your Honor. The defense moves that the charges be dropped as a matter of law because the prosecution has failed to meet its burden of proof."

"Denied." Judge Powell looked at his computer. "I'm going to recess for the day. We'll resume at ten o'clock tomorrow morning."

41

"HE ISN'T HERE"

Lenny was agitated when I met him in the consultation room down the hall from Judge Powell's courtroom. "That wasn't good," he said.

"The prosecution always has an advantage because they go first," I said.

"Why didn't you go after Lee?"

"I could only ask about matters raised during direct. I'll put him back on the stand and do more during our defense."

"You didn't mention any of the other suspects."

"It's better to introduce them to the jury in person than just mention their names. Tomorrow, I'll put Patty Dawson on the stand to talk about Marcus Strong. Then I'll call Davis and Holton. Then we'll bring back Lee and ask him why he didn't seriously consider anybody else."

"What if it isn't enough?"

"I need you to be ready to testify, Lenny."

"You said it was a bad idea."

In most cases, it is. "I may need a short and forceful denial. You'll say that you gave Annie some real pills from the V.A. You have no idea how the tainted pills got into the bottle. Follow my lead, keep your answers short, and you'll be fine."

His voice was far from confident when he said, "I'll be ready."

"The Terminator" was at his desk when I returned to the office at five-thirty. He lowered his mask and said, "I heard you had a rough day in court."

"It happens, T."

"Not to you."

"It happens to all of us. We start our defense in the morning. Have you talked to Patty Dawson today?"

"I checked in a little while ago. She seems content at the Golden Gate Hotel."

"Good. I'll need her to testify tomorrow. Can you pick her up and walk her over to court?"

"Sure."

"Thanks." I started to walk into my office, then I stopped. "You feeling okay, T?"

"Fine. You?"

"Not bad."

"Good." He put on his mask. "You going home soon?"

"I'm going to see Joe Davis. I tried to call him, but he didn't answer the burner phone that I gave him. I want to make sure that he's ready to testify tomorrow."

The lobby of the Padre Apartments was empty when I walked up to the young man at the desk. The brown eyes above his mask looked at me sternly. "No visitors."

I adjusted my mask. "I need to see Joe Davis."

"He isn't here."

"I'll wait for him. It's a legal matter."

His eyes narrowed. "He isn't coming back."

"What do you mean?"

He took a deep breath. "Are you family?"

"A friend."

His voice softened. "I'm sorry to give you bad news, but Joe passed away earlier today."

Dammit. "I'm sorry to hear that. Do you know what happened?"

"He called downstairs around noon and said that he wasn't feeling well. I went upstairs to check on him, and he had passed out in his room. The ambulance got here within five minutes. They took him to San Francisco General, but he was D.O.A."

My head throbbed. "Was it the virus?"

"Might have been. Joe said that he had a sore throat. He had other medical issues, too."

My mind raced as I tried to analyze the impact on Lenny's case. "Has the family been notified?"

"Yes. Joe had a brother in Texas. He said that he would make arrangements. Do you want his information?"

There was nothing that I could do. "Yes, please."

Lenny looked like a caged tiger in the consultation room at the San Bruno Jail at eight-fifteen the same night. "What the hell happened to Davis?"

"They don't know for sure. It might have been the virus."

"You needed to keep him alive so that he could testify tomorrow."

"I can't control everything, Lenny."

"Seems you can't control anything, Mike. Where does this leave us?"

"Unless you want me to ask for a continuance, we'll proceed as planned."

"Without an important witness," he said.

"It may work to our advantage. I'll try to get Patty Dawson to say that 'Go-To' Joe was distributing drugs in the TL. Now Joe won't be able to defend himself."

He stopped pacing. "You think it's going to work?"

"It's the best that we can do, Lenny."

Nady's name appeared on my phone as I was driving north on the Golden Gate Bridge. "You okay?" she asked.

"Been better. How's your mom?"

"Doing a little better. I heard you had a rough couple of days in court."

"Comes with the territory." I summarized the prosecution's presentation.

"You have cards to play, Mike."

"One of them died earlier today. Joe Davis is dead."

There was a brief silence before she said, "That doesn't help."

I tried for a positive spin. "He won't be able to defend himself. I can try to foist the blame over to him, but I'm not sure that the jury will buy it."

"You can be very persuasive, Mike."

"Looks like I'm going to have to be."

It was a few minutes before midnight when I pulled into my parking space behind my apartment. A familiar name appeared on my phone. "Evening, Nick."

"Evening, Mike." Nick 'The Dick' Hanson's singsong voice was always energetic. "How the hell are you?"

"Couldn't be better. You okay?"

"Indeed I am."

"You're up late."

"My kids and grandkids won't let me leave the house. I got nothing else to do, so I check in with my friends." His tone turned serious. "I heard that 'Go-To' Joe Davis died."

Nick knows everything. "It's true."

"I'm sorry. You gonna be able to work around it?"

"Seems I don't have any choice."

"I'll keep my ears open," he said. "I'll let you know if I come up with something."

"Thanks, Nick. Give my best to Nicki."

"Indeed I will."

I walked into my apartment, put my laptop on the kitchen table, and punched in the second number on my speed dial.

Pete answered on the first ring. "I heard about Joe Davis," he said. "That isn't good."

"My witnesses keep dying. You still in the garage?"

"For now."

I visualized my brother sitting in his bomber jacket at a makeshift desk in his garage in San Anselmo, about five miles northwest of my apartment in Larkspur.

"My moles told me that Erickson did a nice job," he said. "You gonna be able to muddy things up enough to get an acquittal?"

"Not sure. Best case may be a hung jury."

"A lot can happen in court."

"True." I waited a beat. "Pete?"

"Yes, Mick?"

"If there's any chance that you can find something that will help me with Lenny's case, this would be a good time to do it."

"I'll see what I can do."

At twelve-forty a.m., I was sitting at my kitchen table and going over the witness list for our defense when my phone vibrated, and Rosie's face appeared on Facetime.

"You look tired," she said.

"I haven't been getting much sleep."

Wilma the cat was curled up on the sofa. The TV was turned to the news, the sound off.

She flashed a confident smile. "I trust that you're ready to rock and roll later this morning?"

"Absolutely."

Her voice turned serious. "I heard about Joe Davis. I hope your defense isn't limited to blaming dead guys."

"We have some other options. My medical expert will testify that Annie Parker died from her heart condition."

"If the jury believes him, you can stop right there."

"Not likely, Rosie. I'll put Patty Dawson on the stand to throw shade at Strong and maybe Davis. Then I'll throw Holton under a bus."

"You going to put Lenny on the stand?"

"If I have to."

"Trials never play out exactly as planned." Her brown eyes gleamed on the tiny screen. "You don't sound wildly confident, Mike."

"I've become more realistic as I've gotten older."

"I hadn't noticed."

"When I was a baby Public Defender, a very smart attorney told me that if the facts and the law aren't on your side, you should muddy the waters enough to get one juror to reasonable doubt."

She smiled. "I remember that conversation."

"It's still good advice."

"I know. Are you going to be able to turn one juror?"

"The same attorney told me that it's a bad idea to make predictions while you're in trial."

42

"A TICKING TIMEBOMB"

The man with distinguished salt-and-pepper hair, Armani suit, and monogrammed Egyptian-cloth white shirt embodied understated confidence. "My name is Dr. Richard Kramer," he said. He nodded subtly at the jurors. "I am a practicing physician and full professor of medicine at Stanford Medical Center."

I was at the lectern. "How long have you been a doctor?"

Rich nodded. "Forty-three years."

"What is your specialty?"

"Cardiology."

Erickson quickly stipulated as to his expertise. *If you ever have a heart problem, Rich Kramer is your guy.*

Rich had grown up around the corner from us in the Sunset. His parents were founding members of Congregation Adath Israel at Twenty-sixth and Noriega, just north of the Sunset Reservoir. His father was a professor of American literature at State. His mother taught second grade at Dianne Feinstein School. Rich graduated from Lowell, UCLA, and USC Medical School. He was in private practice in Palo Alto and later joined the faculty at Stanford, where he was a world-class cardiologist. He was also a generous soul who had graciously agreed to be an expert witness for me from time to time. He could explain complex medical concepts to jurors with a perfect mix of authority and genial humor. I tried not to impose upon him unless it was absolutely essential. After all, he spent most of his time saving lives.

I handed him Dr. Siu's autopsy report. "Are you familiar with this document?"

"I am. It's the autopsy report prepared by Dr. Joy Siu in connection with the death of a young woman named Annie Parker."

"Do you know Dr. Siu?"

"I've met her. She's a fine doctor and an expert on anatomic pathology. I respect her work very much."

I moved closer to the box. "You've had an opportunity to study Dr. Siu's report?"

"I have."

"She concluded that Ms. Parker died of an overdose of fentanyl, didn't she?"

"Yes."

"Do you think that she came to the correct conclusion?"

"Hard to say." He took off his wire-framed glasses and pretended to look at the last page. "Ms. Parker had a dramatically irregular heartbeat. It was a very serious condition that I would describe as a ticking timebomb. At some point, it was going to detonate."

"Is there any way to predict when that might happen?"

"Unfortunately, there is not."

"What would have happened when it did?"

"Ms. Parker would have suffered a severe heart attack. Without immediate intervention, it's almost certain that she would have died."

I handed Rich a printout of an electrocardiogram. I provided copies to the judge and Erickson. I introduced it into evidence without objection and displayed it on the TV.

"Dr. Kramer," I said, "could you please describe the ECG on the screen?"

"Yes. It's an ECG showing a normal heartbeat."

"I take it that this isn't Ms. Parker's?"

"No, it is not." The corner of his mouth turned up slightly. "It's mine."

I introduced an ECG for Annie Parker. Once again, I displayed it on the TV.

"Are you familiar with this electrocardiogram?" I asked.

"Yes." Rich pointed at the screen. "It's an ECG for Ms. Parker taken two years ago when she was admitted to San Francisco General after she passed out on the street. It reveals that Ms. Parker suffered from a severe arrhythmia, or irregular heartbeat."

"Is that always a serious problem?"

"Not necessarily. For some people, it's normal for the heart to beat too fast or too slow. In its most benign form, it means your heart is out of its usual rhythm. It occurs when the electrical signals that coordinate the heart's beats don't work properly. If it causes the heart to beat too fast, it's called a tachycardia. If it beats too slow, it's called a bradycardia."

"How serious was Ms. Parker's arrhythmia?"

"Very." He paused. "If untreated, it was likely to kill her."

I displayed the two ECGs side by side on the screen. Rich walked over to the TV and pointed out the differences, which were plainly visible. Rich's heartbeat showed a consistent pattern. Annie's had almost no pattern at all. The jurors were taking notes.

I moved back to the lectern. "Dr. Kramer, if Ms. Parker had been your patient, how would you have described her condition?"

"Serious enough to be life-threatening. She suffered from a ventricular tachycardia, which manifested itself in rapid, chaotic electrical signals in the lower heart chambers called ventricles. The rapid rate didn't allow the ventricles to properly fill with blood. As a result, the heart couldn't pump enough blood."

"How would you have treated it?"

"Initially, medication along with a program of diet and exercise. If that didn't work, more invasive procedures might have been necessary."

"Did Ms. Parker's medical records indicate that she had received any such treatment?"

"No."

"What happens if it's left untreated?"

"The risk of heart attack, stroke, and sudden death increase exponentially."

"Would taking pain medication such as OxyContin increase the odds of heart problems?"

"Possibly."

"What about fentanyl?"

"Absolutely."

"Do you agree with Dr. Siu's conclusion that Ms. Parker died of a fentanyl overdose?"

"I have great respect for Dr. Siu, but in my opinion, I cannot rule out the possibility that Ms. Parker died as a result of her heart condition."

"No further questions," I said.

"Cross-exam, Mr. Erickson?"

"Just a few questions, Your Honor." Erickson moved to the front of the box. "Dr. Kramer, you can't state with any certainty that Ms. Parker died of a heart issue, can you?"

"No."

"How likely was it?"

"I can't give you an exact percentage, but I would say that the likelihood was at least fifty-fifty, and probably greater."

"But you think Dr. Siu was wrong?"

"I don't know for sure. Ms. Parker's heart condition was very serious."

It's always better for expert witnesses to avoid overstating their conclusions.

Erickson kept his voice even. "You've known Mr. Daley for a long time, haven't you?"

"Yes."

"You have been an expert witness for his clients on several occasions?"

"Yes."

"Mr. Daley worked with you to prepare for your testimony today?"

"He provided Ms. Parker's medical records and the autopsy report. He told me the general nature of the questions that he was going to ask."

"How many hours did you spend preparing for your testimony today?"

"About ten."

"What is your hourly rate for acting as an expert witness?"

"Fifteen hundred dollars an hour."

"I take it that Mr. Daley is compensating you for your time?"

"No."

Erickson appeared surprised. "You aren't being paid?"

"From time to time, I handle matters on a *pro bono* basis for clients who lack the resources to pay my fees."

Erickson threw in the towel. "No further questions."

"Redirect, Mr. Daley?"

"No, Your Honor."

"Please call your next witness."

That went about as well as I could have hoped. On to my fingerprint expert. "The defense calls Mr. Sridar Iyengar."

43

"A PERFECT MATCH"

The slender man with the jet-black hair, bags under his eyes, and severe crow's feet spoke deliberately. "I recently retired after thirty years at the San Mateo County Crime Lab."

I stood at the lectern. "What is your area of expertise?"

"Fingerprints."

"Could you please tell us a little about your background?"

"Certainly." Sridar Iyengar's gray mustache twitched. "I am a first-generation native of San Francisco. My parents were born in India and immigrated to London. They moved to San Francisco and opened a restaurant on Irving Street. I attended Lawton Elementary School, Lincoln High School, and San Francisco State, where I earned a bachelor's and a master's in criminology. I went to work at the San Mateo County Crime Lab, and I stayed there for my entire career." His tone was appropriately humble as he ticked off a half dozen honors.

Erickson spoke from his seat. "The People will stipulate as to Mr. Iyengar's expertise in fingerprint analysis."

Sridar was, in fact, one of California's leading experts on fingerprints. He was also a one-time neighbor, long-time friend, and one of the most meticulous guys I've ever known. His parents came to San Francisco to be closer to Sridar's grandfather, who was a researcher at UCSF. They moved to the Sunset, where they were one of the few families of Indian descent. His mom and dad opened an Indian restaurant a few doors from Big John's saloon, and it became an unlikely hit among the Irish, Italian, and later Chinese families. It was a regular on the *Chronicle*'s list of best restaurants in San Francisco, and its Tandoori chicken was otherworldly.

Sridar and I became friends even though he attended public school and I went to St. Peter's, St. Anne's, and St. Ignatius. During the week, he worked at his parents' restaurant after school. On weekends, he was a scrappy second baseman on our neighborhood baseball team at McCoppin Square Park. I tried to convince him to go to law school, but he believed that he was too introverted for courtroom theatrics. His scholarly demeanor and engaging manner made him an ideal expert witness, and he had become my go-to fingerprint expert since he took early retirement from the San Mateo County Crime Lab.

I pointed at the TV. "Are you familiar with these prints?"

"Yes. The one on the left is a thumbprint of the decedent, Ms. Annie Parker, which the SFPD Crime Lab lifted from a pill bottle found at the scene. The other was taken postmortem. They're a perfect match."

The judge granted my request to have Sridar leave the box and point out the similarities between the prints. He deftly explained that fingerprint examiners use the so-called "ACE-V" method. A stands for Analysis, which involves deciding whether a print is suitable for a Comparison. Comparison is performed by an expert like Sridar who views the known and suspect prints side-by-side and identifies minute characteristics and locations to see if they match. At this time, prints are often compared against databases such as the FBI's Integrated Automated Fingerprint Identification System (IAFIS).

Next comes Evaluation, where the examiner decides if the prints are from the same source, different sources, or are inconclusive. Inconclusive results may come from poor quality samples, lack of comparable areas, or an insufficient number of corresponding or dissimilar features. During the final step, Verification, a second examiner independently analyzes, compares, and evaluates the prints to support or refute the conclusions of the first examiner.

"Mr. Iyengar," I said, "could you please explain how you determined that the prints on the left and those on the right belonged to Ms. Parker?"

"Of course, Mr. Daley." He quickly noted fourteen matching points of comparison. "Bottom line, there is no question that the prints on the bottle were those of Ms. Parker."

I asked Sridar to identify a second set of prints.

The mustache twitched again. "The thumbprint on the left was found on the same pill bottle that I mentioned earlier. The one on the right was obtained at the defendant's booking." He walked us through the same exercise of showing us a dozen matching characteristics. "There is no question that the defendant held this bottle."

"Can you tell us when he held it?"

"No, Mr. Daley. The bodily oils that form fingerprints can remain on a surface for years."

"Did you identify Ms. Parker's or Mr. Garcia's prints on the tainted pills found inside the bottle?"

"It would have been almost impossible to lift recognizable fingerprints off pills."

"Do you have any fingerprint or other forensic evidence that my client put tainted pills inside this bottle?"

"No."

It wasn't a home run, but it may have gotten us a little closer to reasonable doubt. I put up another slide showing two prints. "Do you recognize these fingerprint samples?"

Sridar nodded. "They are partial prints that the crime lab identified on the pill bottle."

"Did the prints come from the same person?"

"I can't tell."

"Were you able to match any of these prints to Ms. Parker or Mr. Garcia?"

"No."

"Or any other person in the FBI database?"

"No."

"What about the pharmacist at the V.A. Hospital who filled the prescription?"

"We did not come up with a match."

"So it's possible that at least two other people handled this bottle?"

"It's likely."

"In fact, it's quite likely, isn't it?"

"Objection. Asked and answered."

"Sustained."

Another inch closer to reasonable doubt. "No further questions."

I stood at the lectern five minutes later. "Could you please describe your occupation?"

Dr. Carla Jimenez removed her mask, adjusted the sleeve of her navy suit jacket, and spoke with authority. "I am a senior forensic DNA Analyst at the Serological Research Institute in Richmond, California. I have worked at SERI for twenty-four years."

"You're a medical doctor?"

"Ph.D. I got my B.S. in chemistry and biological science from San Francisco State. I earned a master's and then a Ph.D. in forensic science from UC-Davis."

"What is your area of expertise?"

"Forensic serology and forensic DNA."

"You've been called as an expert witness before?"

"Many times. I have testified in hundreds of cases in state and federal courts nationwide as well as in federal and military courts."

Rosie described her high school classmate and lifelong friend as the most intense person she'd ever known. The Mission District native graduated second in her class at Mercy High, worked her way through State, and was accepted into UCLA Medical School. She deferred her admission to work in a research lab in the Department of Forensic Science at UC-Davis, where her instructor offered her a full scholarship to earn a master's and then Ph.D. She interned for two summers at SERI, a pre-eminent DNA testing facility. SERI became the go-to lab for DNA analysis in Northern California, and Carla and her colleagues were among the most respected experts in their field. She was testifying *pro bono* as a favor to Rosie.

I moved closer to the box. "You've received a great deal of recognition over the years, haven't you?"

"Yes." She looked at Erickson, expecting him to stipulate to her expertise. Instead, he sat tight, which allowed Carla to impress the jurors. "I am a Fellow of the American Board of Criminalistics in Forensic Biology with subspecialties in Forensic Biochemistry and Forensic Molecular Biology. I am also a member of the California Association of Criminalists, the Northwest Association of Forensic Scientists, the California Association of Crime Laboratory Directors, and the Association of Forensic Quality Assurance Managers."

I don't know what any of those organizations do, but it sure sounds impressive.

Erickson finally spoke up. "We will stipulate that Dr. Jimenez is a highly qualified expert in the fields of forensic serology and forensic DNA."

Was that so hard?

Judge Powell nodded. So did several members of the jury.

I walked over to the evidence cart, picked up an official-looking document, and handed it to Carla. "You're familiar with this report?"

"Yes, I am. It is a DNA analysis of samples obtained on a pill bottle found at the scene of the death of Ms. Annie Parker. The report was prepared by Mr. George Romero of the Forensic Services Division of the San Francisco Police Department's Criminalistics Laboratory."

I held up the pill bottle, which was still encased in a clear evidence bag. "The report refers to this bottle?"

"Yes."

"According to the report, whose DNA was found on the bottle?"

"Ms. Parker's." She glanced at Lenny. "And the defendant, Leonard Garcia."

"Anyone else's DNA?"

"The report indicated that there were traces of DNA belonging to one or more persons other than Ms. Parker and Mr. Garcia, but Mr. Romero was unable to identify those individuals."

"Were you able to verify the accuracy of the matches to Ms. Parker and Mr. Garcia?"

"No, Mr. Daley. Since the bottle was already logged into evidence, I was not allowed to obtain a sample of the DNA found on the bottle."

"Did the report appear to be accurate?"

"Objection," Erickson said. "Calls for a conclusion outside Dr. Jimenez's personal knowledge."

"Your Honor," I said, "Mr. Erickson can't have it both ways. If he isn't going to give us an opportunity to conduct a personal test of the evidence, he shouldn't be able to argue that Dr. Jimenez—whose expertise he has acknowledged—can't comment upon Mr. Romero's conclusions. Moreover, I am not asking Dr. Jimenez to vouch for the accuracy of the report. I am simply asking her to comment as to whether it appeared that it was prepared in accordance with generally accepted procedures."

"Overruled."

Carla held up the report. "As far as I could tell, the report appeared to have been prepared in accordance with industry standards."

"You said that traces of DNA were found on the bottle which did not belong to either Ms. Parker or Mr. Garcia?"

"Correct."

"It's therefore possible that somebody else touched this bottle, right?"

"It's not just possible, Mr. Daley. It's certain."

"And it's possible that the person who touched this bottle may have inserted pills tainted with fentanyl, isn't it?"

"Objection," Erickson said. "Calls for speculation."

"Sustained."

Judge Powell had made the correct call, but I had made my point.

I walked over to the evidence cart and picked up an evidence bag containing Annie Parker's underwear, which I introduced into evidence and handed to Carla. "Are you aware that the San Francisco Crime Lab determined that semen was found on these panties?"

"Yes."

"Are you aware that the Crime Lab also performed a DNA test on these panties?"

"I am."

I pointed at the report. "Did the results of the DNA test appear in this report?"

"They did."

"Did the DNA on the panties match the DNA of the defendant, Lenny Garcia?"

"No."

"Did the DNA match the unidentified traces of DNA on the pill bottle?"

"I don't know, Mr. Daley." She added, "According to the report, the traces of DNA on the pill bottle from sources other than Ms. Parker and Mr. Garcia were so small that a reliable comparison could not be made."

"Did you consider the possibility that the person who had sex with Ms. Parker also gave her some tainted pills?"

"Objection. Calls for speculation."

Yes, it does.

"Sustained."

I hadn't taken my eyes off Carla. "There is a good chance that the person who had sex with Ms. Parker also gave her some tainted pills that night, right?"

"Objection. More speculation."

True again.

"Sustained."

"No further questions."

"Cross-exam?"

Erickson spoke from his seat. "Dr. Jimenez, you have no DNA evidence that the person whose semen was found on Ms. Parker's panties gave her tainted pills, do you?"

"No."

"No further questions."

"Redirect, Mr. Daley?"

"No, Your Honor."

"Please call your next witness."

"The defense calls Ms. Patty Dawson."

44

"HE PREYED ON YOUNG WOMEN"

Patty Dawson gulped her second cup of water. "My name is Patricia Dawson."

I stood about five feet in front of the box. "More water?"

She tugged at the sleeve of the powder blue blouse that she had picked out from the donated clothes closet at the P.D.'s Office. "No, thank you."

"What is your current occupation?"

"I'm between jobs."

"Where do you live?"

"I'm between apartments, too. At the moment, I'm staying in a motel that your office is paying for. Otherwise, I've been staying with friends. Sometimes, I have to sleep outside."

"When was the last time you had your own apartment?"

"About six months ago. I lived at the El Camino Hotel on Larkin Street."

I darted a glance at the jurors who were focused on the young woman whose eyes appeared older than the rest of her delicate features.

"When you were living at the El Camino, did a young woman named Annie Parker live down the hall from you?"

"Yes."

"Did you know her well?"

"Pretty well. We weren't close friends, but we tried to look out for each other."

"Were you employed while you were working at the El Camino?"

"Yes. I worked as a dancer at the Mitchell Brothers Theatre."

There was no need to explain the nature of the Mitchell Brothers' business to a San Francisco jury. "You also had other sources of income?"

"I did." Her eyes locked onto mine. "I was a sex worker."

"Are you still engaged in that type of work?"

"On occasion."

"Was Ms. Parker also engaged in sex work?"

"Yes."

"You and Ms. Parker worked for the same person, didn't you?"

"Yes." Her expression turned grim. "A man named Marcus Strong."

"He arranged clients?"

"Yes."

I moved in a little closer. "Is Mr. Strong available to testify today?"

"No, Mr. Daley. Somebody knifed him in the Tenderloin about six months ago. As far as I know, they haven't caught the person who killed him."

"Was Mr. Strong a good guy?"

Her lips formed a tight line across her face. "No, he was not. He preyed on young women."

"Like you and Ms. Parker?"

"Yes."

"How did you and Ms. Parker meet Mr. Strong?"

"He approached us in the Tenderloin and offered us money and places to live."

"I take it that he didn't do this out of the goodness of his heart?"

"He did it to gain control over us so that we would provide sex to his customers."

"He took a percentage of your earnings?"

"Yes."

"What happened if you didn't hand over his cut?"

"He was physically and emotionally abusive."

"He hit you and Ms. Parker?"

"Yes." She flashed anger. "He liked to say that nobody crossed him more than once."

"I'm sorry. How else did he exert control over you?"

"He drove us to and from our appointments. He took our money. He provided medication when we needed it."

"Did he ever withhold medication?"

"Yes."

"That's dangerous."

"That's the kind of guy that he was."

I asked if Strong also provided illegal drugs.

"He did. Cocaine, crystal meth, and heroin. He got several women addicted to maintain control over them."

"Did he provide drugs to Ms. Parker?"

"Yes. Mostly coke and meth. He gave her Oxy to help her with a bad shoulder."

Erickson interjected in a respectful voice. "Your Honor, I fail to see the relevance of this line of questioning. I would appreciate it if you would ask Mr. Daley whether he's planning to introduce any evidence regarding Ms. Parker's death."

"Your Honor," I said, "I'm getting there."

"I'll give you a little leeway, Mr. Daley, but please get to the point."

"Thank you." *I may need a lot of leeway.* I turned back to Dawson. "Were you aware that Ms. Parker had moved into a tent on U.N. Plaza shortly before she died?"

"Yes."

"Do you know why?"

"She and Marcus had a falling out. Marcus took all of her money and got her thrown out of her room at the El Camino because she couldn't pay her rent."

"Do you know if she had any subsequent contact with Mr. Strong?"

"She told me that he came to see her at U.N. Plaza. He offered to set her up again at the El Camino if she came back to work for him. He also promised to pay for painkillers for her shoulder. She didn't want to do it. She told me that Marcus was really upset."

"Do you know if Marcus Strong provided Annie Parker with OxyContin pills in order to induce her to come back to work for him?"

"It wouldn't surprise me."

"Would you have been surprised if Mr. Strong provided her with pills tainted with fentanyl?"

I expected Erickson to object again, but he stayed in his seat.

"No," Dawson said.

"Do you think Mr. Strong gave Ms. Parker some tainted pills on the night that she died?"

"Objection," Erickson said. "Speculation. Mr. Daley hasn't introduced a shred of evidence connecting Marcus Strong to Ms. Parker's death."

No, I haven't.

Judge Powell's voice was even. "The objection is sustained. Anything else for this witness, Mr. Daley?"

"Just a couple more questions, Your Honor." I turned back to Dawson. "Have you ever met a man named Joseph Davis?"

"Once or twice."

"I informed you earlier today that Mr. Davis died yesterday, didn't I?"

"Yes."

So he can't hurt you. "He was known in the neighborhood as 'Go-To' Joe, wasn't he?"

"Yes."

"Can you tell us why?"

"If you needed drugs, Joe could get them for you."

"Did he ever provide drugs to Annie Parker?"

"Objection," Erickson said. "Calls for information outside Ms. Dawson's scope of knowledge."

"Your Honor," I said, "Ms. Parker and Ms. Dawson lived in the same hotel and were friends. Ms. Dawson has personal knowledge of this information."

"Overruled."

"Joe Davis provided drugs to Annie on a couple of occasions," Dawson said.

"What kind of drugs?"

"Mostly coke. Occasionally meth."

"Oxy?"

"I think so."

"Fentanyl?"

"I don't know."

Fair enough. "It's therefore possible that Mr. Davis provided drugs to Ms. Parker shortly before she died, isn't it?"

"Objection. Calls for speculation."

"Sustained."

I wasn't done speculating. "It's also possible that he provided pills tainted with fentanyl, isn't it? And she put the pills inside a bottle that she had received from the defendant? And the fentanyl killed her?"

Erickson threw his hands up with a melodramatic flourish. "Objection. Speculation. Mr. Daley is testifying. And there isn't a shred of evidence for any of this."

All true.

"Sustained."

Erickson wasn't finished. "Your Honor, I would ask you to instruct Mr. Daley to provide some hard evidence instead of making wild accusations about individuals who are deceased and are not available to defend themselves."

The judge responded with a dry, "Noted, Mr. Erickson. Anything else, Mr. Daley?"

I needed to take a chance to see if she would implicate Holton. "Just one question, Your Honor." I looked at Dawson. "Do you know of anyone else who provided drugs—legal or otherwise—to Ms. Parker?"

"No, Mr. Daley."

"Thank you, Ms. Dawson. No further questions."

After Erickson passed on cross, the judge asked if I wanted to call any other witnesses.

"Yes, Your Honor. The defense calls Brian Holton."

The judge looked at his watch. "It's almost noon. We'll proceed after lunch."

45

"I NEED YOU TO BE BETTER"

Lenny was sweating profusely in the consultation room during the lunch break. "That's the best that you can do?" he snapped.

"I need you to be patient," I said.

"I need you to be better. The jury thinks we're desperately trying to deflect blame."

We are. "I can't generate facts, Lenny. We need to chip away at their case and try to convince at least one juror to acquit."

"They aren't buying it."

"They will." *Maybe.* I handed him a turkey sandwich. "It's going to be a long afternoon. Eat something."

"I'm not hungry. What's the plan?"

"I'm going to put Holton on the stand and accuse him of giving Annie the pills."

"He'll deny it."

"I'll shred his credibility."

"It would be better if you could prove that his fingerprints were on the bottle."

"I can't. Then I'll put Inspector Lee on the stand and accuse him of jumping to conclusions and failing to consider other suspects."

"He'll deny it, too."

"I'll shred his credibility, too."

He exhaled. "You think it'll work?"

"It's our best shot."

"And if it doesn't?"

"I need you to be ready to testify that you didn't give Annie the tainted pills."

"I can do it."

"Good."

The deputy standing guard knocked on the door and let himself in. "Judge Powell wants to see you in chambers right away."

46

"YOU DON'T WANT TO PUT HIM ON THE STAND"

Judge Powell sat at his desk, expression somber. "Something has come up, Mr. Daley."

I glanced at Erickson, who was sitting in the chair next to mine. A surgical mask covered his nose and mouth, but I could see tension in his eyes.

"What's this about?" I asked the judge.

His eyes darted to Erickson, then back to me. "You said that you are planning to call Brian Holton as your next witness."

"Correct."

He looked over at Erickson again, who took the cue.

"You don't want to put him on the stand," he said.

"Yes, I do."

Erickson's tone became adamant. "No, you don't."

"He's been on our witness list for weeks."

"This isn't about your list. His testimony won't help your case."

"Yes, it will."

"No, it won't. He didn't give Annie Parker the tainted pills."

"You don't know that."

"Yes, I do."

What the hell? I looked at the judge. "What's going on?"

Judge Powell nodded at Erickson again. "Would you please enlighten Mr. Daley?"

"Holton is an undercover cop. *Deep* undercover."

Oh crap. "How long have you known?"

"Months."

"When were you planning to tell me?"

"It's complicated."

"Not *that* complicated. He's been on our witness list from day one."

"I was hoping that you wouldn't need his testimony."

The back of my neck was burning. "I do."

"It will only hurt your case if you put an undercover cop on the stand and accuse him—without evidence—of murder. If you don't ask him about his occupation, I will do it on cross. When the jury finds out, it will blow your credibility and your case out of the water."

Yes, it will. "You sandbagged me."

"I did what I thought was right to protect Officer Holton and avoid compromising several highly sensitive ongoing investigations."

"You compromised my client's rights."

"No, I didn't."

"Yes, you did. You have a legal obligation to provide relevant information."

"I'm required to share evidence that may tend to exonerate your client. The fact that Officer Holton is SFPD does exactly the opposite."

"Is that even his real name?"

"I'm not authorized to disclose that information."

"This is wildly unfair."

"This is within the letter and spirit of the law."

I looked at the judge. "This compromises the integrity of this trial. I have no choice but to request a mistrial."

"Denied."

"Mr. Erickson withheld material information."

"That he was under no obligation to provide to you."

I glared at the judge. "You're going to pretend that it didn't happen?"

"I'm following the law, Mr. Daley."

I spent five minutes trying to persuade the judge to declare a mistrial, which likely would have implicated double jeopardy—which meant that Erickson would not be able to refile charges against Lenny.

Judge Powell knew exactly what I was doing, and he didn't budge. He folded his arms and said, "Your motion for a mistrial is denied."

"You're going to be overruled on appeal."

"So be it. I'm doing what I think is right."

And you'll be retired and playing golf by the time an appellate court hears our appeal.

Erickson turned to me and lowered his voice. "For what it's worth, Mike, I know that I've put you in a difficult position. I hope you believe me when I say that I was trying to avoid this conversation. I would encourage you not to put Holton on the stand because it will not help your client, and it will derail several investigations that are in their final stages. We're very close to arresting some really bad guys including the biggest fentanyl distributor in San Francisco."

"I need to think this over."

"Fine."

I turned to the judge. "I'd like a continuance."

"We'll resume tomorrow morning."

47

"I SCREWED UP"

"I screwed up," I said.

Rosie sat in the chair opposite my desk. "Did you tell Lenny that Holton was an undercover cop?"

"Yes. I needed to explain why I wasn't going to call him as a witness. I told Lenny to keep it to himself. We stand to gain nothing if it comes out."

"You think he'll keep quiet?"

I shrugged. "I hope so."

"How did Lenny take the news that Holton was a cop?"

"Poorly." I swallowed. "I should have known."

"You had no way of knowing. I have plenty of issues with the police and the prosecutors, but I understand why they need to protect their undercovers. It's a matter of life and death."

That much is true.

We were in my office at eight-forty-five on Thursday night. Rosie had insisted on coming in despite my protests. Terrence was in his usual spot outside my door. Pete and Nady were on speaker. My mind raced for a solution to a problem that I couldn't fix.

Nady's voice was subdued. "I'm sorry, Mike. I should have known."

"Not your fault. Don't beat yourself up."

When I worked for five long years at a megafirm at the top of the Bank of America Building to make money after Rosie and I got divorced, many of my partners had a nasty habit of taking credit for anything that went right and blaming the nearest associate for anything that went wrong. I promised myself that I would never treat my subordinates that way.

Pete spoke up. "It's my fault. I have connections to SFPD. I should have found out."

"Nobody in SFPD was going to give up the identify of an undercover—not even to you."

"I'll make it up to you."

Probably not this time. "Thanks."

Rosie returned to the matters at hand. "So you aren't going to put Holton on the stand?"

"Correct. If I do, he'll deny that he gave Parker the tainted pills, and he'll reveal that he's an undercover cop. That will kill my credibility with the jury and blow his cover on the street. I'll go back to our original narrative. There's a good chance that Parker died of her heart condition. They have no hard evidence that Lenny gave Parker the tainted pills. There were others more likely to have done so."

"How do you plan on doing it?"

"I'll put Lee on the stand and argue that he jumped to conclusions."

"Are you going to mention Holton's name without calling him to testify?"

"Yes. I'll suggest that he gave Parker the tainted pills. Lee and Erickson will have to decide whether to reveal that Holton is a cop. My guess is that they won't. If they do, I'll pretend that I didn't know and accuse them of withholding evidence. It won't be a good look for them."

"It might not be a good look for you, either."

"If it gets one juror to reasonable doubt, it's worth it. We'll get a hung jury and Erickson will have to decide whether to start over. It will be six months to a year before we get another trial. A lot can happen between now and then."

"If Lenny can survive that long."

"He's tough, Rosie."

"It's starting to look like the Coronavirus may be tough, too."

"A long time ago, you taught me to focus on things that I can control. The virus isn't one of them."

"What if Lee's testimony doesn't go well?"

"I'll put Lenny on the stand to give a solid denial."

48

"YOU DIDN'T CONSIDER ANYBODY ELSE"

"Inspector Lee," I began, "you are the lead homicide investigator in connection with the death of Annie Parker?"

At ten o'clock the following morning, a Friday, Inspector Ken Lee sat ramrod straight, arms folded, demeanor professional, manner confident. "Yes."

I stood at the lectern in the silent courtroom. "You interviewed witnesses in the vicinity?"

"Yes."

"Were there a lot of people in U.N. Plaza?"

"Yes."

"Yet you didn't consider anybody else as a potential suspect, did you?"

He shook his head dismissively. "That's not true, Mr. Daley. We found no evidence connecting anyone other than the defendant to Ms. Parker's death."

"You ruled everybody else out?"

Erickson could have objected on the grounds that Lee had already answered my question, but Lee didn't need his help.

Lee repeated his mantra. "We found no evidence connecting anyone other than the defendant to Ms. Parker's death."

"That's because you rushed to judgment."

"Objection."

"Withdrawn." I moved in front of Lee, making sure that the jurors could see his face. "You were here in court when SFPD's fingerprint expert, Lieutenant Kathleen Jacobsen, testified, right?"

"Right."

I walked over to the evidence cart and picked up the pill bottle. "Lieutenant Jacobsen testified that she found prints other than those of the decedent and my client, didn't she?"

"Yes."

"Did it occur to you that the other person who handled this bottle slipped some tainted pills inside?"

"We found no evidence, Mr. Daley."

"But you didn't even consider the possibility, did you?"

"Objection. Asked and answered."

"Sustained."

I inched closer. "Did you take fingerprint samples from everybody that you interviewed on U.N. Plaza?"

"We obtained prints from at least a dozen people. None of them matched those on the bottle."

"Why didn't you fingerprint everybody you questioned?"

"We couldn't fingerprint the entire Tenderloin, Mr. Daley."

"Which means that you chose to ignore dozens of people who might have touched this bottle?"

"As I said, Mr. Daley, we couldn't fingerprint the entire Tenderloin."

I pushed out a melodramatic sigh. "That's because you had already jumped to the conclusion that my client was guilty."

"Objection. Argumentative."

"Sustained."

I handed him the evidence bag holding Annie's underwear. "You heard Mr. George Romero testify that there were traces of semen on these panties?"

"Yes."

"The semen did not match the DNA of my client, right?"

"That simply proves that your client didn't have sex with Ms. Parker."

"But somebody else did, right?"

"Presumably."

"That person could have given her tainted drugs in exchange for sex, right?"

"Objection. Calls for speculation."

"Overruled."

Lee's tone was dismissive. "We had no evidence of any such barter transaction."

"But you can't rule it out, right?"

"Objection. More speculation."

"Sustained."

Erickson rose to his feet and feigned impatience. "Your Honor, we covered this information during Inspector Lee's earlier testimony. Mr. Daley is simply attempting to muddy the waters by asking Inspector Lee to speculate about wholly unsubstantiated claims."

That's my job.

The judge rolled his eyes. "Let's move along to some new material, Mr. Daley."

"Yes, Your Honor." *I've just started asking Lee to speculate.* "You're familiar with a man named Marcus Strong, aren't you?"

"Yes."

"He was a pimp, a drug dealer, a fence, and an extortionist in the Tenderloin, wasn't he?"

"Yes."

"According to testimony from Ms. Parker's friend, Patty Dawson, Marcus Strong was Ms. Parker's pimp, wasn't he?"

"Yes."

"Ms. Dawson also testified that Mr. Strong was physically and emotionally abusive to Ms. Parker, didn't she?"

"Yes."

"He hit her. He took her money. He controlled her life."

"According to Ms. Dawson."

"Do you have any reason to disbelieve her testimony?"

"No."

Good. "Ms. Dawson also testified that Mr. Strong provided drugs to Ms. Parker, didn't she?"

"Yes."

I eyed him. "But you didn't consider Mr. Strong as a suspect?"

"We found no evidence connecting him to Ms. Parker's death."

"Did you test Mr. Strong's DNA or prints?"

"Both. Neither matched the prints or DNA on the bottle."

"You didn't consider the possibility that the pimp who was beating the crap out of her, taking her money, and keeping her subservient with drugs might have given her some tainted pills?"

Lee finally showed a hint of irritation. "Of course, I did. We found no evidence connecting him to Ms. Parker's death."

"Seems to me that you didn't look very hard."

"Objection."

"Sustained." The judge tried again. "Please move on, Mr. Daley."

"Inspector," I continued, "are you familiar with a man named Joseph Davis?"

"Yes. Unfortunately, he passed away earlier this week."

"You interviewed him before he died?"

"I did."

"What was his occupation?"

"He was a security guard at a liquor store."

"What was his previous job?"

"He was in prison."

"On what charge?"

Lee shot a glance at Erickson. "He delivered drugs to people in the Tenderloin."

"Illegal drugs?"

"Sometimes."

"He knew Ms. Parker, didn't he?"

"According to Ms. Dawson, they'd met."

"He had delivered drugs to her on several occasions, hadn't he?"

"According to Ms. Dawson."

"Yet you didn't consider the possibility that he had delivered some tainted pills to her shortly before she died?"

"We found no evidence that he did." He cleared his throat. "His prints did not match the unidentified prints on the bottle. We also had a DNA sample from Mr. Davis from a prior arrest which did not match the semen on Ms. Parker's panties."

"What about the traces of DNA on the bottle that didn't match Ms. Parker or my client?"

"The traces were too small to get a match."

"So you quickly ruled him out as a suspect, too?"

"We had no evidence connecting him to Ms. Parker."

"He was her drug supplier."

"We had no evidence that he delivered tainted pills to her shortly before she died."

I gave the jury another skeptical look, then turned back to Lee. "You also interviewed a man named Brian Holton, didn't you?"

Erickson started to stand, then he reconsidered.

Lee tensed. "Yes."

"He lived on U.N. Plaza near Ms. Parker?"

He glanced at Erickson, who nodded. "Yes."

"Mr. Holton has also been investigated for potential drug dealing, hasn't he?"

"Yes." Another look at Erickson. "He's never been arrested or convicted."

"Yet you didn't consider the possibility that he may have provided tainted pills to Ms. Parker?"

"We found no evidence that he did."

"Did you bring him in for questioning?"

Erickson pushed his chair back, but he didn't get up.

Lee held up a hand. "I interviewed him. We found no evidence that he had provided any illicit substances to Ms. Parker."

I feigned incredulity. "Really?"

"Really."

"Come on, Inspector."

"Objection," Erickson said. "There wasn't a question there."

"Withdrawn." I was still glaring at Lee. "So you chose to ignore the possibility that he provided fentanyl-laced pills to Ms. Parker, didn't you?"

"Move to strike," Erickson said. "Mr. Daley is testifying."

Yes, I am.

"Sustained."

I waited a beat to give the jury a moment to process what they had just heard. "Marcus Strong provided drugs and beat the crap out of Ms. Parker. Joseph Davis was a known dealer who had previously supplied drugs to Ms. Parker. And Brian Holton was also a suspected drug dealer who lived near Ms. Parker. Yet you didn't consider any of them as suspects?"

"We found no evidence."

"Just coincidence, right?"

Lee didn't fluster. "I interviewed Mr. Strong, Mr. Davis, and Mr. Holton. They all cooperated and admitted that they were in the vicinity of U.N. Plaza on or around the date that Ms. Parker died, but I found no evidence connecting any of them to her death."

"That's because you didn't try very hard."

"Objection. Mr. Daley has presented no evidence that the prints on the bottle and the DNA matched Mr. Strong, Mr. Davis, or Mr. Holton."

"Sustained."

I tried again. "You jumped to the conclusion that my client killed Annie Parker, didn't you? More accurately, you jumped to the wrong conclusion."

"We followed procedure and went where the evidence took us."

"It took you in the wrong direction."

"Objection."

"Sustained."

"No further questions, Your Honor."

"Cross-exam, Mr. Erickson?"

"No, Your Honor."

"Any other witnesses, Mr. Daley?"

I looked around at the jurors scattered in the gallery. Then I nodded at Lenny, who nodded back.

"Your Honor," I said, "the defense calls Leonard Garcia."

49

"I WAS TRYING TO HELP HER"

I stood a few feet from the box. "You knew the decedent, Annie Parker?"

"Yes." Lenny wiped the perspiration from his forehead. "She was living in a tent next to mine on U.N. Plaza." He said that she had been living there for a couple of months.

Follow my lead, Lenny, and keep your answers short. "Did you know her well?"

"Not that well. She kept to herself. So did I."

The courtroom was silent at eleven-ten on Friday morning. Judge Powell rested his chin on his palm, eyes focused on Lenny. The masked jurors were studying every nuance of the nervous man in the ill-fitting suit.

"When was the last time you saw her?" I asked.

"On the night before she died. I asked her how she was doing. She said that she wasn't feeling well, but she needed to meet a customer."

"You also got into an argument with her, didn't you?"

"Yes. I thought that she had taken my phone, and I yelled at her. I made a mistake and I apologized to her."

"Officer Christa Carter intervened, didn't she?"

"She was walking by us at the time. In hindsight, it was probably good that she helped us resolve the situation."

He was holding up pretty well. I walked over to the evidence cart, picked up the pill bottle, returned to the box, and handed it to Lenny. "Do you recognize this container?"

"Yes. It's a bottle for my OxyContin pills which I take for pain in my knees." He confirmed that he was injured in combat in Afghanistan.

"You have a prescription?"

"Of course. My doctor is at the V.A. I have the prescriptions filled there."

"You took the pills in this bottle?"

"Most of them."

"Did you have any adverse reaction?"

"No."

"In particular, did you have any symptoms suggesting that the pills were tainted by an illegal substance such as fentanyl?"

Erickson stood up to object but reconsidered. Lenny wasn't an expert on the composition of the pills. On the other hand, I had framed my question to ask whether he had felt any symptoms, not a confirmation of the chemical composition of the pills.

Lenny shrugged. "The pills were fine."

"You didn't take all of them?"

"No. I gave a few of them to Annie."

"You didn't need them for yourself?"

He paused for dramatic effect—just the way that we had rehearsed. "I was supposed to go to the V.A. the following day to get a refill. I was trying to help her. She injured her shoulder in an auto accident a few years ago. She was in a lot of pain."

"Why didn't she go to the doctor and get her own prescription?"

"She didn't have health insurance, and she couldn't always get to one of the clinics in the neighborhood."

"She needed the pills that night?"

"She was really hurting, and she had to go to work. She said that she was trying to reconnect with her old boss, who would have been angry if she didn't show up on time."

"You mean her pimp?"

"Yes."

"A man named Marcus Strong?"

"She mentioned that his name was Marcus. I didn't know his last name."

"You think she was in danger?"

"Objection," Erickson said. "Calls for speculation."

"Sustained."

I took the bottle from Lenny. "How many pills did you give her?"

"I think there were three left in the bottle."

"You're sure that the pills were, in fact, the ones that were issued to you by the V.A.?"

"Yes."

"You let her keep the bottle?"

"I didn't need it."

"That would explain how your name and fingerprints were on the bottle?"

"Yes."

I went back to the lectern. "Lenny, did you give Annie Parker any pills that were laced with fentanyl?"

His voice was resolute. "No, I did not."

"Do you have any idea who did?"

"It could have been anybody. There is a lot of fentanyl in the Tenderloin."

"No further questions, Your Honor."

"Cross-exam, Mr. Erickson?"

"Just a few questions." He stood, buttoned his jacket, and walked deliberately across the courtroom, where he took up a position in front of Lenny. "When the police first questioned you, they asked if you had given any pills to Ms. Parker, didn't they?"

Lenny looked my way, and I nodded subtly. *Tell the truth.*

"Yes," he said.

"At first you told them that you hadn't, right?"

Lenny swallowed. "Yes."

"That wasn't true, was it?"

"I told them later that I had given her some of my pills."

"Bottom line, you lied, didn't you?"

"Objection," I said. "Asked and answered."

"Asked," Erickson snapped, "but not answered."

"Overruled."

"I was afraid," Lenny said.

"It was still a lie."

"Objection," I said. "Mr. Erickson is testifying."

"I'll rephrase," Erickson said. "You lied when you told the police that you hadn't given Ms. Parker the pills, right?"

"Right."

"And now you're asking us to believe that the pills that you gave her were clean OxyContin pills that you got from the V.A.?"

"It's the truth."

Erickson got into his face. "You just admitted that you lied to the police. Why should we believe you now?"

Stay the course, Lenny.

"Because it's the truth," Lenny said.

"You're saying that you gave Ms. Parker some clean pills, which she took. Then she got some tainted pills from somebody else, which she happened to put inside the very same bottle that you gave her?"

"Yes."

Erickson feigned disbelief. "You really expect us to believe you?"

"Objection," I said. "Argumentative."

"Overruled."

"It's the truth," Lenny repeated.

Erickson spent five minutes hammering Lenny and trying to get him to admit that he had, in fact, given Annie the tainted pills. I objected frequently. Lenny's voice cracked a couple of times, but he remained unwavering in his denials. Out of the corner of my eye, I could see the stone-faced jurors watching in rapt attention.

Finally, Erickson moved within a foot of Lenny. "You gave Annie Parker some pills that were tainted with fentanyl, didn't you, Mr. Garcia?"

"No."

"And because you did, she overdosed and died."

"It wasn't because I gave her some bad pills."

"You'll feel better if you come clean, Mr. Garcia."

"I didn't give her tainted pills, Mr. Erickson."

"Yes, you did."

"No, I didn't."

"Come on, Mr. Garcia."

"Objection," I said. "There wasn't a question."

"Withdrawn," Erickson snapped. "No further questions."

"Redirect, Mr. Daley?"

"No, Your Honor." I had nothing else. "The defense rests."

The judge looked at his watch. "I was just handed a note that I have to hear an emergency motion later this afternoon. I am therefore going to recess until ten o'clock Monday morning, when you and Mr. Erickson should be prepared to deliver your closing arguments."

50

"I NEEDED TO CLEAR MY HEAD"

Joey's blue eyes twinkled as he tossed a dishtowel over his shoulder just the way his grandfather used to do it. His phony Irish brogue also sounded just like Big John when he asked, "What'll it be, lad?"

"Just coffee, Joe."

The brogue disappeared. "You look like you could use a beer, Mike."

"I could, but I can't tonight."

We were the only people in Dunleavy's at eight-forty-five on what would ordinarily have been a busy Friday night. The Warriors game was on the flatscreen, the sound turned down. A hand-lettered sign on the door noted that Dunleavy's would remain closed for a few days.

He poured me a cup of Folgers, took a sip of club soda, and leaned on the bar. "I didn't expect to see you tonight. I figured you'd be at the office working on your closing."

"I needed to clear my head. I've had a couple of long days in court."

"I take it this means that things haven't gone exactly as planned?"

"They never do."

"You'll dazzle them with your closing. Rosie always says that you're the master of improv."

"I'm going to have to be." I looked around at the empty bar. "When are you going to reopen?"

"Not sure." He scrunched his face. "Starting Monday, I'm going to do takeout only."

"Can you make a go of it?"

"Sure thing. Our regulars are very loyal." He winked. "If you're tired of being a Public Defender, you can come over and help me make the fish and chips."

"It'll be more fun than doing a murder trial."

"You're hired."

I grinned. "The Mayor's Office told us that the shutdown won't last more than a few weeks."

"We'll see."

"They said on the news that they may start a program to make loans to small businesses to help them pay their employees during the shutdown."

"A fine idea." His tone filled with sarcasm. "If my guess is correct, most of the money will go to big businesses and fat cats. Besides, I don't take handouts."

"It won't be a handout."

"Yes, it will." He pointed at the photo of Big John above the bar. "Did you ever meet his daddy?"

"When I was a kid. He ran a little grocery in the Mission. He was a good guy."

"Big John told me that Great-Grandpa Johnny refused to take welfare during the Depression, even though he was entitled, and he could have used it. It was a matter of pride—the Dunleavy family didn't take relief." He eyed me. "I feel the same way."

I wondered what I would have done if Rosie and I were still running a two-person law firm in a converted martial arts studio above a Chinese restaurant on Mission Street. "Good for you, Joe."

The backdoor swung open, and Pete let himself inside. He was carrying a stack of empty takeout boxes which he hauled over to the kitchen. "I was able to get twelve dozen," he said to Joey. "Costco sold out, so I called in some favors. This should be enough to get you started."

"Thanks, Pete."

My brother took off his bomber jacket and slid onto the stool next to mine. Without a word, Joey poured him a cup of black coffee.

Pete handed each of us a baggie containing a dozen surgical masks. "You might need these," he said. "They were the last ones left at CVS."

I nodded. "Thanks, Pete. I thought Donna wasn't letting you leave the house."

"I can't even get inside the house except to shower. Donna wants me to stay in the garage until I get tested."

"How did you escape?"

"I offered to make a Costco run to pick up supplies." He rolled his eyes. "You wouldn't believe what's going on. People are hoarding paper towels. As if that's going to cure the virus."

"People are crazy."

"That they are." He turned serious. "I heard you had a couple of rough days in court."

"It's been a challenging week." I told him that closing arguments would start on Monday.

"The jury isn't buying your story that they should blame it on one of the dead guys?"

"It's a long shot. I think I've convinced them that Marcus Strong was a bad guy and Joe Davis was a drug dealer. I suggested that Brian Holton could have slipped Annie the tainted pills. In fairness, I haven't given the jury any hard evidence that any of them had a direct connection to her death."

"The evidence is the evidence, Mick." His mustache twitched as he looked up at the basketball game. "Let me ask around. I owe you one for not knowing that Holton was an undercover cop."

"You don't owe me anything."

"You may not think so, but I do."

"You know anybody working in the Tenderloin?"

"Maybe."

"What about Nick 'The Dick' and his family?"

"Not this time. His kids and grandkids won't let him out of the house, and everybody at the agency is staying out of the TL." He finished his coffee. "Can you stall for a few days if I'm onto something?"

"Probably."

"Can your fingerprint and DNA experts give us a fast turnaround?"

"Sure."

Pete pulled on his bomber jacket. "I'll be in touch."

51

"DUMPSTER DIVE"

My back ached as I stared at my laptop sitting on the butcher block table in the kitchen of my apartment. "Thanks for seeing us on short notice, Carla. Sorry to bug you on a weekend."

"You're welcome, Mike."

On Skype, I could see Dr. Carla Jimenez sitting in her home office in a refurbished Julia Morgan house in the Berkeley hills. In the background I saw medical texts and photos of her husband, grown children, and two grandchildren.

"You were terrific in court," I said.

"It's going to be my last in-person appearance for a while. I promised my husband and my colleagues that I wouldn't go anywhere other than our house and the office."

"How long do you think this virus will last?"

"Hard to say. I've been working with a team at UCSF that's analyzing the RNA, and I've been in contact with the pharmaceutical companies about developing a vaccine. There is some hope that the virus will disappear when the weather warms up, but I'm not making any predictions until I see more data."

I looked at the box in the upper left corner of my screen, where an unshaven Pete was staring intently at his computer. "You at home?" I asked.

"Still in the garage." He confirmed that his wife and daughter were okay.

"You got something for us?"

"I might." His eyes shifted from one side of the screen to the other. "I e-mailed Carla the DNA report for the semen found on Annie Parker's panties. She confirmed that it wasn't a match for Lenny's."

"We already knew that."

"I brought her a few other DNA samples to run."

Contrary to what you see on TV, DNA tests can be completed in a matter of hours if you know the right people who have the right equipment.

I looked at Carla. "Anything we can use?"

"The DNA on the panties matches a man named Kyle Adams."

Huh? I looked at Pete. "Why was the City's Homeless Outreach Czar having sex with Annie Parker?"

He responded with a wry grin. "I presume it was for the same reasons that the rest of us have sex, Mick."

Right. I looked at Carla. "Did the DNA on the panties also match the unidentified DNA on the bottle?"

"The unidentified sample on the bottle was too small for analysis."

Damn. "Can you testify?"

"Remotely."

"We'll work it out. In the meantime, would you be willing to sign a sworn statement with your analysis?"

"Sure."

"I'll e-mail it over to you later today. Carla?"

"Yes?"

"Thanks."

"How did you know it was Adams?" I asked Pete.

We were still on Skype. Carla had signed off.

"I got lucky," he said.

"You don't believe in luck."

"I believe in hunches."

It was a good one. "How did you get a sample of Adams's DNA?"

"Dumpster dive."

"Seriously?"

"Sometimes the traditional investigative methods are the most effective."

"Did you wear a mask?"

"Yes."

"Did anybody see you?"

"I'm a professional, Mick."

Indeed. "Does Donna know about this?"

"Yes. I'm going to be staying in the garage a little longer."

"Did you get any prints from Adams?"

"Afraid not."

"Any other evidence of a connection between Adams and Annie Parker?"

"None."

"Any indication that Adams was providing drugs to Parker?"

"No, although I wouldn't be surprised if he was having sex with other women in the Tenderloin."

Neither would I. "I'll show the DNA report and Carla's affidavit to Erickson."

"It isn't enough, Mick. It proves that Adams had sex with Parker. It doesn't prove that he killed her."

"I'll argue that he gave her the tainted pills."

"On what evidence? His DNA was on her panties, not the pill bottle."

True. "It'll muddy the waters and show that Adams is a bad guy."

"It proves that Adams was sleeping around, which means he's an asshole. It doesn't prove that he killed her."

"Then find me something else that I can use."

"Like what?"

"There was an unidentified print on the pill bottle. I need to prove that it was Adams's."

"How far do you want me to go?"

"Don't do anything illegal."

52

"YOU'RE GOING TO BE EMBARRASSED"

Erickson studied Carla's affidavit. "Dr. Jimenez says that Kyle Adams's semen was found on Annie Parker's underwear?"

"Correct."

"How did you obtain a DNA sample from Adams?"

There was no reason to be disingenuous. "Pete did a Dumpster dive."

The corner of his mouth turned up. "I should have known."

Erickson and I were the only people in the D.A.'s Office at six-forty on Saturday night. As soon as I received Carla's signed affidavit, I texted Erickson and requested a meeting. I wasn't surprised that he was in the office. To his credit, he agreed to see me.

He took off his glasses. "You realize that this is inadmissible."

"I'll file a motion to compel Adams to provide a DNA sample."

"Good luck. Are you planning to put Dr. Jimenez on the stand?"

"Yes, but she wants to testify remotely. I trust that you won't object?"

"I won't. Are you also going to add Pete to your witness list?"

"Yes."

"I will object, but the judge will probably rule in your favor. Adams, too?"

"We'll see."

He considered his options. "Before we go any farther, I will need to validate this evidence and confirm your expert's conclusion on the DNA with George Romero." He cleared his throat. "George doesn't work weekends."

"Understood. I will have no objection if you need a delay to verify the evidence."

He studied the affidavit for another moment. "For the sake of discussion, let's suppose that your brother did, in fact, obtain a DNA sample from Adams which matches the semen found on Parker's panties. What do you expect me to do?"

"Drop the charges against my client."

"You can't be serious."

"It establishes a direct connection between Adams and Parker."

"It proves that they had sex. Last time I looked, that wasn't a crime."

"It is if it isn't consensual."

"Did your brother find any evidence that it wasn't?"

Uh, no. "Not yet."

"It's irrelevant to our case."

"You're going to ignore the direct connection to Parker?"

"It doesn't prove that Adams gave her tainted pills."

"The jury will be able to connect the dots."

"There are no dots to connect." His tone became more emphatic. "Annie Parker died of a fentanyl overdose. This new information—assuming that we can confirm it—has nothing to do with the cause of her death. For all we know, Adams and Parker engaged in consensual sex regularly. Even if it wasn't consensual—which you can't prove—it doesn't provide any evidence that he slipped her some tainted pills."

"At the least, you should find out if he's been having sex with other homeless people."

"That's a separate issue. I would be happy to consider charges if you can provide proof." He lowered his voice. "In all honesty, Mike, I don't think it will help you. Annie Parker was a sex worker. Her sexual encounters are irrelevant to this case. It will probably cost Adams his job, but it doesn't prove that he gave her the tainted pills." He held up a hand. "I understand what you're trying to do, but the jury won't buy it."

"You're going to be embarrassed."

"Adams will be embarrassed."

"What would it take to get you to reconsider?"

"Get me solid evidence that somebody other than your client gave Annie the pills laced with fentanyl."

My mind raced. "There were some unidentified prints on the pill bottle."

"So?"

"Every City employee in his position has to be fingerprinted and drug tested. It'll take Kathleen Jacobsen five minutes to compare the unidentified prints on the bottle with the prints in Adams's file. We can do this the easy way and you can ask Kathleen to compare the prints. Or we can do this the hard way and I will file a motion to compel you to produce his prints. Either way, I'm going to get them."

He smiled. "Or you can just have Pete do another Dumpster dive to get a sample of Adams's prints."

I smiled back. "I'm trying to avoid that."

"It may take me a few days to get a court order to get a copy of the prints."

"I won't object to a delay."

"I'll be in touch."

53

"HE'LL FIND SOMETHING"

At ten-forty-five on Saturday night, I took a sip of Pride Mountain Cab Franc as Wilma the cat curled up under the lamp next to the laptop on the desk in my bedroom. She looked up at me, shook her head, yawned, and closed her eyes.

I shifted my gaze to my computer, where I saw Rosie on Skype. "Such a sweet kitty," she said. Rosie took off the wire-rimmed bifocals that replaced her contacts when she got home from work. I could see the embers in the fireplace behind her. She took a sip of wine and placed the goblet on her desk. "I prefer having our nightly glass of wine in person."

"Me, too. We need to make sacrifices during a medical emergency. Anything else from the Mayor's Office?"

"The official announcement will come on Monday or Tuesday. All City offices will have to go remote by the end of the week. How's your trial?"

"Not great. Closing arguments are Monday." I told her about the DNA test for Adams. "I talked to Erickson. Let's just say that he isn't ready to drop the charges."

"The fact that Adams had sex with Parker doesn't prove that he gave her the tainted pills. It's a bad look for Adams, but it isn't a silver bullet for us."

Ever the voice of reason.

"Is Judge Powell going to let Carla testify again?" she asked.

"I think so."

"Are you going to put Adams on the stand?"

"Yes. I'll accuse him of having sex with Annie, but I have no way of proving that he gave her the fentanyl."

"You got anything else?"

"I asked Erickson to check the unidentified prints on the pill bottle against the prints in Adams's personnel file."

"And if it isn't a match?"

"Pete is looking for other evidence."

"He'll find something."

"Maybe not this time, Rosie."

Her tone was confident. "He always does." She finished her wine. "Get some rest, Mike. You need to work on your closing."

I was entering the Hall of Justice at nine-fifteen on Monday morning when my phone vibrated. I had a text from Erickson.

It read, "Please meet me in Homicide ASAP. Need to talk."

54

"PROFESSIONAL COURTESY"

Erickson's voice was muted as he sat at the metal table in the windowless conference room adjacent to the bullpen where the homicide inspectors worked. "Thank you for coming in."

"You're welcome." *Let him talk.*

Ken Lee sat in the chair next to mine, eyes focused on Erickson. A.C. Brown was standing by the closed door, arms folded.

Erickson glanced at his laptop, then his eyes shifted to mine. "The matters that I'm about to discuss are very sensitive. As a matter of professional courtesy, I need to ask you to keep this information to yourself until I make a public statement."

What? "I'm under no legal obligation to keep anything that you tell me confidential."

"Please, Mike."

"Agreed." *For now.*

He cleared his throat. "At your request, we obtained the fingerprints of Kyle Adams from his City personnel file. The unidentified print on the pill bottle was small and slightly smudged. As a result, the computer didn't identify any matches when we ran it through our usual databases. In an abundance of caution, we asked Lieutenant Jacobsen to perform her own analysis. She confirmed that one of the unidentified prints on the bottle matched Mr. Adams."

Yes!

He glanced at Lee, then he turned back to me. "Late last night, we persuaded Judge McDaniel to issue a warrant to search Mr. Adams's flat. Inspector Lee and Sergeant Brown served the warrant without incident and conducted the search."

I looked at Brown, whose stoic expression didn't change.

Erickson held up an evidence bag containing a plastic bottle about the size of an aspirin jar. "Among other items, Inspector Lee and Sergeant Brown found this container in Mr. Adams's bathroom. Sergeant Brown logged it into evidence and submitted it to Lieutenant Jacobsen for fingerprint analysis. She confirmed that the prints on the bottle matched the prints of Kyle Adams."

So far, so good.

Erickson was still talking. "In addition, Inspector Lee transported several of the pills found inside this bottle to the Medical Examiner's Office for analysis. Dr. Siu determined that they were fake OxyContin pills laced with fentanyl. Dr. Siu also reported that the pills were virtually identical in appearance and composition to the pills in the bottle found inside Annie Parker's tent on the morning that she died."

Even better. My heart pounded, but my expression didn't change. On my first day at the P.D.'s Office, Rosie taught me never to reveal my emotions to a prosecutor.

Erickson's tone remained measured. "As you know, we have a legal obligation to provide evidence to the defense attorney when we believe that it would tend to exonerate his client."

Yes, you do. "I appreciate your honesty and integrity in providing this evidence so quickly."

"It's the law. After we obtained the analysis of the pills and the fingerprints, Inspector Lee and Sergeant Brown brought Mr. Adams in for questioning. Mr. Adams asked to speak to his attorney, and he did not provide any information to us. Just to be clear, Mr. Adams has not admitted that he was having sex with Ms. Parker, nor did he acknowledge providing her with tainted pills. However, we now have reason to believe that he may have been providing pills to Ms. Parker and other women—some of whom may have been underage—in exchange for sex."

"Where is Adams now?"

"He is being detained while Inspector Lee continues to investigate."

"Are you planning to charge him with the murder of Annie Parker?"

"We believe that there is a substantial likelihood that he is responsible for providing the tainted pills to Ms. Parker. We will determine charges, if any, after further investigation. Confidentially, we also have reason to believe that Mr. Adams may be willing to cooperate with us by identifying several of the major suppliers of fentanyl in the Bay Area."

"Are you planning to offer him a deal?"

"We'll make that determination in due course as well."

"You aren't going to give him immunity on Annie Parker's death, are you?"

"Absolutely not."

"I trust that you will not object when I file a motion to drop the charges against my client?"

"I will not, subject to the condition that you will not file your motion or say anything about it until you get the go-ahead from me."

Works for me. "Agreed."

"Please e-mail me a draft of your motion when it's ready."

"I will. I plan to include an affirmative recitation that Lenny is innocent."

"I won't object."

It's a total victory for Lenny. "Andy?"

"Yes?"

"I know that a win in this case was very important to you. I appreciate the fact that you did the right thing."

"A conviction of an innocent man is not a win." His eyes narrowed. "I will get my win, and justice will be served. It's just going to take a little longer than I had hoped."

We need more public servants like you. "Let me know if there is any information that you need from me."

"I will."

"I know that you keep saying that you aren't planning to run for D.A. Please let me know if you change your mind. I think I can muster some support for you at the P.D.'s Office."

"I'm not sure that it's in my political interest to have an official endorsement from the P.D.'s Office."

"I'm not sure that it's in Rosie's political interest for the P.D.'s Office to make an official endorsement in the D.A.'s race. On the other hand, I would be happy to put in a good word for you among my colleagues."

The corner of his mouth turned up. "Thanks, Mike. I'll let you know."

55

"I'LL BE FINE"

At eight-forty-five on Monday night, I waited for Lenny outside the prisoner discharge area on the ground floor of County Jail #2 adjacent to the Hall of Justice. A light rain was falling as a sheriff's deputy escorted him to the release area. Clad in the standard-issue release clothing—slacks and a button-down shirt—he kept his eyes down as he strained to walk the final twenty feet to freedom. He was clutching his wallet and his watch, which had been returned to him. They were the only items of personal property in his possession when he was booked.

The deputy activated the gate, and the lock disengaged. He wished Lenny luck. Then he closed the gate, turned around, and returned to his post.

I handed Lenny a raincoat from the used clothes bin at the P.D.'s Office. "Sorry it took so long to get you out of here. The paperwork took longer than I had expected."

"No worries."

"Congratulations, Lenny."

"Thanks for everything, Mike." His somber expression didn't change as he put the jacket on. "I don't know what I would have done without you."

"I'm sorry that you don't have a bigger welcoming party."

"My sister had to go to work. I didn't expect anybody else."

We walked through the SFPD parking lot to Seventh Street, where I had parked my Prius. We got into the car, and I turned on the heat. I flicked on my wipers, and we headed north on Seventh and under the 101 Freeway.

"Where to?" I asked.

"Perlita said that I could stay with her for a few days." He looked out the window. "I told her that I would stay in her garage. I don't want to expose her daughter to the virus."

"We have people at the office who can help you find a job and a place to live."

"I don't have any money."

"We work with some charitable organizations that provide money to people who are getting back on their feet."

He grinned for the first time since I had met him. "Sort of a Kickstarter for felons?"

"You aren't a felon, Lenny. I'm getting the murder charge expunged from your record. I'll hook you up with a lawyer to help you sue the City for false imprisonment."

"I definitely want to do that." He leaned back in his seat, closed his eyes for a moment, and then reopened them. "How did you know that Adams was distributing tainted pills?"

"My investigator played a hunch. To their credit, Erickson and Lee followed up and got a warrant to search Adams's apartment. They matched his prints to the unidentified prints on the pill bottle."

"You're saying that we got lucky?"

Yes. "I'm saying that we're fortunate that we had an excellent investigator, and the D.A. and the police did their jobs. Justice is being served late, Lenny, but we got the right result."

"I guess. How is Nady's mother?"

"Doing a little better."

"You and Nady were the only people who believed me. I'll never forget that."

"Nady told me that you were telling the truth. That was good enough for me."

I turned left on Harrison and got onto the 101. We drove in silence to the 280, which we took to Daly City.

"You hungry?" I asked.

"Yes." He said that he had lost twenty pounds in jail.

"I'll take you for something to eat. What have you got a taste for?"

"In-N-Out."

"I'm happy to pop for something a little fancier."

"I've been craving In-N-Out for a year."

"Deal."

We drove past the Daly City BART Station and exited the freeway at Sullivan Avenue. We stopped at the In-N-Out next to the Krispy Kreme adjacent to the freeway. I bought Lenny a double-double with fries and a chocolate shake. He ate his burger and fries enthusiastically and thanked me repeatedly.

"We'll go for something a little more upscale after you get settled," I said.

"Sounds good." His tone turned thoughtful after we got back into the car and started driving to his sister's house. "You okay?" he asked.

"Fine. You?"

"Fine."

"You look a little pale."

He took a deep breath. "My throat is sore and my head hurts."

"You want me to take you to the emergency room?"

"No. Just drop me off at my sister's house."

"You sure?"

"I'll be fine, Mike."

56

"YOU DID EVERYTHING THAT YOU COULD"

Three days later, I was driving north on the Golden Gate Bridge through a cold drizzle at six-thirty p.m. when my phone vibrated. I answered using the hands-free. "Michael Daley."

"It's Perlita Garcia."

"Hi."

"Hi." Her voice cracked. "He's gone."

My throat tightened. "Lenny left?"

"No, he's dead."

Dear God. "I'm so sorry. What happened?"

"He woke up with a fever and a cough. I took him to the emergency room where he started having trouble breathing. They gave him antibiotics and some other drugs, but they didn't help, so they put him on a ventilator." Her voice trembled. "He died about an hour ago."

My stomach churned. "Was it the virus?"

"The doctor thinks so. She won't know for sure until they do the autopsy."

"Do you need help with the arrangements?"

"I'll figure it out."

I didn't know what to say, so I went with a lame, "How are you holding up?"

"Physically, I'm okay. Emotionally, not so good. My daughter has a low-grade fever. She's staying at home until I can get her tested."

"Is there anything I can do?"

"You did everything that you could. You got Lenny home, and I'm very grateful."

"You're welcome."

"You need to get tested," she said. "I would tell you to come down to the hospital where I work, but we're running low."

"I'll find one someplace else."

I drove up the hill past the vista point at the north end of the bridge. The rain became harder as I headed into the Robin Williams Tunnel toward Sausalito. On nice days, it was the dividing line between the San Francisco fog and the Marin County sunshine. Tonight, it was cold and rainy on both sides.

"Mike?" she said.

"Yes?"

"Thank you for helping Lenny."

"You're welcome, Perlita. I'm so sorry for your loss."

I punched in Pete's number as I pulled into the carport in front of my apartment building. He answered on the first ring.

"Sorry about Lenny," he said. "Terrence just told me about it."

"Thanks. You okay?"

"Fine, Mick. You?"

"Been better."

"I heard that they arrested Kyle Adams for killing Annie Parker. Do you know if they're going to charge him with murder or manslaughter?"

"As far as I know, they haven't decided yet."

"Nice work, Mick."

"You, too, Pete."

"Where are you?"

"Just pulled into my driveway."

"You're not staying at Rosie's house?"

"Lenny probably died of the virus. I need to get tested. So do you."

"I already tested negative. So did Donna and Margaret."

"How did you get tested so quickly?"

"I know somebody."

You always do.

He added, "I'm not bursting with pride about the fact that I jumped the line to get a test, but sometimes you do what you gotta do. I can get you a test if you want one."

"I don't have any symptoms."

"The doctor told me that people without symptoms are testing positive." He waited a beat. "You want me to get you a test?"

"That's probably a good idea. Is Donna pissed off at you?"

"Yes. We'll deal with it. We always do."

I took a moment to gather my thoughts. "What made you think that Adams was involved in Annie Parker's death?"

"I talked to a couple of my moles at the Mitchell Brothers. They thought there was something odd about him, and he was spending a lot of time at the Theatre. He was hitting up the dancers and offering them meth."

Good hunch. "Pete?"

"Yes?"

"Thanks."

"You're welcome. Take care, Mick."

Nady's name appeared on my phone as I entered my apartment. "You okay?" I asked.

"All things considered, not bad." She sounded tired. "You?"

"Fine," I lied. "How's your mother?"

"Still in the hospital, but it looks like she's going to be okay."

"Good to hear. Any idea when she can go home?"

"Too soon to know. I may get to see her in person in a couple of days."

"Take as much time as you need."

"Thanks, Mike." Her tone turned somber. "Terrence told me about Lenny. I'm so sorry."

"Thank you."

"You got a great result for him."

"It was mostly Pete."

"It was both of you. Can you take some time off?"

"Looks like I'm going to have to. We're closing the office, and I may have been exposed to the virus. No symptoms—yet. I'm going to stay at the apartment at least until I get tested. I'll keep an eye on your cases."

"How long do you think this is going to last, Mike?"

Not a clue. "A few weeks. Maybe a month."

She reported that she and Max would be staying in L.A. until her mom was able to take care of herself. "Thanks for everything, Mike."

"You're welcome." My phone vibrated, and I saw Rosie's name on the display. "I gotta run, Nady. The boss is on the other line."

"Take care, Mike."

"You, too."

57

"IT'S WORKING"

Rosie's tone was impatient. "Hit the button that says, 'Join meeting.'"

I pressed my phone to my ear and stared at my laptop. "I did. Nothing happened."

"Try again."

"Can we just Facetime or Skype?"

"No. You need to learn how to use this technology, Mike."

Wilma was sitting next to my laptop at ten o'clock on Thursday night, bored. "Can you show me how this works?" I asked her.

She responded with a yawn, curled up, and closed her eyes.

Rosie's voice filled with exasperation. "Are you still there?"

"Yes."

"Hit the button that says, 'Join meeting.'"

I did as I was told. A moment later, Rosie's face appeared in a box on the screen. Grace showed up in an adjoining box. She was in her condo in Emeryville and wearing a USC sweatshirt. Tommy appeared a moment later in a Cal hoodie. The Pac-12 was well represented.

Rosie waved. "Can you see me?"

"Yes."

She pointed at her ear. "Can you hear me?"

"Over the phone, but not over the computer."

"Hit the 'Audio' button." Thankfully, she didn't add the words, "You idiot."

I did as she said, and the audio on my computer came to life. I ended the call on my phone, looked at the assembled group on the screen, and smiled triumphantly. "It's working."

Rosie and Grace responded with matching eyerolls. Tommy was more diplomatic and flashed a thumbs-up as his eyes drifted to his phone where he was watching the Warriors game.

"Welcome to Zoom," Grace said. "And welcome to the Twenty-first Century."

"Thank you."

"I'm sorry about Lenny Garcia."

"Thanks."

"Sounds like it was a tough trial. How much time did you spend in the Tenderloin?"

"More than I wanted to." I lowered my voice. "There's an insane amount of fentanyl in circulation, and it's killing people. You and Tommy need to watch out for fake pills. Don't buy anything that doesn't come from a real pharmacy, okay?"

"Okay."

I hoped that she and Tommy got the message, but you never really know.

"You healthy?" she asked.

"I think so."

"You should stay home for a few days."

"I'm not going anywhere until I get tested. Are you and Chuck okay?"

"Fine. Pixar told everybody to work remotely for at least a few weeks."

"How are you going to do meetings?"

She pointed at the screen. "Zoom."

I looked at her image in the corner of my screen. "You think it's going to work?"

"We'll get used to it."

I have doubts. "Can you mute people if you don't want to hear what they're saying?"

"Yes." She grinned. "I gotta run. The Uber Eats guy is here. I love you."

"I love you, too."

Her box disappeared.

I looked over at Tommy, who was sporting the beginnings of his first beard. "All quiet in Berkeley?"

"Not bad." His eyes darted from the basketball game to me. "A couple of people in my dorm tested positive. The university moved them to a separate floor. If it gets worse, they're talking about sending everybody home and doing classes remotely."

"You might be more comfortable in your own bedroom." *And you'll have your own bathroom.*

"We'll see."

When I was a freshman at Cal, the last thing I wanted to do was to stay with my parents.

Tommy turned away from the screen, and I heard a voice behind him ask if he wanted to go out for food. He turned back to me and said, "I gotta run, Pop."

"Take care, Tom."

"You, too." His box disappeared.

Rosie leaned closer to the screen and took a sip of wine. "How do you like Zoom?"

"I'll get the hang of it."

"It's the future."

"I hope not."

"It's going to be the future for at least a few weeks. I just got the official word from the Mayor's Office. They're going to shut down city offices, schools, courts, restaurants, gyms, and all businesses deemed 'non-essential.'"

"What does that mean?"

"I'm not sure, but it includes us—for now."

"I'm going out on a limb here, but I'm guessing that people will continue committing crimes during the lockdown. Some of them are going to need Public Defenders."

"We'll figure out a way to deal with it, Mike. We have no choice."

"The courts are already backed up for months."

"It's going to get worse. They want us to do status conferences, motions, arraignments, and even prelims by Zoom."

"We can't do trials by Zoom."

"There aren't going to be any. It hasn't been announced officially, but all pending trials are going to get an automatic delay for at least three months, maybe longer."

"They're going to make our clients sit in jail until the virus passes?"

"You got any better suggestions?"

"Uh, no." I waited a beat. "I can go in to the office and keep an eye on things."

"Absolutely not. You've been exposed. Terrence has agreed to monitor everything. He's going to wear a mask and avoid contact with anybody. I'll go in every few days to make sure that stuff is getting done. How's Pete?"

"He tested negative. So did Donna and Margaret. They're hunkered down at home."

"How did he get tested so quickly?"

"He knows somebody."

She grinned. "I'm not surprised. Can he get you a test?"

"Working on it. I don't feel great about jumping the line, but I'll feel worse if I accidentally infect you and the kids." *Or if I die.* "Is your mother okay?"

"Fine. She's getting everything delivered from Amazon, Safeway, and DoorDash. Tony is dropping off fresh fruit and vegetables. I talk to her a couple of times a day on Zoom. She's very tech-savvy."

"More than I am."

"You'll get the hang of it. She's even playing mahjongg online. Tommy helped set up Ann-Helen, Mercedes, Flo, and Char on Zoom."

I winked. "What about the, uh, usual refreshments?"

She gave me a conspiratorial grin. "Their dispensary does home delivery. It's good stuff, and the delivery person is a nice young woman from St. Peter's."

"Your mom has a way of making new friends."

"She does." Rosie reported that Tony's market would remain open. "He's asking his customers to wear masks and pick up orders at the curb."

"And Rolanda and Zach and the baby?"

"All fine. They're camped out at their house for the duration. I approved Rolanda's request to extend her maternity leave for another three months. After the paid leave expires, she'll go on unpaid leave. Zach's law firm is also transitioning to working remotely."

"How is a big law firm going to do that?"

"They're very resourceful when they need to protect their billable hours."

True. I told her that I talked to Nady. "Her mother is doing better, but I have no idea when she'll be able to return to the office."

"You'll continue to cover for her?"

"Of course."

"Thanks, Mike." She took another sip of wine. "I'm worried about the kids."

"So am I. There's no playbook for this, Rosie. Hopefully, things will return to normal pretty soon."

"Let's hope so. Is Joey going to keep Dunleavy's open?"

"He's going to do takeout for the time being."

"You think Dunleavy's will survive?"

"They'll be fine. Joey is very adaptable, and Big John paid off the building years ago."

"Maybe it's better that Big John isn't around to deal with this."

"Maybe." I thought about my uncle standing behind the bar, a dishtowel over his shoulder, a Guinness in front of him.

Rosie lowered her voice. "Do you think we'll need to postpone Grace's wedding?"

"Not a chance. It isn't until December. Things will be back to normal by then." I winked. "Or I suppose we could do it on Zoom."

"Absolutely not, Mike." She took a deep breath. "I'm so sorry about Lenny. It's so sad. You and Pete did a phenomenal job."

"It seems like a bit of a hollow victory now."

"You proved that Lenny was innocent—before he died. It isn't a perfect victory, but it's far from hollow. Did you find out anything else about Kyle Adams?"

"He's been arrested in connection with the death of Annie Parker. Charges still to be determined. And it seems that Parker wasn't the only person with whom he traded pills for sex."

"That's sick."

"It is. Andy Erickson told me that Adams was also selling pills on the side. Evidently, he needed the money to cover the costs of his own cocaine habit and some gambling debts. I don't think his father's money or his connections to the mayor will help him. I suspect that he'll be spending a long time in one of our finest state prisons, although he might get a lighter sentence if he gives the D.A. the names of his suppliers."

"That's likely to piss off some nasty people."

"He should have picked his friends more carefully."

"You don't think they'll put him in witness protection, do you?"

"Highly unlikely." I looked at her. "We were fortunate that Andy was handling this case. He did the right thing and investigated when we connected Adams to Annie Parker."

"He's a solid guy—for a prosecutor."

"We need more people like him."

"We do. You got any good news?"

"I got Patty Dawson a slot in a residential treatment program."

"That's great. You think she'll see it through?"

"Hard to say."

She finished her wine. "You holding up okay, Mike?"

"Just tired. And worried about the kids. And you. And me."

"Take some time off."

"I need to monitor Nady's cases."

"They'll keep for a few days. Besides, if you come into the office, you're violating an official City policy." She grinned. "I know that you're a stickler for rules handed down by the Mayor's Office."

"Yup. That's me. Always coloring inside the lines."

She turned serious. "I don't want you coming into the office until you're rested and tested, understood?"

"Understood." I looked at her eyes, which were beautiful even on a Zoom screen. "You're going to work from home?"

"As much as I can."

"You want company?"

"After you're tested." Her expression softened. "What is it, Mike?"

I felt a lump in my throat. "I miss you, Rosie."

"I miss you, too."

"This is a hard time to be by myself."

"It's hard for me, too."

I pointed at Wilma. "Well, I'm not completely alone. Wilma is good company, but not as good as you."

She gave me a reassuring smile. "We'll get through this, Mike."

"We always do."

"I'll call you in the morning."

I corrected her. "You mean you'll *Zoom* me in the morning."

Her smile broadened. "I don't think 'Zoom' is a verb."

"It will be—just like Google." I looked into her eyes. "I love you, Rosie."

"I love you, too, Mike."

A Note about Fentanyl

In the course of researching this story, I had to learn a lot about fentanyl, which is widely available and all-too-frequently leads to tragedy. In 2021, the Center for Disease Control reported that 108,000 people died from drug overdoses (up from 94,000 overdose deaths in 2020). Of the 108,000 deaths, more than 80,000 involved opioids, and more than 71,000 of all opioid deaths involved illegally manufactured fentanyl.

Fentanyl is so pervasive we must assume that any drug (legal or otherwise) is tainted unless it is prescribed by a doctor and delivered by a licensed pharmacist in a bottle. Although **DOUBLE JEOPARDY** is a story about the prevalence of fentanyl in a homeless encampment in San Francisco's Tenderloin, the fentanyl epidemic has become a tragic problem in every community. Fentanyl deaths have become all-too-common among high school and college students. Given the nature of our modern world, many people (especially younger ones) order drugs (and, it seems, everything else) online or via social media. Procuring drugs in this manner (except from a licensed pharmacist) is especially dangerous and, in many cases, deadly.

I would encourage you to educate yourself about fentanyl, and I would also suggest that you talk about the dangers with your family and friends. This is extremely serious stuff, and

I hope that you will become informed and take necessary precautions.

For more information, I would suggest that you take a look at the following websites:

- Center for Disease Control. Fentanyl Facts.
  https://www.cdc.gov/opioids/basics/fentanyl.html

- Song for Charlie. Facts About Fentanyl.
  https://www.songforcharlie.org/facts-about-fentanyl

- NPR. Overdose Deaths Continued to Rise in 2021, Reaching Historic Highs.
  https://www.npr.org/sections/health-shots/2022/05/11/1098314220/overdose-deaths-continued-to-rise-in-2021-reaching-historic-highs

Thanks for listening. Take care and stay safe.
Sheldon Siegel
Marin County, California. Fall 2022.

Acknowledgments

As I have noted in the past, I am extraordinarily fortunate to have a very supportive and generous "board of advisors" who graciously provide their time and expertise to help me write these stories. As always, I have a lot of thank yous!

Thanks to my beautiful wife, Linda, who reads my manuscripts, designs the covers, is my online marketing guru, and takes care of all things technological. I couldn't imagine trying to navigate the chaos of the publishing world without you.

Thanks to our son, Alan, for your endless support, editorial suggestions, thoughtful observations, and excellent cover art and formatting work. I will look forward to seeing your first novel on the shelves in bookstores in the near future.

Thanks to our son, Stephen, and our daughter-in-law, Lauren, for being kind, generous, and immensely talented people.

Thanks to my teachers, Katherine Forrest and Michael Nava, who encouraged me to finish my first book. Thanks to the Every Other Thursday Night Writers Group: Bonnie DeClark, Meg Stiefvater, Anne Maczulak, Liz Hartka, Janet Wallace, and Priscilla Royal. Thanks to Bill and Elaine Petrocelli, Kathryn Petrocelli, Karen West, and Luisa Smith at Book Passage.

A huge thanks to Jane Gorsi for your excellent editing skills.

A huge thanks to Linda Hall for your excellent editing skills, too.

Another huge thanks to Vilaska Nguyen of the San Francisco Public Defender's Office for your thoughtful comments and terrific support. If you ever get into serious trouble, he's your guy.

Thanks to Joan Lubamersky for providing the invaluable "Lubamersky Comments" for the fourteenth time.

Thanks to Tim Campbell for your stellar narration of the audio version of this book (and many others in the series). You are the voice of Mike Daley, and you bring these stories to life!

Thanks to my friends and current and former colleagues at Sheppard, Mullin, Richter & Hampton (and your spouses and significant others). I can't mention everybody, but I'd like to note those of you with whom I've worked the longest: Randy and Mary Short, Chris and Debbie Neils, Joan Story and Robert Kidd, Donna Andrews, Phil and Wendy Atkins-Pattenson, Julie and Jim Ebert, Geri Freeman and David Nickerson, Bill and Barbara Manierre, Betsy McDaniel, Ron and Rita Ryland, Bob Stumpf, Mike Wilmar, Mathilde Kapuano, Susan Sabath, Guy Halgren, Ed Graziani, Julie Penney, Christa Carter, Doug Bacon, Lorna Tanner, Larry Braun, Nady Nikonova, Joy Siu, and DeAnna Ouderkirk.

Thanks to Jerry and Dena Wald, Rabbi Neil Brief, Gary and Marla Goldstein, Ron and Betsy Rooth, Jay Flaherty, Debbie and Seth Tanenbaum, Jill Hutchinson and Chuck Odenthal, Tom Bearrows and Holly Hirst, Julie Hart, Burt Rosenberg, Ted George, Phil Dito, Sister Karen Marie Franks, Chuck and Nora Koslosky, Jack Goldthorpe, Peter and Cathy Busch, Steve Murphy, Bob Dugoni, and John Lescroart. Thanks to Lloyd and Joni Russell and Rich and Leslie Kramer. Thanks to Gary and Debbie Fields. Thanks to Marge and Lori Gilbert. Thanks always to the wonderful Mercedes Crosskill.

Thanks to Tim and Kandi Durst, and Bob and Cheryl Easter, at the University of Illinois. Thanks to Kathleen Vanden Heuvel, Bob and Leslie Berring, Jesse Choper, and Mel Eisenberg at Berkeley Law.

Thanks to the incomparable Zvi Danenberg, who motivates me to walk the Larkspur steps.

Thanks as always to Ben, Michelle, Margie, and Andy Siegel, Joe, Jan, and Julia Garber, Roger and Sharon Fineberg, Scott, Michelle, Kim, and Sophie Harris, Stephanie, Stanley, and Will Coventry, Cathy, Richard, and Matthew Falco, and Julie Harris and Matthew, Aiden, and Ari Stewart. A huge thanks once again to our mothers, Charlotte Siegel (1928-2016) and Jan Harris (1934-2018), whom we miss every day.

A Note to the Reader

I tend to get ideas for my stories from the news. Then I try to put Mike and Rosie into situations where they have to deal with difficult issues and see how they react. Some of my readers have observed that I seem to find new ways to torture Mike and Rosie in each book. That's the whole idea! It's what makes the books interesting to read and challenging to write.

In recent years, a lot has been written about the homeless situation and the fentanyl epidemic in San Francisco. These are profoundly serious problems without easy solutions. **DOUBLE JEOPARDY** is the story of how Mike and Rosie deal with those issues.

As if that wasn't enough, I decided to set DOUBLE JEOPARDY at the beginning of the Covid era, which created issues for everybody and generated unique challenges for defense attorneys and everyone involved in the criminal justice system. I was hoping to avoid dealing with the Covid era altogether, but it seemed appropriate to do so in this story. I hope that this will be my last book set in the Covid era.

I hope you liked DOUBLE JEOPARDY. I enjoy spending time with Mike and Rosie, and I hope that you do, too. If you like my stories, please consider posting an honest review on Amazon or Goodreads. Your words matter and are a great guide to help my stories find future readers.

If you have a chance and would like to chat, please feel free to e-mail me at sheldon@sheldonsiegel.com. We lawyers don't get a lot of fan mail, but it's always nice to hear from my readers. Please bear with me if I don't respond immediately.

I answer all of my e-mail myself, so sometimes it takes a little extra time.

Many people have asked to know more about Mike and Rosie's early history. As a thank you to my readers, I wrote **FIRST TRIAL**. It's a short story describing how they met years ago when they were just starting out at the P.D.'s Office. I've included the first chapter below and the full story is available at: www.sheldonsiegel.com.

Also on the website, you can read more about how I came to write my stories, excerpts and behind-the-scenes from the other Mike & Rosie novels and a few other goodies! Let's stay connected. Thanks for reading my story!

Regards,
Sheldon

Excerpt from FIRST TRIAL

Readers have asked to know more about Mike and Rosie's early history. As a thank you to all of you, I wrote this short story about how Mike & Rosie met years ago as they were just starting out at the P.D.'s Office. Here's the first chapter and you can download the full story (for FREE) at: www.sheldonsiegel.com.

1
"DO EXACTLY WHAT I DO"

The woman with the striking cobalt eyes walked up to me and stopped abruptly. "Are you the new file clerk?"

"Uh, no." My lungs filled with the stale air in the musty file room of the San Francisco Public Defender's Office on the third floor of the Stalinesque Hall of Justice on Bryant Street. "I'm the new lawyer."

The corner of her mouth turned up. "The priest?"

"Ex-priest."

"I thought you'd be older."

"I was a priest for only three years."

"You understand that we aren't in the business of saving souls here, right?"

"Right."

Her full lips transformed into a radiant smile as she extended a hand. "Rosie Fernandez."

"Mike Daley."

"You haven't been working here for six months, have you?"

"This is my second day."

"Welcome aboard. You passed the bar, right?"

"Right."

"That's expected."

I met Rosita Carmela Fernandez on the Wednesday after Thanksgiving in 1983. The Summer of Love was a fading memory, and we were five years removed from the Jonestown massacre and the assassinations of Mayor George Moscone and Supervisor Harvey Milk. Dianne Feinstein became the mayor and was governing with a steady hand in Room 200 at City Hall. The biggest movie of the year was *Return of the Jedi*, and the highest-rated TV show was *M*A*S*H*. People still communicated by phone and U.S. mail because e-mail wouldn't become widespread for another decade. We listened to music on LPs and cassettes, but CD players were starting to gain traction. It was still unclear whether VHS or Beta would be the predominant video platform. The Internet was a localized technology used for academic purposes on a few college campuses. Amazon and Google wouldn't be formed for another decade. Mark Zuckerberg hadn't been born.

Rosie's hoop-style earrings sparkled as she leaned against the metal bookcases crammed with dusty case files for long-forgotten defendants. "You local?"

"St. Ignatius, Cal, and Boalt. You?"

"Mercy, State, and Hastings." She tugged at her denim work shirt, which seemed out-of-place in a button-down era where men still wore suits and ties and women wore dresses to the office. "When I was at Mercy, the sisters taught us to beware of boys from S.I."

"When I was at S.I., the brothers taught us to beware of girls from Mercy."

"Did you follow their advice?"

"Most of the time."

The Bay Area was transitioning from the chaos of the sixties and the malaise of the seventies into the early stages of the tech boom. Apple had recently gone public and was still being run by Steve Jobs and Steve Wozniak. George Lucas was making Star Wars movies in a new state-of-the-art facility in Marin County. Construction cranes dotted downtown as new office towers were changing the skyline. Union Square was beginning a makeover after Nieman-Marcus bought out the City of Paris and built a flashy new store at the corner of Geary and Stockton, across from I. Magnin. The upstart 49ers had won their first Super Bowl behind a charismatic quarterback named Joe Montana and an innovative coach named Bill Walsh.

Her straight black hair shimmered as she let out a throaty laugh. "What parish?"

"Originally St. Peter's. We moved to St. Anne's when I was a kid. You?"

"St. Peter's. My parents still live on Garfield Square."

"Mine grew up on the same block."

St. Peter's Catholic Church had been the anchor of the Mission District since 1867. In the fifties and sixties, the working-class Irish and Italian families had relocated to the outer reaches of the City and to the suburbs. When they moved out, the Latino community moved in. St. Peter's was still filled every Sunday morning, but four of the five masses were celebrated in Spanish.

"I was baptized at St. Peter's," I said. "My parents were married there."

"Small world."

"How long have you worked here?" I asked.

"Two years. I was just promoted to the Felony Division."

"Congratulations."

"Thank you. I need to transition about six dozen active misdemeanor cases to somebody else. I trust that you have time?"

"I do."

"Where do you sit?"

"In the corner of the library near the bathrooms."

"I'll find you."

Twenty minutes later, I was sitting in my metal cubicle when I was startled by the voice from the file room. "Ever tried a case?" Rosie asked.

"It's only my second day."

"I'm going to take that as a no. Ever been inside a courtroom?"

"Once or twice."

"To work?"

"To watch."

"You took Criminal Law at Boalt, right?"

"Right."

"And you've watched Perry Mason on TV?"

"Yes."

"Then you know the basics. The courtrooms are upstairs." She handed me a file. "Your first client is Terrence Love."

"The boxer?"

"The retired boxer."

Terrence "The Terminator" Love was a six-foot-six-inch, three-hundred-pound small-time prizefighter who had grown up in the projects near Candlestick Park. His lifetime record was two wins and nine losses. The highlight of his career was when he was hired to be a sparring partner for George Foreman, who was training to fight Muhammad Ali at the time. Foreman knocked out The Terminator with the first punch that he threw—effectively ending The Terminator's careers as a boxer and a sparring partner.

"What's he doing these days?" I asked.

"He takes stuff that doesn't belong to him."

"Last time I checked, stealing was against the law."

"Your Criminal Law professor would be proud."

"What does he do when he isn't stealing?"

"He drinks copious amounts of King Cobra."

It was cheap malt liquor.

She added, "He's one of our most reliable customers."

Got it. "How often does he get arrested?"

"At least once or twice a month."

"How often does he get convicted?"

"Usually once or twice a month." She flashed a knowing smile. "You and Terrence are going to get to know each other very well."

I got the impression that it was a rite of passage for baby P.D.'s to cut their teeth representing The Terminator. "What did he do this time?"

She held up a finger. "Rule number one: a client hasn't 'done' anything unless he admits it as part of a plea bargain, or he's convicted by a jury. Until then, all charges are 'alleged.'"

"What is the D.A. *alleging* that Terrence did?"

"He *allegedly* broke into a car that didn't belong to him."

"Did he *allegedly* take anything?"

"He didn't have time. A police officer was standing next to him when he *allegedly* broke into the car. The cop arrested him on the spot."

"Sounds like Terrence isn't the sharpest instrument in the operating room."

"We don't ask our clients to pass an intelligence test before we represent them. For a guy who used to make a living trying to beat the daylights out of his opponents, Terrence is reasonably intelligent and a nice person who has never hurt anybody. The D.A. charged him with auto burglary."

"Can we plead it out?"

"*We* aren't going to do anything. *You* are going to handle this case. And contrary to what you've seen on TV, our job is to try cases, not to cut quick deals. Understood?"

"Yes."

"I had a brief discussion about a plea bargain with Bill McNulty, who is the Deputy D.A. handling this case. No deal unless Terrence pleads guilty to a felony."

"Seems a bit harsh."

"It is. That's why McNulty's nickname is 'McNasty.' You'll be seeing a lot of him, too. He's a hardass who is trying to impress his boss. He's also very smart and tired of seeing Terrence every couple of weeks. In fairness, I can't blame him."

"So you want me to take this case to trial?"

"That's what we do. Trial starts Monday at nine a.m. before Judge Stumpf." She handed me a manila case file. "Rule number two: know the record. You need to memorize everything inside. Then you should go upstairs to the jail and introduce yourself to your new client."

I could feel my heart pounding. "Could I buy you a cup of coffee and pick your brain about how you think it's best for me to prepare?"

"I haven't decided whether you're coffee-worthy yet."

"Excuse me?"

"I'm dealing with six dozen active cases. By the end of the week, so will you. If you want to be successful, you need to figure stuff out on your own."

I liked her directness. "Any initial hints that you might be willing to pass along?"

"Yes. Watch me. Do exactly what I do."

"Sounds like good advice."

She grinned. "It is."

There's more to this story and it's yours for FREE!

Get the rest of **FIRST TRIAL** at:

www.sheldonsiegel.com/first-trial

About the Author

Sheldon Siegel is the New York Times best-selling author of the critically acclaimed legal thrillers featuring San Francisco criminal defense attorneys Mike Daley and Rosie Fernandez, two of the most beloved characters in contemporary crime fiction. He is also the author of the thriller novel The Terrorist Next Door featuring Chicago homicide detectives David Gold and A.C. Battle. His books have been translated into a dozen languages and sold millions of copies. A native of Chicago, Sheldon earned his undergraduate degree from the University of Illinois in Champaign in 1980, and his law degree from Berkeley Law in 1983. He specializes in corporate law with the San Francisco office of the international law firm of Sheppard, Mullin, Richter & Hampton.

Sheldon began writing his first book, Special Circumstances, on a laptop computer during his daily commute on the ferry from Marin County to San Francisco. Sheldon is a San Francisco Library Literary Laureate, a former member of the Board of Directors and former President of the Northern California chapter of the Mystery Writers of America, and an active member of the International Thriller Writers and Sisters in Crime. His work has been displayed at the Bancroft Library at the University of California at Berkeley, and he has been recognized as a Distinguished Alumnus of the University of Illinois and a Northern California Super Lawyer.

Sheldon lives in the San Francisco area with his wife, Linda. Sheldon and Linda are the proud parents of twin sons named Alan and Stephen. Sheldon is a lifelong fan of the Chicago Bears, White Sox, Bulls and Blackhawks. He is currently working on his next novel.

Sheldon welcomes your comments and feedback. Please email him at sheldon@sheldonsiegel.com. For more information on Sheldon, book signings, the "making of" his books, and more, please visit his website at www.sheldonsiegel.com

Connect with Sheldon
Email: sheldon@sheldonsiegel.com
Website: www.sheldonsiegel.com
Amazon: amazon.com/author/sheldonsiegel
Facebook: www.facebook.com/sheldonsiegelauthor
Goodreads: www.goodreads.com/sheldonsiegel
Bookbub: bookbub.com/authors/sheldon-siegel
Twitter: @SheldonSiegel

Also By Sheldon Siegel

**Mike Daley/Rosie Fernandez
Novels**
Special Circumstances
Incriminating Evidence
Criminal Intent
Final Verdict
The Confession
Judgment Day
Perfect Alibi
Felony Murder Rule
Serve and Protect
Hot Shot
The Dreamer
Final Out
Last Call
Double Jeopardy

Short Stories
(available at sheldonsiegel.com)
First Trial
The Maltese Pigeon - A Nick "the Dick" Story

David Gold/A.C. Battle Novels
The Terrorist Next Door

Made in the USA
Las Vegas, NV
12 October 2022